The
Intended

A Pirate's Confession

The Intended

A Pirate's Confession

Sten Eirik

**TOP HAT
BOOKS**

Winchester, UK
Washington, USA

First published by Top Hat Books, 2014
Top Hat Books is an imprint of John Hunt Publishing Ltd., Laurel House, Station Approach,
Alresford, Hants, SO24 9JH, UK
office1@jhpbooks.net
www.johnhuntpublishing.com

For distributor details and how to order please visit the 'Ordering' section on our website.

Text copyright: Sten Eirik 2013

ISBN: 978 1 78279 572 8

A CIP catalogue record for this book is available from the British Library.

Design: Stuart Davies

Printed in the USA by Edwards Brothers Malloy

We operate a distinctive and ethical publishing philosophy in all
areas of our business, from our global network of authors to
production and worldwide distribution.

CONTENTS

In memory of
Eva and Karl-Fredrik Gustafsson,
my parents

and my grandfather
Eirik Hornborg

For my family

People find safe places in which to
stand in the territory of memory – at
first islands, then archipelagos, and
then continents – that provide them
with platforms for speaking of what
hasn't been spoken about.

Michael White,
*Narrative Therapy: the
Scaffolding of Therapeutic
Conversations*

There remained only his memory and
his Intended.

Joseph Conrad,
The Heart of Darkness

ॐ ॐ

The monarch of Sweden smiles at harlequins and diablos, sheiks and shepherdesses. King Gustav III is in his element, surrounded by charade and make-believe. A quarter to midnight, the witching hour. Even the lowest rank can hide behind the opulence of a mask. The highest can pass for beggars. Wolves in sheep's clothing. In the wings, an arsenal of painted scenery on wheels.

On the stage of the Royal Opera, the orchestra strikes up the first dance of the evening. King Gustav's annual costume ball. Masked dancers take their positions for the quadrille. Gilded wall brackets shimmer with the waxy radiance of tapers.

King Gustav knows his enemies. He's aware that they want him dead. An hour ago, he was handed the latest note cautioning him about a revolution brewing within his inner circle. Not as in Paris, fuelled by the masses, but rather by a stealthy elite made up of those with whom his governance has fallen out of favour. Crown Equerry von Essen has advised His Majesty not to attend onstage. King Gustav gave a quick laugh, saying "Shall my enemies know me as a coward?" It is the same courage that earned him the reputation as a fool in the war on Russia. Even to the extent of a mutiny by his officers.

To his left, the King's roving eye lingers on a figure cloaked in a black domino with a rounded hat, also black, wearing a white half mask. It's not the figure itself that catches the King's eye, but his recognition that this one is more or less a duplicate of several others, like a dark thread woven into the costumed festivity.

"How unsubtle," muses the King to himself, without alerting his body guard. "If they were here to take my life, would they dress so conspicuously?" Two things are insufferable. Fools and poor taste. "If these men be murderers, they are fools. Should I fear a fool?" He turns to his escort, the unfailing von Essen, and they exchange a smile.

A glove touches his right shoulder lightly. King Gustav turns the other way, believing that his young aide Pollett may have nudged him. He doesn't hear the soft summons, "Bon soir, bon masque."

He doesn't see the black domino looming directly behind, the glove withdrawing from his shoulder as the man makes way for a killer.

J.J. Anckarström has failed twice before. Of shorter stature than his compatriots, he now takes a step forward, expecting the King to turn. But King Gustav seems engaged with Pollett. Even here, Anckarström feels overlooked by his sovereign. He takes aim and fires his pistol into the body regal.

King Gustav stumbles, wide-eyed, clutching von Essen's arm. Only a few minutes remain before the stroke of midnight. For a few minutes more, it is March 16, 1792.

ISLANDS

ജ രു

GUSTAVIA
(1792)

℘ ೧

St. Barth was only a minor gem in the dazzling necklace of the West Indies. From the royal thrones of Europe, she appeared merely as a speck overshadowed by Antigua and Martinique, Barbados and Guadeloupe, from whence came the cotton and the tobacco, and sugar to make Europe sweet.

After the Seven Years' War, King Louis XV was content to give away the whole of Canada if he could keep his darling Indies. By the 1780's, having an island in the Indies was simply *comme il faut*. Everyone ought to have one.

But King Gustav of Sweden was without. He had learned that national wealth was no longer a matter of military might alone, but depended also on trade routes and natural commodities. The Swedes had been ogling the island of Tobago but it wasn't to be. Tobago was the only redeeming piece from France's settlement with England, so King Louis was not about to part with it. King Gustav, therefore, must settle for this obscure jut of rock named St. Barth and he decreed that a town be erected forthwith bearing his name.

೧ ℘

"Här bor man ovanpå ett enda stort skelett," says the magistrate, peering impishly at Olof.

His words bring a smile to their faces, some merely obsequious, some with a rush of anticipation at the promise of another bold story. Old Cederhök is an authoritative voice and when he speaks, other conversations retire sheepishly.

But the magistrate has realized that one of his dinner guests is left out. "I will use my English, such as it is," he says, raising his glass in a toast, "lest our good neighbour from St. Maarten should feel altogether forsaken." From the far end of their table, on Mrs. Cederhök's left, Mr. Fenwick grins at him graciously, returning the toast.

"*Mina vänner*, that is to say my friends," quips Cederhök, "the English I know is not so poor as to confound you, nor yet so clever as to confound you."

The powdered faces flanking the riches of the table break into a round of well-sated laughter, one to another, some with delight at the magistrate's wit, some to demonstrate that they're indeed capable of his English, and a few merely to keep in step with other dancers more nimble than they.

Old Cederhök lays one hand lightly on Olof's shoulder. "And to you, let this be a lesson in the English tongue, which you shall require when you leave us for America."

"*Prata på, bäste herrn,*" replies Olof. "*I Svea rike är det bara* 'le français' *som är god nog, men man får nöja sig med gemenare tal i kolonierna.*"

At these words it is again Fenwick, the visitor from St. Maarten, who is the odd man out, knowing not a whit of Swedish. It may be for the best since those words, properly apprehended, would convey that nothing less than *le francais* will do in Sweden, whereas in the colonies one must settle for the commoner's speech. Olof glances around the table, plucking a twinkle from the eye of the local Swedes.

Old Cederhök taps him affectionately on the shoulder. "You have no respect, son. You'll do well in America."

Further merriment around the table.

"He had top military honours from Berlin, you know," boasts the magistrate. "In Finland he fought well for his King. It earned him the rank of officer. All in the family, of course. His father served in the Royal Suédois in France. Now then, let me tell you what I set out to say. It will make you humble. The island of St. Barth, you see, is built on flimsy. The entire town of Gustavia, I say this whole colony, is girded round with another colony."

He pauses to observe this conceit taking hold in his audience. "We dwell on top of a colony of sea-creatures. These little animals build their colony in coral. The Indies are everywhere the same. This island, this rock upon which we tread our daily path, is nothing more than coral. We devour our roast and wash it down with a good claret..." He lifts his glass to the entire company and the sparkling crystal is raised all around the table as they finish their wine. "...with a good claret, I say," continues Cederhök, licking his chops, "but underneath of us is toil and trouble, the grinding of waves and the sucking of mussel and sea urchin to undo the brave work of the coral builder. Every day is a contest. Are we sitting on a rock? No, sir, not at all. We're sitting on a precious balance, I say, between those little builders in the deep and their destroyers."

Cederhök leans back on his chair, satisfied with the pregnant hush he has instilled in each and all.

At length, he leans towards Olof. "So, my dear son-in-law, could you make head or tail of it?"

Olof shakes his head, blond curls dancing on his forehead.

"You exaggerate," comes the rumbling voice of Doctor Henckell.

All eyes turn with fresh anticipation to the doctor's prodigious figure, improbably supported on the dainty bow-legs of the chair. The magistrate raises a bushy white eyebrow.

"We're not a coral reef," continues Doctor Henckell. "We are solid in the middle, solid porphyry. We're a buckle of volcanic rock. What does coral have to do with it?"

The dinner guests turn slowly back to Cederhök. They know that, whatever his reply, he will get the final word.

"More than you imagine, Doctor. Much more. This solid rock, as you will have it, is not the ground we walk upon. Between you

5

and the rock is limestone and what, I ask, is limestone? A pressured *mélange* of crushed sea-shell and mussel and coral, a cousin to the very coral of which I've spoken. This limestone, too, is visited by wind and water, bravely built since the dawn of ages, warped and gouged into caves where the winds make mischief and fool the sight of God."

Cederhök's bony hand clutches the edge of the table as he leans forward, his chin aimed squarely at Doctor Henckell. "Must you take each matter so literally!" he hisses. "Is it the scalpel, or what makes you surgeons so impoverished in the realm of higher thought?"

"Your skill at twisting the plainest matter inside out is admirable," replies Henckell calmly. "No doubt, you made a formidable young barrister."

Doctor Henckell's ample frame is rocked with silent mirth as he catches the eye of Mrs. Cederhök. The fact of the magistrate's imminent retirement is no secret.

But on the lady's left side, their English visitor rises to his feet. "I should like, if I may be allowed, to commend you, sir, on your mastery of English." He directs himself down the full length of the table to old Cederhök. "I'm obliged also for your kind consideration in speaking my language among these most excellent countrymen. I'm honoured to be in town on this gay occasion and owe you all a debt of gratitude for allowing my native tongue to intrude briefly upon the festivity. I shall take it kindly if you cease this courtesy and revert to your own accustomed speech."

Those guests with a grasp of English are moved to acknowledge his graciousness with a round of light applause. Again, the remainder jump quickly in, concerned about appearing not so much ill-bred as obtuse. The good servant Nils is on hand with two trays of rum toddy. He deposits them on the side buffet, flanked on either side by a wall bracket with wax taper.

"Well now," chimes Mrs. Cederhök, "look at the sky! Henrik,

may we stretch our legs?"

Old Cederhök has regained his equanimity. "To the terrace! And watch yourselves on the threshold!"

ॐ ॐ

THE CASTAWAYS
(1795)

ℰ ℭ

"Man alive!"

Captain Woolsley's words rippled through the noonday heat. Though his voice was made thinner and almost inconsequential on that great, heaving hulk of creaking timbers, there was not a head that did not turn.

The Captain had stationed himself at starboard gunwale, the better to observe a wayward little vessel down below. While the northeasterlies were giving him good speed towards the West Indian isle of St. Kitts, Woolsley had had a full quarter hour to study the bobbing prow of the little skiff.

Now the siesta was broken. Hearing the Captain's voice, His Majesty's garrison of eight dropped their game of checkers and shouldered their muskets. The deckhands came shuffling from their sluggish nooks, while the mate scuttled down from quarter-deck carrying the Captain's spyglass.

From where she rested at the quarter-deck gunwale, Glenda could not hear the conversation but it soon became apparent that Captain Woolsley and his first mate were not of one opinion. She had come to know Woolsley as a portly, weathered old seadog who did not always take kindly to Benny's Irish temper. But the first mate was not one to look for trouble and when his ill manners led nowhere, he soon became repentant and made the meekest, most irresistible amends. Captain Woolsley would have pardoned his first mate's Irish insolence, even had the Lords of Trade and Plantations posted a ban against it. Those two, engaged in another fruitless pantomime, brought a smile to Glenda's lips.

"Good Lord," remarked Devon. "Six weeks away from

England, but it's like we haven't left! Every day we're reminded again of the upstart Irish."

"Dear cousin, don't be harsh," smiled Glenda. "There's no harm in it, I promise. Their differences are of that friendlier sort that appears between husband and wife. And besides, have you on this vessel found anything matching this for amusement?"

Devon refused a smile. "He's our Captain."

"Then take me to the Captain," said she, extending her hand. "I should like to know more."

Devon straightened his double-breasted jacket and ran a hand over his braid of hair. "I will have a word with him. Keep yourself safe." Speaking thus, Devon launched himself across the quarter-deck with great strides and positively lunged his stockinged legs down the half dozen steps to mid-deck.

Glenda watched her cousin's bravado and felt the faint flutter in her heart. Maybe he would get his wish with her. There was nothing lacking, certainly, in his persistence. If her mother had sway, Devon would surely triumph. His was the more monied side of the house of Heywood and, to boot, young Devon Heywood was bound for a future in cotton.

Glenda could not be certain as to what she was witnessing. From the elevated quarter-deck, her view of the heaving skiff showed a narrow crescent of its interior, from which two or three dark heads were emerging. On deck, cousin Devon had now made himself a party to the disagreement, pacing with sublime exasperation beside Woolsley and Benny.

Mr. Fenwick, the merchant from St. Maarten and slovenly as ever, was joining the others at the gunwale. At mealtimes, he had often addressed Glenda and her cousin. On Devon he had lavished long dissertations about the new economy of the Indies and, of course, the troublesome climate. Despite his dishevelled appearance, Fenwick had impressed them as a true gentleman.

Glenda's eye was drawn again to the greenish brine as a dark figure rose to his feet at the prow of the skiff. Lurching side to side, he appeared to support himself with one hand on the edge of the boat. The other arm was raised in a salute and, in his hand, a large crucifix. It took no great effort to surmise that Woolsley and Benny were divided over what to do with these castaways. Glenda made her guess as to what each of them was advocating.

A drumming of heels on the wooden stairs announced Devon's return. Even before he reached her, he was trumpeting his despair.

"I've beseeched the Captain but to no avail. He will offer them refuge."

Glenda gazed again toward the flashing crucifix and the half dozen bodies prostrate in the other boat. "Your upstart Irishman is not of such a poor opinion, then?"

Devon did not deign to reply. He was studying the little skiff that rode the waves thirty paces to starboard.

She nodded toward the water. "Is he not a man of God, marooned by ill fortune? Can you doubt the sight of the holy rood on such a rough journey as theirs?"

From the deck, a hawser was hurled into the air, unfurling with a sparkling splatter on the billows below. A couple of deckhands arrived with a second hawser, which they launched after the first.

"My lady," came the Captain's voice from below, "I must ask that you retire from deck." Woolsley had turned to face her, shading his eyes with one hand. "I gave your mother my solemn oath that I should keep you from any peril. We cannot leave this priest to perish, but you must remain within doors."

Glenda waved. "You are my Captain."

Woolsley returned her greeting before he trained his eye once more on the men from the water. They appeared too weakened to climb, because each of the hawsers now held one man who clung inert to the hemp as it was being hauled back up the gunwale. The priest was on one of them. His long black robe fell freely around his legs; it did not appear to be wet.

Glenda could not take her eyes off the scene until she was tugged firmly away by the hand at her elbow. Devon escorted her to the aft companion where they could watch unseen.

"I had supposed that your Irishman might argue a little kindness toward a fellow Catholic," quipped Glenda with a sidelong glance. "The Captain, meanwhile, has missed his opportunity to rid the world of one more papist."

From behind, Devon's arm arched protectively across her bosom. "The Captain is too general with his kindness. Believe it, cousin, I shall make a report."

Glenda slapped his arm lightly. "Please, good Devon, don't be a tattle. You could bring misfortune on his head."

From their shaded retreat, they peered toward mid-deck. The gaps in the upper railing afforded them a glimpse of what passed below. Two more castaways had arrived on deck. Another two were on their way up, leaving the skiff empty and skittish, still moored to the ship's hull. One of these two must be more dead than alive, for the hemp was slipping, bit by bit, through his fingers and it seemed certain that he should plunge back into the waves. Even so, His Majesty's guard held their muskets at the ready.

Glenda could glimpse the Blackrobe approaching Captain Woolsley and his first mate with a sombre greeting. His hand emerged from inside the long robe, no longer with a crucifix but with a flintlock pistol. His arm swung wide and, from a distance of three feet, fired the weapon at Benny's curly head.

Glenda wrenched her eyes away with a gasp. In the patchy view between the balusters, she had escaped the sight of blood, catching only a hint of Benny's head and shoulder tossed sidelong out of sight.

"My God," she whimpered feebly.

"By heaven, don't look," stammered Devon. "Woolsley is going to get it."

With a single sweep, the Blackrobe's other arm had followed the first, holding a second pistol to the Captain's left ear. The deckhands, recovering from the shrill clap of the gunshot, had stopped in their tracks. Even the King's soldiers, muskets levelled from their chins, froze at the trigger.

"The ship is ours," pronounced the Blackrobe. "Drop your firearms."

Beside them, Benny's shattered skull was draining slowly across the mid-deck boards. The castaways had thrown off every semblance of fatigue. Even the last arrival was slamming his heels onto the deck and produced from his baggy breeches a pistol, as had each of the others. Behind the King's soldiers, Mr. Fenwick had his pistol trained on their backs. After a moment's deliberation, the soldiers complied with the Blackrobe's demand.

Devon whispered at Glenda's ear. "They've taken command. Fenwick was an impostor."

Refusing to look, Glenda pressed her forehead on the rim of the dark wainscoting. "In Thy great mercy, Lord Father, preserve the Captain from harm."

"You would do well, cousin, to start with our own salvation. I'll fetch my pistol."

She ignored him and went on fiercely whispering her prayer.

The Blackrobe remained at Woolsley's side, as unflinching and confident of his design as though he were cut in stone. The blackened orifice of his flintlock gaped at the Captain's head. Woolsley remained impassive. From beneath the salty drip of his eyebrows, his gaze was trained on the man they had known as Mr. Fenwick.

The castaways were busy rounding up the ship's crew with gruff and harsh prodding, while the Blackrobe shouted a few directives to guide their work. Two of the newcomers made their way to quarter-deck to take the helm and place the ship on her new course.

CR ℘

OLOF'S LOVE
(1792)

ℬ ℭ

The conversation swells generally and more casually in Swedish among the dinner guests. Twenty chairs scrape the unpainted pine floor as they are pushed, bit by bit, from the table. Miss Fridell, the school mistress, gathers her wide, starchy skirts and rises on stiff legs while Hansson, her escort, offers his arm.

Olof slips around behind them, dodging Pastor Snell and his wife in order to reach Cecilia. She is still conversing with the young clerk who has been her company at dinner.

"Cecilia."

She turns to look at him. The thick, flax-coloured hair pulled back from her ears shows a longer neck, suggestive perhaps of a greater sophistication than he remembers of her from home. It will be four years almost to the day. Cecilia Cederhök. The girl who had to leave school when her father was appointed to the Indies.

"Allow me." He speaks in his native tongue, offering his arm.

Cecilia turns back to the young clerk with a sweet smile.

The clerk glances from Olof to Cecilia, shrugging his shoulders. "*Mon plaisir.* You are perfectly *charmante.*"

Cecilia touches her white fingers to his hand. She rises from the table and, negotiating the chair with her skirt, tucks her hand under Olof's arm as they follow others toward the terrace.

The French window spills a flurry of waistcoats, crinolines and bright voices onto the terrace. Old Cederhök leads his guests into the pelting sun.

Cecilia slips a closed parasol from her wrist. "The ladies can't keep their eyes off you," she whispers. The parasol bursts like a blossom above her face.

"Never mind," he says. "I have you."

Cecilia tips her forehead against Olof's shoulder. They stroll among the parasols and conversations, enveloped by the soft breeze that keeps the terrace so temperate. From where they stand, Olof's eye drifts up the hillside. Near the top, the lush greenery ends and, over the craggy crest, a flagpole flies the yellow and blue of Sweden. Olof strains to catch a glimpse of the gunnery but only a wedge of the timbered roof is visible from this side of town.

"Fort Gustav," comes a familiar voice. "A garrison of sixty."

Olof turns back to see a rust-brown velvet sleeve ending in a white lace ruffle, from which pudgy fingers proffer a rum toddy.

"Your health, sir, and to your stay in Gustavia."

Olof accepts his rum toddy from the Englishman and, with a gracious tilt of the head, they salute each other and drink a toast. Olof's eye lingers again at the top of the hill.

"You're a military man?" pursues Fenwick.

Olof recognizes this as being a question. "Your pardon, sir?" he replies.

"Are you an officer?" asks the man. And after a moment, "An officer? The King's army?"

Olof nods and gives a smile. *Svea livgarde.* What is it in English?

"I am major. High major."

The Englishman looks perplexed.

"In the Royal Guard," mumbles Olof. "I was high major."

"High-ranking major, yes. Let me see." An epiphany illumines the ruddy face. "Lieutenant-major maybe?"

"Maybe," says Olof with a shrug.

"Indeed? *Lieutenant-major* Crohnstedt!" salutes the stout Englishman, taking another swig of his toddy. "She's a fine little fort. Much improved now, under His Swedish Majesty. Very much improved."

"Yes," replies Oluf with as much *bonhomie* as he can fit into one foreign three-letter word.

With an expert's sleight of hand, Fenwick extends his rust-velvet arm to whisk another toddy from Nils' ambulating tray. With a grin that pulls his bloated face into bulges and crinkles, he offers the cup to Cecilia but she declines. Without missing a beat, he tilts the cup to his own lips instead. "How's your English, sir?" he continues, cheeks already showing some colour. "Spoken English, sir. You're going to need it in America."

The stout, dishevelled gentleman is chuckling now, not derisively or even specifically, but more comprehensively at the pleasure of the afternoon, the transparency of sky and shimmering sea with its darker fringe of palm trees stretching in the distance below the magistrate's terrace. Olof joins in the laughter. It is exploratory laughter; a vague affirmation between men who barely understand one another's words.

"Ah, look where our Captain hides!"

Old Cederhök is approaching, brandishing his walking stick. "My Cecilia's not laughing. What, then, could be making you gentlemen so merry?"

The Englishman seems to have a toast for everything. "Will you take a glass with me, sir? Our host and his most excellent daughter." He sips his toddy with the magistrate.

Cederhök presses a kiss on his daughter's forehead. "Mr. Fenwick, what is your business with my son-in-law?"

"Not yet, sir, not yet son-in-law," quips the Englishman. "Not till the week is up." He tips his cup for a last drop.

Cederhök turns to Olof, an impish sparkle beneath the bushy eyebrow. "*Honom skall du se upp för, min käre Olof. Han är Västindiens värste rackare.*"

Olof lets out an amused chortle, at which Fenwick turns on his host.

"Have you slandered me, sir, in a tongue where I'm not able to defend my good name?"

The magistrate steps bow-legged in front of Fenwick, bony knuckles dug into his side. "I'm cautioning my own kin against the greatest scoundrel in the West Indies. I'm a man of jurisprudence. I have a nose for scoundrels."

A ripple of polite amusement stirs across the bright terrace.

Cederhök remembers his daughter. "Cissie, is your heart content?"

Cecilia raises her hand to brush Olof's cheek. "Oh father, yes. But the week is too long."

Fenwick's gaze lingers above the magistrate's shoulder, with a frown as though his sense of humour had suddenly died.

Cederhök turns halfway to trace the other's look.

"Begging your pardon, sir," croaks Fenwick. "I'm struck by your colours flying on the hill. They are at half mast."

Cederhök turns back to him, giving a groan.

"Has there been a death?" asks Fenwick.

The old magistrate takes him by the arm and steps to the edge of the terrace.

Olof and Cecilia saunter a few paces behind. Olof peruses the winding street below, the cobbled path climbing through a patchwork of tiled rooftops from the harbour to the heights.

The old man's bony fingers pinch Fenwick with unexpected fervour. "The king," says he. "The King of Sweden."

"Has died?"

"Has been shot."

"King Gustav is dead?"

CR SO

THE PIRATE
(1795)

℅ ℞

Devon was returning from his cabin, having armed himself with his pistol. As he entered the hallway, he became sensible of a scuffle, a bodily struggle, and loud protestations coming from his cousin. He turned the corner to discover Glenda thrown against the wall. Her contorted face was wedged between the wall and a powerful forearm belonging to the Blackrobe's man, who had his swarthy face pressed into her bosom.

"Get away from me..." she wailed, tugging in vain at the black, curly hair.

Devon's pistol went straight to his shoulder and he spread his feet for a steady aim. Defying the spasm in his throat, he blurted out:

"Say your prayers, pirate."

The looming attacker had Glenda by the waist and wrenched her body around. She ended up between them, her auburn hair tumbling derelict upon her shoulder, eyes moist and wide.

"Have no fear," promised Devon. "He's mine." He steadied his arm with the other hand. He was a good marksman and the attacker's shaggy head made an ample target above Glenda's rumpled figure.

But before Devon could pull the trigger, another pistol jabbed him at the base of the skull. "You're interrupting, sir."

There could be no mistaking the Blackrobe's voice. Devon noticed his poor cousin had turned her eyes to a place behind his shoulder.

"You'll be no good to her once you're dead," cautioned the Blackrobe in his ear.

Devon thought better of it and lowered his arm, dropping the weapon.

What followed was even more unexpected. Still ensconced behind Glenda, the big lout bawled at the Blackrobe. "Enough now, for Christ's sake!"

"As you were!" insisted the other.

But the man released Glenda and stepped out from behind. A nasty scar shimmered along the bridge of his nose.

"Or die like a dog!" continued the Blackrobe through clenched teeth. "D'ye hear, now do your best with her!"

The pistol's barrel was quivering at the back of Devon's head. Should the Blackrobe decide to kill his man, so went Devon's prayer, may it please God to remind the Blackrobe that his pistol was not now at the right place.

The splayed fingers of Glenda's hand went up in a wordless plea.

"*Sancta Maria*, do what you will!" growled her attacker, facing the Blackrobe. "I don't play till the work is done."

The Blackrobe's pistol went off with a deafening report. Teetering on the edge of comprehension, Devon felt the barrel still nudging him, finding himself no less alive than before. Panting piteously, he could only conclude that the Blackrobe must have had both of his pistols out.

Glenda had covered her face. The wainscoting showed a hole next to the pirate's elbow and the man looked back at his chief in disbelief.

"Come, Raoul, be quick," said the Blackrobe.

The pirate whose name was Raoul turned to Glenda and began to pick at her dress again. At his wit's end, Devon was about to hurl himself upon his adversary. But the steady jabbing from the pistol's point was enough to stay him. Those square, rapacious fingers had hiked Glenda's skirts waist-high and, despite her most earnest tears, were now groping at her garter and the soft, untouched flesh beneath.

It wasn't hers, thought Glenda to herself. Couldn't be her flesh when soiled by these vile caresses. She belonged far away. These guileless limbs were nothing to her, splayed against the wall by the lumbering blackguard who employed one arm across her neck while the other was undoing his breeches.

Her cousin stood by like a ghost, drained of all life. Glenda glimpsed the Blackrobe's face, as he observed them with an odd pinched grin upon his lips.

"You will hang for this," barked Devon.

The Blackrobe gave a soft snicker and turned on his heel, releasing Devon.

At the fall of his footsteps, Raoul looked up from his labours. "Mother of Christ," he blurted, "are you laughing?"

His chief was removing the priest's robe and flung it into a corner.

"I'll not work for you!" continued Raoul to the Blackrobe, tossing Glenda hard upon the floor. "You play when you should be at your work."

From the foot of the companion-ladder, the chief locked eyes with his shipmate. "Then let's not laugh," they heard him say. "Let's not laugh again."

The light streamed down on his slender frame. Taking hold of a rung, he vanished up the ladder.

CR ഏ

A KING'S SHADOW
(1792)

℘ ☙

"It was in March, not three months past."

Fenwick shakes his head. "I've heard nothing."

"You know the islands. The news goes wherever the wind happens to blow."

They stand together, gazing at the masts in the anchorage. Pastor Snell's little girls run shrieking with laughter.

"A week ago," says Cederhök in a flat voice, "our doorstep was draped in black. Every home in Gustavia. Every doorstep in Sweden. We put it away only to allow Sunday's nuptial."

"Who is the felon?" asks Fenwick.

"A captain of the Royal Guard. A strange, solemn fellow. I knew him vaguely. Indeed, there's no living soul that knew him more than vaguely. The hearts of men know a common pulse, but Anckarström was out of step. In sooth, I'm not the one to speak of this. I have my news from Olof."

The magistrate beckons to Olof and Cecilia. "I say, come talk to us about the murder."

Olof approaches with an air of distaste.

"How now?" asks the magistrate. Then to Fenwick, "Poor lad. You know, six weeks at sea."

"Sir," begins Olof, "I can only repeat what I spoke to you at my arrival."

"Let me see," continues Cederhök from memory. "Anckarström had been dismissed from the Royal Guard. He vowed to have justice. He has confessed to a previous attempt that failed?"

The magistrate interrogates Olof with the pomp befitting a court room. The adjacent guests are listening and edging discreetly closer.

Olof nods affirmatively. "Anckarström had arrived at the Opera with a pistol inside his costume."

"His Majesty's annual costume ball," explains the magistrate.

In his stuttered English, Olof outlines how Anckarström had found the ball poorly attended and no comrade to cover his escape, so he gave it up. But it was only a postponement.

Fenwick is one step ahead. "He had the same chance again this year."

"Trusting and generous to a fault," adds Hansson ruefully, "that was King Gustav. His greatest pleasure was to mingle with the people. He wanted no barriers, only good taste. His was a heart to melt the very glacier of Sweden."

Doctor Henckell has stepped closer. "It is why he had to die."

Old Cederhök is not about to let the doctor stand unchallenged. "He was a champion of culture and *beaux arts*," argues the magistrate, leaning hard on his cane. "He brought the gentler charms of France to Sweden. I say that's where he made his enemies. That was their worst charge. That he had turned vikings into fops."

"Pish!" blurts the doctor. "Three years after the Bastille and still we must hear of the gentle French?"

"Every nation has its rabble," croaks Cederhök.

"King Gustav loved the rabble," protests Hansson. "It was the rabble *rousers* he couldn't abide. He was getting ready to take back Paris."

Even Pastor Snell has left his wife's side to join in the debate. "Yes, he was going to liberate Louis XVI and the queen," says the Pastor. "So he was clearly not a revolutionary."

"His Majesty would stop at nothing," resumed Cederhök. "When his officers quit at Anjala, he was ready to lead the army single-handedly into Russia." He gives a nod to Olof. "You were there, were you not?"

"Yes."

"Then speak up, my son."

Olof gives a sigh, as though he's been over this too often already.

"Recovering from six weeks at sea," repeats the magistrate by way of excusing Olof's reticence.

"I don't like to remember," says Olof. "We had fought very well but a few of the officers had enough. The mutiny spread like wildfire, rumours jumping tent to tent. In the morning, His Majesty had no officers left."

"Olof was not yet of that rank," explains old Cederhök.

Hansson is fuming. "His Majesty's officers are paid in peacetime when they're no earthly use. Why, then, should they desert in war?"

Olof shoots him a look. "I cannot speak for every man, sir, but a war on Russia would've been unconstitutional. Some said the king was a warmonger who wanted to outshine Karl XII. They said King Gustav would've led his battalions into slaughter just to restore the glory of the Karolin troops."

"And who," asks Fenwick, "would lay this charge?"

Hansson, a devout royalist, is quick to reply. "The aristocracy. Yes, the landowners, the barons and counts who had always been rulers of the land. King Gustav chipped away at their power. Think of the war. He took from their wealth to pay for it. They hated him enough to wish him dead."

"And this murderer," asks Fenwick, "did he act alone?"

Olof shakes his head. "It was a conspiracy. When I sailed from Stockholm, there were fresh suspects every day. The list is long, but only two have confessed. Count Horn and Count Ribbing."

Miss Fridell puts her hand to her mouth. "Ribbing?"

"Yes, him."

"Ludvig Ribbing?"

"Yes, *mademoiselle*, the same."

The school mistress pinches her lips together, inhaling noisily. "Such a fine boy." Her voice has a tremor. "A sweet boy."

Hansson takes her hand between his. "He was your pupil?" She shakes her head. "Not mine. Master Ludvig had a private instructor. But he learned horseback riding from my father." A look of great perturbation sits on Hansson's brow. The easy conversations have foundered. Wavering slightly on his cane, even Cederhök seems at a loss.

But Hansson's tongue cannot keep still. "To plan a murder so monstrous! Such villainy, surely you must've seen the badness in the boy? I say, hang him high!"

Miss Fridell looks up to meet an imperious stare from Hansson. He has made himself a stranger. With a great sob, she wrenches her hand away from him and stalks off to the house. Always the good hostess, Mrs. Cederhök hobbles after.

Hansson stands with his arms at his side, staring morosely in front of him, trapped in the precipice between King Gustav's honour and his own affections for Miss Fridell.

Fenwick is squirming and wiping his forehead with a kerchief. "I'm so sorry," he says.

"Not at all," assures Cederhök. "Nothing to do with you."

Fenwick reflects for a moment. The old magistrate has, in fact, taken the wrong meaning from his words, mistaking his way of general condolence for an acceptance of personal blame. He turns to his aged host, this time with unaffected remorse. "Yes, I'm sorry I asked about the murder."

Clearly, Cederhök has laid his funereal drapes too soon into the attic. Out of doors, on this sunwashed terrace, they still darken the air.

CR SO

ADRIFT
(1795)

℘ ☙

From the ship's hold, barrels and iron-girded chests emerged on deck, hoisted from the dark by Woolsley's crew and hauled by His Majesty's reluctant soldiers to the gunwale. All this while, a low-slung schooner was quickly overtaking them. With a white froth about her bows, she crossed their wake and approached on the port side.

Glenda saw three dark figures perched in the shrouds while the topsails were sheeted home, followed by one of her jibs. Behind these, a huge black flag came into view at the top of a halyard tied to her mainsail. This was the flag Glenda had seen only in her worst imaginings, or posted on a scaffold at the Dock in Wapping. Hovering within its baleful quadrangle was a crude travesty of a skull, at once naive and horrifying.

Glenda held her cousin's arm in a desperate clinch. "I'll not go without him. He's sure to perish in your little boat."

Towering behind them, big Raoul gave Devon a nudge that sent him crashing down the steps to middle-deck. Glenda, whose clenching hand was locked in a spasm, went stumbling after. Devon helped Glenda to her feet as the schooner came up broadside of them.

From the other ship, a wiry old seadog tossed a hawser to his comrade on Woolsley's deck. Another hawser was tossed further aft and, with little slack, made fast at the gunwale. On the pirate ship, other men appeared on deck with sacks of grain which they tied to the gunwale on a short lanyard and dropped over the side in order that the two bulwarks might ride up against each other without damage.

This was in preparation for the transfer of booty and

prisoners. A few of the schooner's crew climbed onboard to help out. Each chest or barrel had to be rolled, wrestled and levered onto the planks laid between the two vessels.

From the forward companion-way came the Blackrobe's voice. "Ho, Papa!"

The same wiry old geezer waved, his grizzled hair blown by the wind.

"We done well!" continued the pirate chief.

"Where's your robe?" asked the older man.

His chief signalled that it was gone. "Never the same thing twice." He stepped over to where Woolsley was sitting. "This way, sir."

Captain Woolsley did not wait to be prodded or pushed. With his hands bound behind him, he strained forward over his round belly and struggled to his feet.

"Your captain will join us," announced the pirate chief as Woolsley came toward Devon and Glenda.

Big Raoul guarded them with a sly, musing eye.

Devon called to the pirate chief. "Pray, take me along! If she must go, then let me go too."

The chief gestured to Raoul and they steered the other captives across deck to the opposite gunwale. Devon made a show of protest but a hard boot in the small of his back persuaded him to go along.

The skiff which had carried the castaways was now packed with Woolsley's crew. Another boat had been found and it, too, would be loaded with mariners and the King's men once the booty was safely stowed in the schooner.

"Sir," said Glenda, her two hands clasped in supplication, "I cannot imagine what kind of a man you are, but don't do this." Her voice was trembling. "Don't put my cousin in the boat."

The pirate made no earnest reply. He merely turned his whiskered face to her and said, "How can this be so much worse than what awaits *you*?"

At his words, Glenda fell silent and remained speechless throughout. She clung to dear Devon's face until she was roughly dragged from him and, through bitter tears, watched him swing his leg over the side and climb into the boat with the rest. Recharging one of his pistols, the pirate chief leaned over the gunwale, speaking to the men below.

"God be with you. As He is my witness, you're no enemy of mine. If any among you should prefer to take a ball from my pistol, let him speak now."

A concerted silence ensued. The boats rolled side by side on the greenish brine.

"Very well," said the chief. "*Bon voyage.*"

The hawsers were released and tossed into the boats. As Woolsley's sails billowed before the wind, the little vessels were left in the wake, becalmed on the slow swell of the ocean.

Glenda watched her cousin's face recede into the bright haze and blurring at last so that, with her keenest effort, she could no longer discern his features. Her tears were spent. Something else had come instead. A deep devastation chilling her to the bone. A shrillness at the back of her head saying this was not so, this was a mistake that would correct itself the next moment.

After some time, she heard the chief's voice in her ear. "We're ready for you now."

Glenda turned her head. Big Raoul was on his way to the schooner with Woolsley. The chief stood next to her. She lifted her eyes to his, giving him the full flash of her anger and trying to speak to him. No words would come. She couldn't begin to say what she had to say to him. Her impasse was broken by a sudden swoosh overhead, followed by a muffled snap.

The chief reached for her arm. "The sails will burn."

He whisked her across middle-deck. The chief's men had emptied a barrel of pitch and set it on fire. She looked up to see another flaming shaft rip through the foresail, while flames were climbing all around the mainmast. Watching for danger from above, her feet tripped over something soft. Lurching forward perilously, she looked back to see the bloodied mess that had been Benny, the Irish mate, splayed on the deck.

"God, oh God," she moaned, taking her eye quickly away.

They arrived at the opposite side and the chief held out his arm as support while Glenda hoisted herself, sitting, onto the gunwale and waited for the two bulwarks to grind together again, so that she could ease herself down to the level of the schooner.

"Stand by to go about!" yelled Raoul.

Glenda found herself crouched against the wooden carriage of one of the cannons. She heard the sheets groaning in their blocks as the schooner veered away from Woolsley's ship. Confusion ran like a shudder through the sails. Then the jib flapped and filled on the other tack, and the mainsail began to draw.

They were eastward bound, topsails up and gathering good speed. Woolsley's ship was not so fortunate. The wind savaged the flaming canvas and, before they lost her on the horizon, they saw the charred skeleton of her mainmast pitch and vanish.

CR SO

IN THE WHALE'S BELLY

ℬℛ

Even as fear continued to gouge at her stomach, Glenda could feel sleep overtaking her. She had thought she would not, could not. All these hours, she had held her Bible clasped tightly to her ribs, never once thinking to read from it or use it in any way other than to press the four corners unrelentingly into her abdomen.

Across from her, the lantern's greasy glow kept oscillating between one corner of the cabin and the other. Glenda had fixed her eye on this natural oscillation of light and shadow, emptying herself of all those other thoughts until nothing else was real and the lantern, swinging to the roll and pitch of the schooner, was putting her to sleep.

To be sure, Glenda remembered the events of the day but only at a distance, unreal like a morning remembered when waking from a late afternoon nap or after prolonged and bitter weeping. Through the curving hull, the sea spoke in a strange, hissing tongue, rocking their vessel to starboard and to port, pitching her down the slide with a sudden rush and lifting her bows with a strict jolt at the far end of the trough. Free of the influence, the lantern and hammock swayed against the pitch of the cabin. Their pendulous constancy was mesmerizing and Glenda cleaved to it willingly. Through the hull came the enthralling voice of the sea, syllables of water hiccuped in her ear. Words buried in water, secrets waiting to surface. No single word could be spelled, yet their gurgling, hissing cadence was seething with the most dire intimations. The sea had his lips pressed to the barnacled hull.

A shadow on the wall made Glenda turn her head. She was looking at the old man, whom they called Papa, the same who had questioned the pirate chief about his black robe. Leaning on a post, he was observing her, his wizened face impassive as the woodwork. He had an uncanny stillness, appearing to have no more breath than the post itself.

"How long have you been here?" she asked.

He made no reply at first, as though he hadn't quite finished his inspection of her.

Glenda turned away, fingering her Bible nervously. As he came close, she braced herself. A small tin pot alighted on her lap.

"Captain wants to see you."

Glenda felt her heart pounding. Maybe it would all come to an end now. The other captives had been safe to release, but she and Captain Woolsley must not be heard from ever again.

She looked over at the old man, but his eyes told her nothing.

"Eat."

She looked down. The pot had warmed right through to her skin. Inside was a lumpy brew speckled with peas and chunks of onion and ham.

"What is it?"

"Eat."

Glenda studied the muddy concoction. She must concede that the fumes in her nostril were not at all disagreeable. It came down to a struggle between her aching stomach and the perils of accepting any sustenance from this scraggy old ruffian.

"It won't kill you," said he. "Thistle soup."

Glenda deliberated briefly, then gave a little twitch of a smile and lowered the pot to the floor at her feet. If she was about to be shot, Glenda decided, thistle soup wouldn't matter a jot.

Still clutching her Bible, Glenda followed him through the narrow doorway. She was walking now without difficulty; the rough sea was subsiding. Ahead of her was the 'tween-decks passage, wide and murky, barely tall enough for her to stand erect. In the dim light, Glenda could distinguish several sagging hammocks in a row and, in the centre, the massive shaft of the mainmast. The other pirates were nowhere about, but the odd word or two came sifting down from the main-deck.

Old Papa walked ahead as they crossed 'tween-decks to the main hatch. She would be dead, Glenda reminded herself, before she could feel the chill of water. She and Woolsley would be shot like the Irish first mate, which was all quite fine with her. She'd rather die suddenly by a pistol than by the degrees of drowning.

A few paces before the mast, Papa climbed some steps which brought him up the main hatch and Glenda followed after, the Bible nestled to her bosom.

The sun had set, leaving a spectral glow across the sky. Already there was a chill in the air; Glenda pulled the shawl more snugly about her shoulders. The pirates were stirring all around.

"*Capitain*," called old Papa.

Glenda presumed he was French, though it wasn't quite the accent she had heard in Europe.

The wide horizon was gone. A narrow cove enveloped them on all sides. She could see dark rocks silhouetted against the vivid sky, and a smattering of trees. Straight on their bow was a timbered house.

"We'll be stopping here." This was the other voice, the chief.

She turned her head and there he was, right behind her. His eyes were pale but very frank, almost rude. She looked back towards the island and said nothing.

"It's all for the best," he continued. "You'll be provided for."

At his presumption, she could hold her tongue no more. "For the best, is it? My cousin's drowned. Captain Woolsley's mate most cruelly shot and murdered. All for the best. A private appointment awaits me on St. Kitts and, I can tell you, if I've not landed within the week my employer will make inquiries."

At this outburst, a few of the pirates stopped in their tracks and looked on. Old Papa arrived on deck, escorting Captain Woolsley. The pirate chief eyed Glenda with no word of reply. His gaze, though neither hostile nor scornful, was most unrelenting. As Glenda's eye wandered from his face to the shore behind, she noticed they were drifting sideways on the calm water. They must be at anchor.

"You had other plans," affirmed the chief. "Ah, but life won't hear of plans. Mischief, all mischief."

He pointed to starboard, offering her his hand. But his didactic rejoinders had been too much. Glenda's hand shot suddenly for his face and struck him on the mouth. It was heard clear across the deck and brought colour quickly to the pirate's cheek.

Now, she thought, he would draw his pistol and fire, at close range, and that would be it. The men, too, were waiting for his next move. But he made none, not even to hold his jaw. He stood there, hand on hip, his eyes downcast with the sunbleached hair in his face.

"I have my own two feet," said Glenda, her voice almost a whisper. "I shan't need your help. Not ever."

So she walked to where he had indicated, past a few squint-eyed pirates. In the baffled silence, Glenda's boots on the wide planks gave the only sound. As she reached the gunwale, sure enough, a skiff came into view. Glenda gathered her long skirts and put one leg over the edge. She found a foothold beside the cannon in a scupper-hole and took hold of the shroud with both hands while she eased herself down to the skiff. Her lip was wet with tears. The oarsman was ready to give her a hand until she could sit.

Meanwhile, old Papa had ushered Captain Woolsley to the gunwale. They came climbing after, followed by the pirate chief and two of his men. The oarsman held his oar up to the schooner's hull and pushed off.

CR ഇ

SERENADE FOR CECILIA
(1792)

℘ ℭ

They have been too immersed in the royal murder to heed the first few drops. Of a sudden, the rain is upon them, beating thunderously on rooftops and paving stones, into pails and reservoirs, through the massive, gleaming foliage of trees which none of them can name.

The ladies shriek with alarm. The magistrate's terrace is transformed into a minor stampede of light-hued frocks and waistcoats. The gentlemen awkwardly assume parasol duty, in order that the ladies may employ both hands to hoist their ballooning crinolines above the puddling rain. Charging thus along the slight incline towards the French window, everyone stumbles to safety in Cederhök's drawing room.

Shaking the rain from their parasols and wigs, the guests laugh and tap their buckled shoes noisily. Accompanied by Pastor Snell, Cederhök is one of the last to hobble in from the downpour. He pulls the kerchief from his pocket and spreads it over his wig, patting lightly with his hand.

His guests look agitated and amused in equal measure. A new exhilaration has sprung from the bodily exertion of their escape.

Cederhök rubs his hands together. "*Gott folk,* we've had a most excellent stretching of legs, but may we not stretch them more musically?"

Voices are raised in delight and approval. While the rain drapes a sombre curtain around them, a fresh exuberance kindles within. Nils walks around the room, lighting a wax taper in each wall bracket. In the damp air, the scrubbed wooden floor smells wholesomely of lye, mingling with the agreeable scent of burning wax to inspire a good humour in each and all.

By Cecilia's chair, Olof leans the dripping parasol against a wall of blue-and-white East India damask. Her hair glistens with beads of rain as she sits back and lifts her gaze to his. Her breath comes fast and, above the neckline, her white bosom heaves marvellously. Olof brings his hand to her cheek, running a finger along the jawbone from ear to chin.

He has desired her from afar. He has nursed her father's affections for four years. On the winter campaigns to Karelia and Lake Ladoga, he curled up on a horsehair mattress in his canvas tent, with only the memory of Cecilia to warm him. He desires her now with a vast certainty, made sweeter still by the prospect of imminent fulfilment. At the Swedish church, Pastor Snell will join them together for ever.

From the nook by the fireplace, a burst of violins turns everyone's head. One of the violinists is Hansson. He is joined by Afzelius, the music teacher, and Funck, a sugar merchant and proprietor of a billiards hall at the waterfront. Their tuneful threesome brings everyone to their feet.

The musicians lead off with a bright allemande. Mrs. Cederhök and Miss Fridell get into line with the other ladies, and Olof drops off Cecilia at the end of their line. Across from them, the men take their positions, winking and signalling each to each. Taking their cue from the head of their line, the couples greet each other gracefully with bowed head and bended knee. Hard heels treading the wood floor make some commotion, but the violins rise over the top of it.

As Olof and Cecilia lock arms briefly for a wheel, she whispers, "Never another, only you." She smiles and his hand tightens round her wrist.

Already the dance is at an end. Cecilia is close enough to kiss, yet coy enough to make him wait. From Olof's lips comes a soft tune, syllables of song closing the gap between them.

"As a shepherdess garb'd for the holiday,

On her knees by the jumping brook
Doth plunder the grass for buds of May
To adorn and anoint how she looks. "

Finding his voice quite serviceable, Olof steps away to give himself more compass, now serenading the entire room.

"And ne'er would taint with a flash of pearl
That fragrant, blossoming round
Where the bird-cherry, clover and lilac unfurl,
In a wreath so handsomely bound;

So simply and sweetly from Flora's fest
My nymph attired her hair,
Invited by Mollberg to come as a guest
On his picnic in country air. "

His lips are pursed for the next syllable but none comes to him.

It's no matter. Cecilia is too overcome to blush. She has known nothing of his singing voice.

The audience, also, is charmed. Mrs. Cederhök leads the applause, followed by her husband and guests. Olof takes a quick bow, gracious though not theatrical.

"Whence do you know this piece?" asks Afzelius, his curiosity laced with disdain.

"A little book from the pen of..."

"Bellman?"

"The very man." Olof pulls the slim folio from his jacket to read the name from its cover. "Carl Michael Bellman."

"I knew it," blurts Hansson from the chair beside Afzelius. "Is he not more famous for drinking and debauchery?"

But already the guests are nattering amongst themselves, about Olof's impromptu entertainment or the delicacies of the table. Hansson leans back beside his fellow musicians, obliged to postpone any further dispute.

The dancers are warm and limbered when the musicians turn to the more languid strains of a gavotte. The silken crinolines brush the floorboards, catching a radiance from tapers along the wall.

With her hand on Olof's, Cecilia promenades down the middle. She catches her mother's eye. Mrs. Cederhök looks very pleased, her lips pursed with emotion at the thought of Sunday's nuptial.

Olof speaks above the rich, reverberant strings. "Soon as we're married, I'll bring you to America."

"I know that," she smiles, looking straight ahead.

"You'll have the finest house in Boston."

Cecilia laughs brightly. "Pretty dreams!"

"Not a whit," he whispers. They are near the end of their promenade. "And in that house, we shall have all night to do whatsoever we may please."

Cecilia cannot look him in the eye. Her hue deepens to a blush, as they drop their hands and part, each returning to the sides. When the dancers finish with a courtly flourish, Hansson rises from his chair, taking the violin from his chin.

"Dear hosts, what say you? Are we permitted a cotillion?"

This, of course, provokes a new excitement, being as the cotillion is of such scope and elaborate form as is rarely seen except in the courts and chateaux of old Europe.

The magistrate looks at his wife and they smile. "Away with the chairs!" he decrees.

It is a day of bright and splendid prospects. A day for the cotillion.

CR SO

LA FOURCHUE
(1795)

ℰᏅ ᏮᎹ

As they walked up from the shore, Glenda's anger gave way to surmise. An uninvited curiosity took hold of her. The two-storey house loomed before them, about a quarter of a mile from the shore. It was built very smartly from dressed timbers, with handsome shutters on all the windows. The peak of the roof stopped short of the end walls so that, in lieu of gables, the roof sloped to all the four walls. Adjacent the house, and almost as high as the lower storey, was a reservoir made of bricks and mortar. A solid barrier of tall, dark greenery covered the gentle slope beyond.

Captain Woolsley was close by her side, hands tied behind his back. "The knave!" he was whispering. "But you gave him something to think about, m'lady. That you did!"

Glenda took him by the elbow and held it tight. Trudging on, she was able to eavesdrop on a couple of pirates walking close behind them.

"He'll want the booty on shore before dark."

"Bugger!" snorted the other. "You worry too much, Matt. He's got somethin' else to think about. The only gold on his mind is that one there."

She heard them chortling, each to the other.

"Did you hear what Raoul had to do?" said the first one.

"Aye, and at gunpoint too!"

"Let no woman interfere with a man's work, that's in the articles."

"Aye, and always was."

Glenda stole a glance behind and saw, a few paces away, the two pirates glaring at her.

Turning her attention to the house again, Glenda's eye paused at one of the shutters. Two or three broken slats had left a gaping hole. And having discovered the broken shutter, it was as if the entire frame of the house began to unravel before her eyes. Part of the roof must have lifted in a high wind, leaving a gaping aperture into the upper storey. The brown paint was peeling badly; chinks and hairline cracks crisscrossed the timbers everywhere. The doorway was without a door. Everything was beginning to appear utterly derelict. Near a corner of the house, stones had been laid in a circle and used as a hearth, now covered in ashes.

"The place is a ruin," mumbled Woolsley in her ear.

Glenda strained to see through the gaping doorway. All was dark inside. She stepped closer, but a hand came down firmly on her shoulder.

"I'll show you inside," she heard the pirate chief saying.

That's when he put the blindfold on her.

CR SO

Glenda awoke with a deep sigh of gratitude. She couldn't remember how she had gotten to sleep after stumbling about in the musty void of her blindfold, seeking to familiarize herself with the room. Somehow she must've found her way back to the bed assigned to her by the pirate chief. Somehow she must've gotten herself into the bed, with the covers pulled up about her chin. Somehow she must've let go of all those dark thoughts and intimations stalking her mind.

One thing Glenda remembered with perfect clarity. She had been certain that it was all over, that she would need to struggle no further, that she would not wake to see another day. Yet here she was, stretching and yawning and with a gush of gratitude. For what, indeed? Was her attachment to life so desperate that she would welcome another day, no matter what her prospects? Or was she capable of such obstinacy that she could still hope for something good, whereof her present state was merely an interlude?

She sat up in bed, adjusting the blindfold where it was pinching her ear. She hadn't even removed it to sleep. The chief had only truly frightened her once. It was his dire warning about the blindfold. Glenda hadn't wanted to make her situation any more perilous than it was already. But now? The prospect of staring into this coarse brown cloth all day brought her to the verge of panic. Surely, if she carried it in her hand, she could pull it back over her head at the first sign of someone approaching.

She remembered coming up a staircase, tripping. Stumbling. Maybe the upstairs was safe. Maybe no one would bother her up here. Glenda lowered her feet to the floor and stepped away from the bed. She reached for the blindfold but curbed her hand suddenly.

She knew that he was in the room. It was not by his breathing. She listened for it but the only breathing to be heard was her own. So she stepped away from the bed. Following a wall, her hands discovered a heavy drape and, further on, some form of upholstered seat. She settled herself on it, quiet as a mouse, her hand clutching the polished armrest.

The deafening rain had stopped, leaving a limpid silence. She strained to catch the lightest pad of a foot, the slightest stir of cloth, the most minute displacement of air. He seemed to exist outside the realm of these things and yet he was there. She could not be mistaken. Drawing a deep breath, she decided to find him, instead, by his smell. Her nostrils filled with fragrance from steaming earth and the sodden leaves, great glistening boughs of soursop and sycamore, plantain and sapodilla shedding their vapour through unglazed windows. In all this, not a trace of man.

But he was watching her, nothing could be more certain.

"What do you want with me?" she said, frightened by her own

whisper.

From the shore, a dog answered her with a single yelp. The room was silent. She was not yet sure how big a room it was. She had not thought to pace the distance along each wall. Her sense of the room was intuitive, like her sense of him. With a pang of frustration, her hands started again toward the blindfold but stopped. He had been emphatic about the blindfold.

"What have I done?" she whispered. "Are you angry?"

She listened for a sign. Outdoors, the rainwater was still dripping into his reservoir. She jumped. Out of nowhere, she could feel him very close. Her heart pounded, her thoughts racing without direction.

"Holy Father," she blurted, spilling her anguish at random, "keep your loving hand over me this day and every day. Help me to know what is wanted of me. Make your mercy to shine on me and on my persecutors, O Lord. Help me to deserve your love and, holy Father, bring my dear cousin safe to a friendly shore. Amen."

In their stifling closeness, she was now aware of his breathing. From the unknown beyond the blindfold, his hand was suddenly at her neck. She gave a great gasp, almost a sob, her chest heaving like a cornered animal. The pirate's hand grasped the lacing of her bodice and began to pull. With no thought to the consequences, Glenda grabbed his wrists with her two hands and pitched him away from her. She realized that she hadn't really budged him; he was merely letting her have her way with his arms. She was still perched on the seat, every muscle strung to a pitch.

Again his fingers reached for her dress; again her hands lashed out at him. Glenda's heart was near bursting. Her blindfold was soaking through with tears.

"Fear not him that can destroy the body."

These words came unannounced. At last her captor had spoken, but to what end? Glenda could not conceive of it. His words rang through her head, shattered by a vicious jolt. Grabbing her dress with both hands, he ripped the fabric from her shoulders. Glenda let out a shriek and threw herself headlong off the seat. Landing hard on her knees, she scrambled on all fours with her skirts dragging. The torn bodice exposed the skin far down her back. Believing herself to have gained a bit of distance, Glenda reached for the blindfold and ripped it from her eyes.

Unaccustomed to the light or even the sight of this house, Glenda squinted toward the upholstered seat. He was on it, observing her with an expression of weariness. She remained on the hemp carpet, staring at him through swollen eyes. Her body was shaking, as from an ague. Neither of them spoke. They remained looking at each other.

Rainwater dribbling into the reservoir.

At length, the pirate got to his feet and walked quickly out of the room. Glenda sank backward onto the hemp and curled up on her side, still shivering. She reached for the moist blindfold. She began pulling it back over her eyes.

CR SO

FOPS' FAIRWAY
(1792)

℘ ℭ

Not everyone wants to stroll down the hill. Mrs. Snell bustles about with her children, making sure that each has taken old Cederhök's hand and bid him a proper adieu. Then the good Pastor gathers them under his wing and they climb merrily into his carriage, parked beside the magistrate's reservoir.

Miss Fridell, on the other hand, has seated herself at the French window. She is still fanning her face, winded from the dance, most especially the quadrille.

"I'll stay behind and lend some *assistence*," she says to Mrs. Cederhök hovering around Nils who, from the looks of it, needs no supervision in restoring the rooms to their former condition.

Hansson is, once again, agonizing over his own divided loyalties. Enviously, he eyes the boisterous expedition now heading down the hillside. Then he looks back at Miss Fridell and the quivering fan that hovers in front of her nose like a hummingbird. His mind is made up. This opportunity for a *tête-à-tête* may not present itself again. It may afford him a means to repair the rift between them. He casts a final, wistful glance after those carefree souls who have nothing quite so deliberate on their minds.

Nils walks by with a liqueur for Mrs. Fridell. She'll surely not refuse it. Hansson reaches for Nils' tray. Winking at the good servant, he relieves him of the little glass and walks resolutely towards the French window.

Meanwhile, Cederhök leads his gallants down the cobbled street. It winds quite steeply down the mountain, flanked on either side by wooden houses built on a tall foundation of brick and mortar.

Afzelius and Funck stroll together, engrossed in the finer points of French music. Behind them comes the ambling hulk of Doctor Henckell. He walks alone because of a generally held perception that he occupies the space of two and, more importantly, that he has little patience with the stupidity of his fellow men. He is followed by Olof and Cecilia walking arm in arm, accompanied by Fenwick. Lagging behind are two younger couples, meandering and dallying coyly in the evening air, among them the young clerk who was Cecilia's escort at dinner.

Cederhök's cane keeps a steady beat upon the paving stones. "Look," he calls to Olof, pointing his cane across the rooftops. "That's what we call *snobbrännan* and you'll see why."

Fenwick is sufficiently in his cups, by now, to have risen above the sort of loose blather for which his drinking is famous. Instead, he turns to Olof with a serene smile, his eyes glazed as though from the glory of some angelic chorus in his head. "And that means Fops' Fairway," he intones in Olof's ear.

Taking Cederhök's pointer as a guide, Olof looks down toward the shore. Daylight is receding behind a string of little islets. In the waning light, the anchored ships appear almost black, schooners, clippers, brigantines with their sails tucked to the yards and flying the colours of Sweden and many great nations of Europe. At last, the sea breeze breaks the swelter of the pelting sun, gently massaging the dark fronds of palm trees on the waterfront.

Cecilia gives Olof's arm a squeeze. "Fops' Fairway is for good society," she explains. "So many pretty things to see. So much of the French!"

Olof notices the levelled boardwalk that runs along the waterfront between the wharf and the edge of town. It's a wide boulevard unto itself, bustling with people at this hour of the evening. Olof leans close to Cecilia. "There's ten in Boston to each one down there!"

Cecilia titters with fresh delight.

Her father is hobbling along, calling to them over his shoulder. "You know, Fenwick, it's remarkable. The Swedes landed in '85 and look what we've done. Gustavia has come of age. She's a prospering, world-class city."

A caustic rumble comes from Doctor Henckell. "Well, well!" he huffs derisively. "World-class no less."

Afzelius and Funck look up from their musical musings, anticipating another good joust between the magistrate and the doctor. But by now, Cederhök doesn't dignify the doctor's comment with so much as a grunt.

Olof kisses Cecilia's ear. "We'll build the biggest house in Boston," he whispers, "to hold all the pretty things you want."

Cecilia squeezes his arm with a secret thrill. She folds her parasol and tucks it under her arm. Dusk is settling softly on their shoulders.

"More than anything," she whispers, "I want to give you a son."

They eye each other with a deep, unspoken hunger. Then Fenwick's rust-brown sleeve is, once again, at Olof's shoulder, the stiff lace ruffle prodding his cheek.

"You say King Gustav's murderer was a captain in the Royal Guard?" says Fenwick, the words slithering from his mouth in a sodden stream.

Olof merely nods his agreement.

"And are you not a lieutenant-major, sir?" continues Fenwick with a great sense of purpose.

"I am, sir," replies Olof.

"In the Royal Guard," pursues Fenwick foxily.

Olof is content to nod.

"And do not officers know one another? What I mean is, officers of similar rank are wont to become acquainted." Fenwick pauses momentarily to ward off some inward distraction. "How well did you know this murderer?"

Olof returns Fenwick's gaze. "If you had met Captain

43

Anckarström, sir, you would hardly wonder why he had few friends. I'm proud to say I kept my distance."

Cederhök has shortened his steps to drop back with his daughter and soon-to-be son-in-law. "Cecilia, my one and only," he croaks, "you look as if someone just gave you the moon and stars." He glances at Olof. "Did you?"

"I made her a promise."

"That's what I like to hear," says Cederhök in Swedish, massaging the front of his gold-embroidered vest. "Remember, a promise is nothing until it's kept, at which time it's a promise no more. Did you see Mrs. Snell with those children? The patience of an angel, that woman."

The waterfront esplanade is obscured by the rooftops as they approach the foot of the hill.

"Her husband seems a good man," says Olof, his arm around Cecilia's waist.

"He is as you say," rejoins Cederhök, "which makes the thought of Sunday all the happier. Of all God's servants, he'll be the one to hear your vows."

By now, some of Fenwick's earlier, self-effacing magnanimity is wearing off. "I know you're talking about me," he pouts, "but what's Pastor Snell and angels and Sunday got to do with it? Can you not speak a language more pleasing to the human ear?"

The magistrate pats Fenwick good-naturedly on the shoulder. He addresses Olof again, but includes the Englishman willingly. "And when will you whisk this daughter away from her old father?" he asks.

"I have a passage to Massachusetts, sailing a week today."

"What's your hurry?" huffs Fenwick.

"None other, sir, than the promise of tomorrow." Olof glances at Cecilia. "I have so much to look forward to."

"And so do I," adds Cecilia. "We'll be three weeks at sea, will we not?"

"If the winds are kind," replies Olof.

"I'll have a word with them," croaks Cederhök. "They'd better know whose daughter it is they're puffing about."

"I would heartily advise against it," says Doctor Henckell with a smirk. "Every blast of wind is haunted, you know. For each felon you've sent to the gallows, there's a ghost with perfect recall and a knack for foul weather."

There is between the doctor and the magistrate a sport which obliges Cederhök, now, to concede a point. He shakes his head, smiling, and trudges on.

On the evening air comes a rhythmic wafting of music. They begin to look around. Along the wharf, many a proprietor or merchant is taking the air, strolling under the palm trees in a wide straw hat and dark waistcoat over knee-length breeches so impeccably white as to signal that their owner has others to do his chores for him. Some have a lady on their arm, some have one or two on each arm. Their path is straight and determinate, formed by the yielding and subservience of others; of those clerks and shipwrights and cotton pickers who bend their head and step out of the way and wipe their soiled hands on the aprons, or those urchins and ragamuffins who run aimlessly with the stray dogs or sit endlessly by a picket fence or tree, staring at anchored ships.

All this meets Olof's eye when they step into *snobbrännan* and suddenly the name has justified itself. All increments of human existence, from hope to despair, from strutting to grovelling are to be found in this little colonial outpost. Leering behind the small-town bustle is a parade of vanity. Two vanities. The one is invited by greed and wealth. The other needs no invitation; it's forever gnawing at the flesh, waiting to ravish the wretched of the world.

"That's the negroes," says Funck of the music.

"Let's find them," exclaims Cecilia.

Cederhök nods his approbation and they turn to the right along the wharf. The two younger couples have vanished by now, lingering in someone's garden or sneaking a visit to one of the waterfront billiard houses. Cederhök and his stalwarts press on. Their eyes are trained on a row of shacks and warehouses, but Olof is distracted by four black men walking in the other direction, in dirty tattered cotton and chained together at the waist. Each of them has his arms raised high, using his hands to balance a large parcel on top of his head. The sullen overseer walks behind, brandishing a four-foot cane which he applies liberally to their bare calves and their torsos. At each blow, the slave reacts with a jolt of pain, careful not to withdraw his hands from their task lest he should incur more dire punishments.

Afzelius points to a warehouse. "Over there."

Olof turns his eye from the slaves. Next to a shed, in the violet light, he can see arms waving and bodies stretching to the music.

"Yes, they're negroes," says Cederhök.

Olof observes the dark, agile bodies. He turns abruptly to Cecilia. "Did you know, in America the slave trade is being abolished."

"God be praised," she answers him. "At least, all are not slaves," she adds, indicating the dancers.

Funck is already studying them. "But how can they dance while their brothers walk in chains?"

"Are you asking compassion from negroes?" croaks Cederhök. "It's a human quality. You won't find it in other creatures."

Henckell locks eyes with him. Through syllables of stone, the doctor peers down his nose at the magistrate. "So it's the negroes now, not the white man, who must put an end to slavery?"

Fenwick, ignorant of Henckell's Swedish rebuttal, rallies behind the magistrate. "Like children," he chimes in, "they cannot choose but be happy."

"If negroes be like children," adds Olof, "then the throne of England is itself perverted."

In his present state, Fenwick is prone to flares of patriotism. He stares at the young Swede with a look of cunning which cannot disguise his failure to apprehend Olof's meaning. Cederhök looks askance at his young protégé.

"In your country, sir, is it a felony," continues Olof, "for a grown man to use a child for carnal advantage?"

Fenwick sputters in outrage. "We're not so backward, sir!"

"Yet your monarch has done it, for he took a negro to be his paramour and queen."

"Queen Charlotte is no negro," blurts Fenwick, "Retract or I shall have you at pistols here and now!"

Olof steals another glance at Funck, a furtive scrutiny of that broad-boned, shallow face and the short bang of hair trimmed very squarely across the forehead. It's sufficient to sustain Olof's ire.

"Shoot my English tutor, if you must," he continues. "For it was he that taught me the queen is a Moor and her nose is too flat and broad at its base. Now if negroes be like children, as you say, then King George has robbed the cradle!"

Fenwick tries to expunge the inebriated muddle from his brain but it's too late. Again he sputters and fumes unintelligibly, petering off into private mumblings.

Olof catches the doctor's eye and there's a sparkle between them. The old magistrate eyes Olof with equal measures of reproach and esteem.

After a politic pause, Doctor Henckell adds, "It appears the negro has found favour with Swedish royals too."

All heads turn.

"Oh," says Fenwick, suddenly revived and slavering for vindication. "How so?"

"I had a letter from Stockholm saying that King Gustav's sister has given away her child."

Funck's jaw has dropped and Fenwick is already nodding maliciously.

The good doctor delivers his medicine. "The father was the king's servant Badin, a certified Moor."

These tidings settle with a silent *frisson* among the strollers. Slowly, almost in spite of themselves, they've been edging closer to the music.

An array of tin pans has been assembled. Two black men are using a stick in each hand to beat the rhythm for their dancers. Seven or eight dancers, men and women, hopping on one foot and on both together, toward each other and away, their dark feet flat to the ground, arms flailing, songs and shouts bursting from their throats; cotton skirts twisting and spiralling above their thin ankles, their men cavorting and stretching lean, naked torsos in arcs of pure joy to the unrelenting drums. A rhythm so compelling and exuberant that everyone within its compass is obliged to respond. To stand still and merely observe is not a state of rest, but of active resistance.

Yet, as Olof glances at his compatriots, not a one is tapping his toe or swinging his arm. Neither is he. But the dancers pay no heed. They're accustomed to these white men who prefer to watch.

"No counterpoint, no glissandi, no pizzicati," snorts Afzelius, leaning to Funck.

"No structure," synopsizes the other. "Purely primitive."

Cederhök is getting impatient with their nitpicking. "I say, they're a spirited lot. Let's not be too harsh."

"Sweden is no worse off for having negroes," offers Olof. "They know their place. Obedience is in their nature. It's the French who strut their finery in our streets as though they were the masters and we the barbarian. Even His Majesty the King, God rest his soul, spoke Swedish only when required. But Sweden is for Swedes. It is not New France."

Notwithstanding, Cecilia's mind is on negroes. "One day slavery will end, will it not?" she says, glancing up at her father.

Cederhök's hand tousles her flaxen locks. "No doubt," says he. "But what is cruelty? You must measure it by the injury suffered."

The tin clatter of the drumming has intensified, the beats melding in a rolling, undulating wall of sound. The dancers reach above their heads, spreading their fingers and stretching again and again toward the drooping black of the palm trees, thrusting their bellies forward, gyrating and parading their limbs in the most shameless way.

Olof and Cecilia find each other's eye, reading the other's mind. It is what they'll do. In their big house in Boston. This is what they'll do.

"You see, negroes are not easily injured," explains Doctor Henckell.

Olof looks over at him. "I had thought you sympathized with emancipation."

Doctor Henckell smiles confidently. "Of course. I make no secret of my politics. Negroes are entitled to their freedom. But I'm also a doctor medicus. My study is organs and anatomy. It is a medical fact, sir, that negroes have thicker skin and a higher pain threshold. They're less nervous or ambitious than we are, and therefore not easily injured. Where the injury is less, so is the suffering also less and, therefore, the cruelty."

The dancers are whirling in Olof's ear, grunting and shouting. He looks over at them, losing himself in the dense flurry of their legs, drowning in the darkness of their bodies. He finds himself nodding now, nodding his participation. At his elbow, Cecilia tightens her hold. And with a single mighty drumstroke, the dancing is over.

The night is deep and still. The dark-hued women squat on the ground with their men, laughing.

CR SO

THE FLESH
(1795)

℘ ℭ

Glenda could hear the pirates moving about downstairs.

Yesterday had been quiet; after their scuffle, the pirate chief had not returned. She had lain on the floor, she knew not how long, slipping in and out of sleep as though she were hoping, again and again, that sleep might whisk her magically away from this house. She had forced herself to endure the stale moistness of the blindfold. Once it showed her no more hint of daylight, she had groped her way into bed. There she remained, not wrapped in sleep's sweet oblivion like the night before, but tossing and turning fitfully while her thoughts travelled the same worn loops over and over.

She had been dozing since dawn, so had no clear sense of how long the pirates had been up. There were loud voices; at one point she thought she recognized the throaty snarl of the pirate who had walked behind her yesterday, complaining about the chief's treatment of Big Raoul. What were they up to now? Perhaps the booty was coming ashore. And where was Woolsley? She hadn't seen her dear captain since they arrived, yet there weren't many places to hide a body on this desert island. Was he still living? Why hadn't she heard from him all day yesterday?

Glenda rolled over on her side. She hadn't been out of her dress since the day before they were captured. It was rumpled and soiled with perspiration and now the back of it was torn almost to the waist. This couldn't continue.

She sat up on the edge of the bed. This mustn't continue. Where was her trunk? Her clothes? Had they removed it from Woolsley's ship or had it burned with the rest? This had to end. Glenda took hold of the blindfold and slipped it off, slowly as if any suddenness would ignite a hidden powderkeg.

Her eyes narrowed as the bright room opened before her. She gazed in wonder at what had, in effect, been a well-appointed drawing-room. On the wall facing her was a window, flanked by heavy burgundy drapes to the floor. Beside it was a French window with louvered doors on the inside. The doors had been left open so that she could see through dusty glass panes to the blue horizon.

The wall on either side of her had two windows, again sumptuously draped with floor-length burgundy. The far right drapes had been drawn in front of the glass so that the corner offered a slight reprieve from the sun. Many of the panes were broken. Between the windows, she noticed a couple of framed portraits and a framed street scene, all in water colours. Above and below, the handsome gold-and-crimson wallpaper had become stained and speckled from rain or mildew. Between the two windows on either side of her was a wall-mounted oil lamp, one of them having been knocked about and hanging askew by a single nail.

Contained within this faded elegance was a suite of furniture, some of brass, some of gilded wood, all in the best of European taste though in varying stages of disrepair. Beneath the far window was the upholstered settee, missing a leg. One of the gracile chairs had had its gold-on-green fabric altogether spoiled by rain. A small chandelier still hung from the painted wooden ceiling, but no one had bothered to replace the candles.

Glenda observed all this with mixed emotions. Her good upbringing was repulsed by the shoddiness of this pirates' lair. In spite of the mildew and decay, however, she had to admire the remains of good taste. It was a pitiable scene, almost woeful. Whose furnishings were these? Did they belong to the man who had blindfolded her two days before? Or were they merely his booty, their rightful owner now resting fifty fathoms deep with a pistol ball in his chest?

Glenda rose from the bed. Taking the blindfold in one hand, she crossed to the French window, keeping herself well out of sight. From behind the louvered door, she peeked through the glass. Directly outside, she could look down on the bricked enclosure beside the house. It was half full of water and Glenda realized that this was a reservoir for rainwater, fed from the eavestroughs. As she strained to find a downspout that would empty into the reservoir, Glenda saw instead some wooden joists protruding outside the French window. Evidently there had been a balcony but very little remained. The fallen timbers had collapsed into the reservoir, having long since settled on the bottom.

Beyond the reservoir, she glimpsed a steady traffic of pirates. They were toiling with barrels, caskets and large sacks but they were leaving, not approaching. Glenda stepped over to the other wall. She nestled close to the burgundy drape but recoiled instantly, blowing the foul, mouldy stench from her face.

Through the window, she could see the men lugging their riches to the shore. Glenda was altogether perplexed. The skiff was heading out, riding low under a fresh load of booty.

"You're a wilful woman."

The words came out of nowhere. They made Glenda's blood run cold, she was so unprepared. Her head turned and there he was, sitting quite properly on an upholstered footstool near the headboard where she had been tossing and turning. They eyed each other.

She forced herself to draw a breath. Her hands were shaking. "What do you mean?" she began.

He made no reply, nor the slightest move.

She brought the blindfold obediently to her head.

"Yes," he said. "But not yet."

Of a sudden, Glenda had no strength to stand. Her legs folded and she landed on a chair. The blindfold fell from her fingers.

"Have you been sitting there?" she asked.

He nodded in reply.

"Sitting by the bed while I slept?" she whispered in disbelief.

Her stare could bring no reply from his lips. She looked quickly away from him. "Are they going to harm me?" she said, startled at her own words.

"No," he answered.

Glenda was gazing through the far window, breathing once again. "What about you?"

There was no immediate reply, so she looked back and found him shaking his head side to side.

"Then what do you want with me?"

He leaned forward, his elbow on his knee. "You must learn obedience. I want to be an example to my men, or I would've struck back at you."

His voice had a coiled fierceness that sent a shiver down her spine. She concluded that he was not from the Americas, since his speech had neither the beauty of English nor the frivolity of French nor the impatience of the Spaniards.

"Remove your garments," he ordered.

Glenda looked over at the bed and around the room. "Remove them from where?" she inquired most earnestly.

If he perceived the humour in this, he didn't show it. "From your person."

At this, all other conjectures fled her mind. Indeed, she felt as though her mind itself had taken its leave. Nausea tugged at her stomach.

"But, sir," she said weakly, "I asked if you were going to harm me."

"You did, yes."

"And did you reassure me?"

The pirate chief nodded impatiently.

"And will you go back on your word so soon?" she asked, her eyes wide with fear.

"No, I will not," he said. "Now don't keep me waiting."

Nothing was making any sense. Glenda couldn't muster a single useful thought. This was, in truth, far worse than a ball from his pistol.

"I'd rather be dead," she blurted. "If you'll have no pity on me, at least consider my mother. She was left alone in the world when my stepfather fell off a horse and broke his neck. She has no one to care for her except me."

"And should you, then, be traipsing half around the world, with your poor old mother all alone?"

His question came so directly and was so precisely to the point that she caught her breath, unable to find an easy reply.

"You will do as I've asked or I'll have my men do it for you. The choice, of course, is yours."

Glenda stared at the pirate chief. She could hardly see him for tears. He rose suddenly from his footstool.

"I will," she whispered, swallowing hard. "I will do it. If you'll have the kindness to leave."

Glenda waited for the man to walk away. He made no such move. The silence was ringing in her ears. In the distance, pirates were hollering and clamoring. Glenda wiped the tears from her eyes to see him more clearly. He was moving to the bed. She took a deep breath. With both hands, she reached for the burgundy drapes and drew them closed, darkening the corner by the French window. She hadn't even bathed herself in days. She moved to the next window and closed those drapes, crossing the room to do the same at the opposite wall. After all of the drapes had been closed, she glanced back at the bed. The pirate chief was reclining comfortably in the shadows. She concluded that nothing further was to be hoped for. Reaching for the small hook and eye at the neckline of her dress, she began to undo it.

"The blindfold," came the pirate's voice.

She paused for a moment, then stooped to retrieve the detestable rag from the floor and pulled it back over her eyes.

"It will make it easier," she heard him saying.

Her hands were working their way down the back of the dress. "For you or for me?" she asked, turning to him as though she'd been able to glare at him. She heard nothing in reply.

In her heart, Glenda was already praying to her good Lord and Saviour to preserve her from the evils looming in her mind. If the worst came to pass and her chastity was to be taken from her, she was determined to endure it with all possible dignity. She cleaved to the memory of martyrs who, reputedly, had remained chaste of mind and spirit regardless of the abominations perpetrated on them. Such would be her strength and resolve that this pirate should hold no sway, should mean nothing to her, should appear in her mind even as a moth flitting and fretting around the burning lamp. She would burn as the lamp, scorching him body and soul.

Glenda pulled the woollen dress off her shoulders. As it fell to the floor, she stood stock-still, cheeks burning, her arms like a shield across her bosom, trying to guess his first move.

The room seemed very still, even serene. But she wasn't going to be fooled. She began to unfasten the cane hoops, three on each hip, which had bolstered the ballooning skirts of her dress. She dropped them onto the floor and straightened her back, listening for the slightest movement from the pirate. She could still orient herself by degrees of light and shadow filtering through the blindfold. By her reckoning, the bed must be directly on her right.

"Are you satisfied?" she blurted at last.

Nothing but silence.

"Sir?" A pause. "Will you leave now?"

The muffled din of the pirates came in from the shore, but the immediate confines of these four walls were as silent as though there had been no house at all.

"Will you leave now?" she pleaded.

When nothing could fetch her an answer, Glenda unlaced her corset and stepped out of her boots. She had to assume that silence meant approval, that he wasn't going to call on his men. She turned towards the French window, keeping her back to the bed. Cousin Devon's dear face leapt into mind, not as she had seen him last but as a young boy of thirteen or fourteen. They had been playing in his father's greenhouse and, without warning, their games became too earnest and Devon lost his composure and pressed his mouth upon hers, tearing her white dress and pinching her little breasts. Poor Devon had been too mortified to look upon her again for two years or more. At last, Squire Heywood had sent a letter to her mother, apologizing roundly for his ill-bred boy. Shortly thereafter, cousin Devon had come to call on her again, impeccably mannered. Glenda had been quick to forgive him, perchance too quick, for he had become the most importunate wooer a woman of good breeding could endure. His boyhood advances were the only attempt on her chastity until that brute, whom they referred to as Raoul, had cornered her aboard Woolsley's ship.

Glenda slipped the camisole off her shoulders. There would be nothing now to prevent the pirate's gaze from devouring every morsel of her white skin. The cool breeze from a broken window stroked her bare bosom, bringing blood to her nipples. Glenda listened for the lightest pad of his feet. He would surely demand more than a hind view.

She was fighting the awful tremors in her heart, the sickening blankness in her head. She must not swoon or she would put herself helplessly at his disposal. Resolutely, Glenda untied her knickers and stepped out of them. He couldn't fault her now. At long last, Glenda had done his bidding. She was wearing nothing but the blindfold.

Something crashed onto the floor and she jumped with alarm. She heard footsteps and pressed her eyes shut inside the brown cloth. But before she knew it, his steps were gone and the door slammed hard behind him.

Glenda opened her eyes. She could see nothing. She lifted the blindfold from her face and looked around. The room, too, was dark though daylight seeped around the heavy drapes. The bed was empty; she was alone. Her garments littered the floor. She was wearing nothing. He had seen enough.

Maybe he was keeping his promise, she thought. Maybe he believed that no harm had been done.

ॐ ॐ

THE MEETING OF MINDS

℘ ℭ

Her flaxen hair is tangled now and dull. From behind, the boy has gathered his fist full of her hair and gives a pull, forcing her head backwards. This folding of her neck pries her lips apart...

Leclair winced, pressing his eyes shut. When he looked again, he could see better. In the window, their schooner rode at anchor in the narrow inlet and, between the mizzenmast and mainmast, he saw a stretch of horizon; the clear, unsullied blue which had first brought him to these islands. It was best forgotten. Since then, a welter of booty and captives had passed through his hands. These four or five years, many a woman of quality had fallen prey to the untrammelled appetites of his robbers. In their triumphal, rum-oozing debauchery, they had shown him time and time again how the light turns to darkness, how light was a mere phenomenon, a thing of gossamer that fades as suddenly from the human heart as it fades from the horizon.

"Where are we?"

At the sound of her voice, he turned.

She was sitting now on the edge of the bed, one leg crossed over the other. Last time around, he hadn't stayed to get a look at her collarbone. It seemed to him the most naked part of her whole body. It suited him well. Her shoulders, though delicate, were broad and finely pronounced, hitched to one another by the contoured arches of her collarbone. She was leaning forward slightly, supporting her hands on the edge of the bed, her breasts drooping long and narrow.

"Sir, where have we landed?"

Her hair had come unpinned on one side and trailed down across the blindfold. He wanted her like this. To meet with her like this, again and again.

"Not far from St. Barth," came his reply.

"And what about St. Kitts?"

He pushed the burgundy drape away. A shaft of sunlight struck her face and she recoiled as from a slap, wrapping her arms about her.

"No one can see you."

She crouched forward over her knees.

"There's only a reservoir under this window," he reminded her.

Still she cowered silently.

"St. Kitts is behind us," he added. "Two score miles out."

Slowly she sat up, still hugging herself protectively.

"I want to look at you," he said. "I'll answer any question so long as you show yourself to me."

Slowly, reluctantly, Glenda straightened her back. He caught his breath at the lustrous white of her breasts emerging from behind the shielding arms.

"Now set your feet apart."

In Glenda's face, even with eyes covered, he could see the struggle raging in her soul. Her jaw was tightly set against the insult of his demands, her lower lip pinched to the upper lip in a dire scowl.

"Think of yourself as a painter's hussy. I have no brush, no canvas, no skill, but it'll hurt you no more than if I did."

Glenda lifted the right leg away from her left, planting her feet side by side on the floor. At once he could see the bushy darkness between her thighs. A fearsome, aching sadness rose in his chest. The humid heat became difficult to breathe.

"I want us to meet like this."

"And how will you pay me?"

Her question caught him off guard. "Pay you?"

"To pose for your painting."

"I said it before," he replied. "What you ask, I'll answer."

Glenda leaned towards him, the blankness of her blindfold

staring him in the face. "I need clothes. Where's my trunk?"

That was a good question, for which he knew no answer.

"Alright then," she resumed after a silence. "Will you take me to St. Kitts?"

He contemplated the question. Crossing to another window, he paused by the oil lamp on the wall. Glenda's head was slightly cocked, tracing his footsteps.

"Will you not keep the bargain?" she asked.

He looked over at Glenda.

"You promised," said she, "to answer each of my questions."

Reaching for the window frame, he took a shard of broken glass between the thumb and fingers of his hand and pulled it, coaxingly, away from the weathered wood. "What would you be doing on St. Kitts?"

Glenda seemed suddenly weary, slumping forward with her elbows on her knees so that he could see the fine ridge of her vertebrae trailing between the shoulder blades. Her voice was flat. "My employment is to tutor a young girl and her baby brother, ten and six. Pray, let me sail tomorrow. I'll say nothing to anyone."

"And what will you profess to these children?" asked the pirate. "Will they learn Rousseau?"

She was shaking her head with hard-won patience. "Rousseau what?" she replied. "Did you understand my question? Why won't you answer?"

He stepped over to the bed. Instantly, she ducked her head and flattened her torso to her knees to hide herself.

"Because it pleases me," he said, placing a serrated edge of the broken glass on the soft contour of her spine.

She gave a quick shudder.

"Because Rousseau will deliver Europe from her monarchs," he went on.

Without breaking the skin, he guided the fractured glass along the vertebrae of her spine. Beneath his touch, he could feel her wincing.

"Because Rousseau will rid Europe of rank and privilege. Because the education of a child is a political matter. Whatever education cannot amend, violence will."

Just above her sacrum, he lifted the glass shard away from her skin and tossed it on the bed.

His captive was very still.

"The royal houses of Europe love nothing so much as outshining each other in gold and finery. Rousseau calls it the dungheap. Have you read Rousseau?"

"He's well known in England," she said softly, "though not well liked."

"I expect so. Most of your English philosophers are a scurvy, stone-hearted lot," said her tormentor, stepping towards the French window. "They expend themselves on proving that the world is an illusion. Very clever, for if the world's an illusion, why bother about the poor and needy people who inhabit it? But clever's not enough, says Rousseau. And you know, he's right. Clever's not enough. If the heart is well, so is the mind and all that comes of the mind. But the education of the mind must proceed with due regard for the needs of the heart. Teach those children well. Don't add to the dungheap."

When he turned to face her, their eyes met. The blindfold was on the floor.

"Are you what you claim to be?" she said at length.

"And what is that?"

"You don't speak like a pirate."

Again, she had disobeyed him. He felt a compulsion to wound her.

"I'll show you what I am."

He crossed back towards the bed. She didn't shrink from his approach, perhaps because she had the use of her eyes. Sitting quite upright, she was watching him come closer.

She was talking back. "Lecture me, if you must, on how I

should conduct my own work. But why do you reserve for yourself a full suit of clothes and allow me nothing to cover myself?"

He had stopped directly in front of her, his waist at the level of her face. He reached for his belt and unbuckled it. "Am I wearing too much?"

"I beg you." She hid her face upon her knee. "Please do not."

He watched her for a moment, his anger subsiding. Then an impish sparkle in his eye. "You asked what I am. I would've showed you."

She made no reply. Her white body was coiled over her legs, taut and unyielding.

"I'm a robber," he said, less harshly. "Where did you learn what a robber is? How a robber should speak? The world has a wound, you see. You're not a part of it yet. But you're more than what you seem." He was willing, now, to wait for her reply.

Nothing came from her. He understood, with perfect calm, that he was standing too close, too high above her. He walked to the door. Her collarbone was hidden.

"Don't lie back," he mumbled. "The glass will cut you."

She looked like a swan sleeping.

CR ൽ

Barrels and crates are stacked up everywhere. Olof's nostrils are numbed by the foulness of bilge-water; he can hear it lapping softly underneath the crates. From above comes the occasional laugh or holler, but no more screams or pistol shots. The carnage must have come to an end. He has no idea how long he's been huddled behind the sugar crates. Now he must find a way to learn what has happened up above.

As Olof gropes along in the dark crawlspace, he tries to imagine what he's going to find. A warm drip catches him on the cheek and he jumps back. He wipes it off with his index finger, then rubs his thumb against it. There's no smell of oil or tar, but it's smoother and more viscous than water. He puts it to the tip of his tongue, then spits quickly. Someone's blood.

He can hear it dripping now, and almost trickling, onto the barrels. Again, the nausea wells up in his throat and he has to gasp for air. He hastens his step, not knowing what he'll do once he gets there. He had scrambled on hands and knees across these same trunks and caskets, bruising his arms on iron girths and hinges. His hiding place must be well forward of the main mast, somewhere below the galley. He is retracing his steps, treading carefully to avoid any tell-tale noise.

From far above comes a muffled crash of something heavy, followed by faint rounds of laughter. Amidships, he recognizes the black oblique of the stairs and, holding his breath, creeps up through the hatchway.

Ascending through the hatch, the first thing that meets Olof's eye is the round gaze of the ship's doctor. The doctor's stare is fixed at the deck from an elevation of a few inches, his ruddy cheek flat against the boards. The man is prostrate in his own blood, his throat slashed and still throbbing.

Olof glances quickly down the low corridor of the berth deck, charging and priming his pistol. He doesn't want to fire it, thus drawing untimely attention. He's standing somewhat aft of the main hatch. It hasn't been opened, though the pirates can be heard shuffling to and fro overhead. They'll be climbing down for booty any minute. About fifteen feet away, one of the ship's crew has fallen back against the main mast, pistolled right between the eyes. The man is mostly on the floor, only his head and shoulders propped upright, his arms limp and toes turned out.

Olof steps off the stairs and goes to the dead man, stooping to pick his cutlass from the floor. As he straightens up, he finds himself looking down the barrel of a pirate's pistol.

He has no idea where this bearded fellow was hiding; in fact, the pirate looks just as surprised. If the man's pistol goes off, Olof will be dead or, at the least, all others will be alerted. It may be his saving grace that the fellow has already tasted too much rum. With a spin of the wrist, Olof delivers a perfect butcher's stroke of the cutlass, severing most of the pirate's hand from his arm. The pistol lands with a thud, still attached to the man's fingers. The pirate has found no sound for his amazement and, before he does, the same cutlass runs him through. The broad blade enters the pirate's chest but gets stuck.

Olof rushes the pirate now, knocking him off balance. The man gives a howl for help, reeling backwards, stumbling and mincing his steps. They lunge across the deck in a macabre *pas-de-deux*, the prodding cutlass ever outpacing the pirate, who is given no chance to recover his balance. With a slam, he runs the pirate against a bulkhead. The cutlass breaks through to the wood behind. The pirate goes limp, collapsing on the floor.

Olof stands awhile, breathing hard. All is quiet. Crouching, he walks through the shadowy waist of the ship, stepping over another sailor whose head is nowhere to be seen.

At the companionway, Olof checks his pistol once again. Then he climbs the stairs to gun deck. His entire body is possessed of the darkest dread. At every step and every twitch of the eye, he expects a pistol's flame. But none appears. On gun deck, the corridor is quiet. All the noise and clamouring comes from outdoors, at middledeck.

He runs to the second door on the left and swings it open. But Cecilia is nowhere to be seen.

CR ഉ

A NEW DRESS

ၜၪ ၛ

The following day, Glenda had still heard nothing from Woolsley, but the pirate chief walked into her room late morning. She was as fully clothed as the torn dress would allow. The blindfold hung off a corner of the footstool by her bed.

Mercifully, the intruder said nothing about removing her clothes or about the blindfold. His mind seemed to be on other things.

"Put your boots on," he said. "We're going for a walk."

At this Glenda was gratified, though she took pains not to reveal it to him. She sat down on the bed and began to lace her boots. "May I speak with Captain Woolsley?"

"All in good time," he answered.

"But you've kept me now the better part of a week without any word from the Captain. Where is he?"

Leclair turned his back on her. "Get your boots on," he said and left the room.

She sat for a moment, staring at the open door. Then she tied her boot and began lacing the other one. Best not to make a fuss now. Already, the heat was pouring through the broken window panes. Lacing her boots was enough to bring beads of sweat to her forehead.

"And where is my trunk of clothes?" she called through the doorway.

No one answered. Glenda got up and went to the mahogany bureau. On the floor was a crumpled, woven tablecloth. She held it up at arm's length, examining it, shaking the dust from it. It was quite long and narrow, so had probably lain as a runner on top of the bureau. It would have to do, she thought. She held it up to the unglazed window and shook it again, harder, then laid it around her shoulders to cover the torn bodice.

Outside her door was a small landing with another door, which was closed. She couldn't help but wonder what was inside. Or *who* was inside. Could Captain Woolsley be so close? Had they been wall to wall with each other and not known it? Glenda was fighting a strong compulsion to walk over and try the door. But she knew that this would be what her captor meant by wilful. His punishment would be quick and terrible. Glenda was better off nurturing that gentler disposition with which he had greeted her today.

She went downstairs, those same stairs which she had climbed blindfolded on their arrival. These rooms she had not seen before. Apparently, they served as a collective den to the other pirates. The sole vestige of their former glory was the wallpaper, slashed and hacked and begrimed with use, some sections peeling and curling, with each season, further down the wall. But between these ravages were a few patches that remained intact, where she could still see the cream-and-gold vertical stripes and tiny white fleurs-de-lis.

Three of the robbers had their backs against the wallpaper, squatting on the floor. Glenda didn't recognize any of them. They looked up from their chowder, or whatever they had in their tin cups, to watch her go by. Glenda didn't feel any immediate danger in their eyes, but no welcome either. She headed for the door, stepping over blankets and sacks. Whereas the room upstairs must've been the parlour, this may have been a sitting room. Two doorways communicated with the rest of the downstairs. The pirates were tracking her with their eyes, even while they resumed their slurping.

Glenda was glad to step out into the white light. Leclair waited beside the stone-built hearth at the corner. There was a deep iron pot now, with a small fire underneath.

"I'll walk you out to the point," said the pirate chief and sauntered off.

Glenda followed a short distance behind him. They were walking back towards the ship; underfoot was mostly rock, with patches of a sparse grass and thistle. The sky was clear, with not a breath of wind.

"Do all of you live in there?" she asked.

Leclair shook his head. "Do you think we're tramps?"

Glenda was observing the back of his bleached hair. Hadn't he talked to her of a wound? His words came back, about the world and the wound and how she was not yet a part of it.

"They live on St. Barth," said Leclair at length. "Every last one of them. Matt is a boat-builder. Big Raoul is married with five children. Bruno will pick cotton, go on the fishing boats or whatever he can get. And so forth."

"And you?"

Leclair turned to face her, walking backwards a little ahead of her.

"No. Not me," he said. "The house is where I live. For a time. But the others come here to avoid trouble, like officers asking about Woolsley, that sort of thing."

Glenda walked quietly, looking down at her feet. Leclair kept a little ahead, still facing her.

"Is Captain Woolsley alive?" she asked.

"Questions, questions, questions." Leclair turned his back on her.

They had veered left along the north side of the inlet. Glenda watched her step carefully on the smooth rocks by the water's edge. They were skirting the little harbour, now approaching the headland. The heat was redoubled on these rocks, burning on her cheeks.

"This is what I'll do," said Leclair, speaking over his shoulder. "I shall ask ten thousand pieces of eight for the life of your captain. And we're going away to stow the treasure and settle all of our accounts."

A smile came to Glenda's lips; Woolsley was alive.

"So your treasure is not on the island?"

Leclair shook his head secretively. "We'll be gone for a day or more. On the way, I'll put you ashore at Gustavia. You and Papa. He'll purchase you a dress. Once we've divided the booty, I'll be back for you."

Glenda was almost dizzy with the news. She would be allowed to leave, not forever, not even for a week, but for a whole day.

Leclair was pointing across the blue water. "Gustavia," he said. "Just a few miles off."

There was a haze on the water, obscuring the rugged shore of St. Barth. Glenda closed one eye to see clearly, but the distant hillside was dark and secretive.

"It's behind the mountains," he added. "I'm putting my trust in you. If you run away, I'll come for you. I'll find you out. I'll kill you, that's certain."

Glenda's thoughts were racing. She felt elated. Suddenly, she didn't know how to look him in the eye.

"What's your name?" said he.

She shaded her eyes with one hand and peered towards Gustavia.

"Burchill," she answered. "Miss Burchill."

❧ ❧

For the short run past the harbour of Gustavia and up the coast, Leclair thought it best to fly the Union Jack. Most any of his flags would go unnoticed except, of course, the flag of Sweden. British and American ships had been among the most regular visitors since '85, when Gustavia had first opened her harbour to free trade.

Nevertheless, to drop anchor in Gustavia's bustling harbour, even for fifteen minutes, with a ship's hold brim-full of loot, half of it belonging to the merchants on shore, was a bit of a dare. In fact, Big Raoul gave orders to drop anchor just before they reached the old Carénage, where the inner harbour was. He was cursing Leclair up and down for making this detour on account of a woman's dress; he had insisted they keep to the north shore and put in at Bay St. Jean, where Papa could find her a mule or an oxcart for the short ride to Gustavia. But Leclair had been stubborn of late.

Here they were, all thirteen of them, with Fort Gustav's garrison breathing down their necks from the hilltop on their port stern. From his seat on one of the forward cannons, Leclair turned his head. "Ho, wait!" he yelled.

But Raoul ignored him, his broad jaw clenched in defiance. The anchor had gone; the windlass was spinning. Emilio had his spike ready to lock up the windlass.

"That's a wharf as good as any," rumbled Raoul, pointing to starboard.

On their starboard bow, the west arm of the Carénage jutted toward them, marking a gateway to the inner harbour.

"I'm stopping here. Let her get off and walk."

Leclair walked towards Raoul, his eyes drawn to slits.

Glenda was emerging from below deck when she discovered the two of them facing each other. Their silence was explosive. Mercifully, Bruno and Matt came slipping down the shrouds, having sheeted home the topsails.

"So we walk from here?" said Papa, crawling down the hatch to fetch his purse and coat.

"A wee walk will do you good," hollered Matt after him.

Matt walked over to the rowboat and prepared to launch it. His resoluteness was a show to distract Leclair and Raoul from each other. It worked.

Leclair turned his back on Big Raoul. "Papa has your money," he said to Glenda, "so don't try anything."

Pierre and Whiskers had come down from the mainmast.

Joining Matt, they levered the skiff over the gunwale and dropped it.

Glenda glanced back at Leclair but she had no idea what to say. She didn't want to feel beholden to him, though she did. She certainly wasn't going to thank him for restoring something which, if it weren't for him, she'd still have in her possession. Besides, she wasn't sure of his motives. She had stitched together the back of her dress using a large awl which Papa had found for her. It was a crude job, to be sure, but at least she didn't look like somebody's alehouse wench.

Papa climbed over the gunwale with surprising agility. Emilio hopped after and, from the boat, offered Glenda his hand. Holding the skirts away from her feet, she crawled over the edge, clinging to the shrouds for as long as she could and trusting Emilio's arm for the rest. Bruno handed them the oars, while Glenda settled herself in the stern.

The pirate schooner was drifting sideways, circling her anchor. At first, the little skiff was dragged right along but, after a few good strokes of the oars, Emilio got clear of the ship. The wharf was directly on their bow, water rippling and bubbling under Glenda's feet. She didn't look back to see Leclair but she knew he was standing there; she felt his eyes burning the back of her neck.

Behind Emilio's labouring shoulders, Glenda saw Papa slumped at the bow. She would be alone with the old man for the day. They'd barely exchanged a word; not on this voyage, not at the house on La Fourchue, except to drop off a slice of grilled iguana or a cup of turtle broth, not in the entire week since the capture. Was Leclair testing her? Was he a poor judge of her or was she perhaps a poor judge of him? Or was she a poor judge of Papa? What was Leclair expecting her to do? Was she to walk at Papa's side all day long like the good little daughter?

Glenda gazed above Papa's head at the crowd along the water-front. Here was her chance. Who could know if Leclair would

ever give her such another one? She could dash off into the
bustle on the sidewalks, but what was Papa capable of? She
knew, now, what Leclair would do. She had to believe, on the
evidence of the past week, that he was a man of his word. He
would take her life with no more remorse than pistolling an
iguana for his lunch. This was a thought that sent a shudder
through her. How was one to deal with men of his calibre?

The skiff arrived at a set of steps dug into the high wharf.
Papa stepped ashore and Emilio turned the boat, pushing with
one oar while pulling with the other, until the stern had come
half circle and Glenda could climb out on the wharf.

"Come to Funck's Billiards," said Papa. "I'll be looking for
you tonight."

Emilio nodded, reaching forward to plunge the oars in again.
"Look out you don't lose her," was all he said.

Glenda could hear that Emilio wasn't exactly envious of
Papa's assignment. The skiff slipped away across the water while
Glenda followed Papa up the three steps onto the wharf which
would lead them into the heart of town. So unaccustomed to
noise had Glenda become, that it quite overwhelmed her at first.
Labourers and gentry hurrying hither and thither. Handsome
two-storey buildings, interspersed with palm trees and
tamarinds, lined the esplanade as far as her eye could follow.

"There's all kinds of dressmakers down this street," said
Papa. "Let's go."

Speaking thus, the old man trudged off at a brisk pace, with
Glenda following on his heels. She was excited now, observing
the boisterous citizens of Gustavia, feeling herself a part of their
activity. She imagined to herself that she was a convict on a day's
leave from her dungeon. In her mind's eye, some gallant rescuer
was already preparing to burst suddenly into her life and whisk
her away from this nightmare.

"You don't say much," remarked Glenda as they walked
along.

Not surprisingly, Papa made no answer at first. After a full minute, he surprised her all the more by saying, "Leclair doesn't want you talking to us."

Glenda nodded. So that's how it had been decreed. "We can't be spending all day together and saying nothing," she answered. "Can we?"

Papa shrugged his shoulders indifferently.

"Alright then," she went on. "I'll begin by saying thank you. You're very kind to accompany me."

Papa didn't look particularly pleased with this little pleasantry, but neither did he look displeased. As on previous occasions, he had a gift for concealing himself. He pulled a curved dirk from inside his shirt.

"Now look," continued Papa without warning. "I've got this old blade and it's better than a shark's bite." He pointed across the esplanade.

Glenda saw a painted sign suspended from an iron bracket above a bakery.

"If you stopped me here and asked me to stick this dirk in the pretzel over there, I'd do it. I'm not going to. It'll draw attention, and a pity to spoil such a comely sign. But if that pretzel were running down the street and it was you, it'd be a different story."

Glenda walked silently beside him. For someone who didn't say much, he certainly knew how to make his point and memorably too.

"Do you understand?" he asked, tucking the dirk away.

Glenda gave a nod.

"Good," said he and trudged on, content to say nothing further.

Glenda was not content. She understood, now, why Leclair hadn't chosen a chaperone from among the younger fellows. They might more easily fall prey to her conversational and womanly charms. Papa seemed blissfully devoid of such compulsions.

They had now arrived at a street corner where the sign read *'Holländaregatan'* which, of course, Glenda had to spell to herself rather than try to speak. Nevertheless, she thought she saw the word 'Holland' in the name and wondered whether she was mistaking Sweden for Holland.

Before she could solve this conundrum, Papa was at her shoulder, pointing up the side street. They had found the dressmaker. A squat, matronly woman in her forties came to the door and ushered them into the shop.

By the far wall was a fine gentleman in white pantaloons, his wig tied handsomely at the back. He was in the company of a young nymph, impeccably apparelled, who was either his daughter or his *maîtresse* or both. They were having a quiet *tête-à-tête,* apparently deciding between some dark damask cloth and a plain, sepia-colored linen.

Mindful of her own appearance, Glenda felt an urge to turn and run from the shop. Instead, she steeled herself and went to the opposite wall, which was covered with shelving. Glenda approached this cornucopia of buttons, hooks, eyelets, fringes and lace.

"This is Madame Hulot," she heard Papa saying. "She'll help you."

Glenda turned to the Madame, who had her hands clasped and was smiling ear to ear.

"Yes, *mademoiselle*," said Madame Hulot in a broken English, "what can I make for you?"

"My daughter needs a dress," began Papa.

"Three, actually."

He looked over at Glenda. Glenda was nodding, wearing her most earnest expression.

"You need three?" inquired Madame Hulot.

Papa turned back to her, chuckling. *"Crisse!* These young girls, eh! She thinks I'm made of money."

The gentleman across the room glanced in Papa's direction.

Madame Hulot gave a little giggle.

"But you *are*, Papa," said Glenda in a cherubic tone of voice. "With all that gold and silver on your ship."

Madame Hulot's eye shifted to Papa, her smile tinged with apprehension.

"Oh please, can't you spare enough for three dresses?" said Glenda imploringly.

She had Papa sweating now, so much in fact that he was obliged, quite against his nature, to paste a broad, apologetic smile on his face. "I'm a seaman," he said, turning to Madame Hulot, "and when she was little, she always thought the ship belonged to me."

Papa looked hard into Glenda's eyes. "It's not mine," he croaked, making his point without much subtlety.

Glenda was enjoying herself, thinking of all those pirates sailing off to somewhere in order to haggle over their share of the treasure.

"You're so mean! And you're just pretending to be my father," she burst out. "God preserve me from a father like you!"

At the far wall, both pairs of eyes were following the spectacle.

Madame Hulot was astonished too, her eyes gaping as wide as her jaw.

Papa grabbed Glenda by the arm. "She's an orphan," he went on. "I took her in when she was just a wee thing." He was dragging her to the door. "It's not been easy," he mumbled, leaving the shop with Glenda in tow. "*À bien tot!*"

Glenda was content to let him have his way. She hadn't found a way to make him give her what she earnestly needed, but she also feared the dirk inside his shirt. As they stumbled out onto the esplanade, his fingers were still locked around her wrist. He hurried on towards the centre of town.

"I'm sorry," she said. "I spoke carelessly but it's true I need more than one dress."

"You're not getting so much as one," hissed Papa. He let go of her wrist. "I should cut your throat to stop you talking so much."

Glenda thought about that. It was past noon already and the sheltered Carénage was humid and sweltering. Glenda's dress cleaved to her skin, smelling of the whole week she had spent on La Fourchue.

"You should be in the theatre," quipped Glenda, trying to coax him out of his fearsome sulk. "They believed your every word."

Papa was not in the mood to return her compliment. "Mother of God, it's the dirk next time," he mumbled through clenched teeth.

෴

SURPRISE ENCOUNTER

ℰᏬ Ꮯᴙ

They had reached the inner margin of the Carénage.

Old Papa turned left on another esplanade, another name that Glenda couldn't pronounce, following the water's edge towards the other side of the harbour. Over yonder, rows of clapboard houses could be seen littering the hillside and behind them the mountain, dark and forbidding in the simmering haze.

Glenda had to admit to herself they were off to a poor start. Perhaps she had been imprudent to attempt something quite so theatrical. Trying to cajole Papa into spending the gold for three dresses had accomplished quite the opposite. Would she be leaving Gustavia, now, in her musty old tatters and nothing else? She felt the adventurousness draining from her and, in its place, a sombre despair. She couldn't afford any more mistakes with Papa. Leave him out of the equation, she thought. Don't try to sway him to anything. Just wait for him to look the other way and - poof! - she'd be gone.

As she was ruminating thus, she became aware of the peal of a church bell. It was a slow, dolorous clanging, well suited to her new mood. She looked up and saw, directly on the waterfront, a paltry-looking wooden church.

She hastened her step and, as suddenly as the ringing had appeared to her, it now ended.

"Watch yourself," growled Papa in her ear.

Glenda was about to reply when she heard, spilling from the church, a sound sweeter than any other. The congregation within had lifted their voices in a hymn which, since childhood, had been her favourite.

"I swear to you, I'll do no mischief!" she called out. "Just give me five minutes in a house of worship."

Without warning, Papa's bony arm was around her neck. "Remember what they did to our Saviour on the cross," he hissed fiercely.

Glenda felt the nudge of his dirk against her ribs.

"They stuck a blade in him," continued Papa.

With astonishment, she felt Papa's nudge growing to a rough poke and, as it broke through the fabric and her skin, it became a stab. Just deep enough to bleed. He clamped his hand over her mouth, while she struggled to shield herself.

"A peep out of you and I'll use the blade as deep as she'll go," said Papa.

Glenda became still. Slowly, the old man released his hold. She straightened her dress and stepped through the white-washed doorway, conscious of the sudden wetness inside her bodice.

The gloom baffled her eyes at first. She didn't wish to sing; the listening was enough to give her comfort.

God himself is with us: / Let us now adore Him, / and with awe appear before him.

The melody unfurled with grace and dignity, the sopranos winging their way to lovely, pristine heights while the basses strode stalwartly below, bearing the entire edifice of song on their broad, reverberant backs.

Slow and majestic and joyful, this song was like a procession. As a little girl, she had imagined it thus, sitting in their pew in Lancashire. The stride of a king, of the King of kings. It was the unhurried, unending march of her Lord. The king of thorns, king of sorrows, so named by mortals who attributed to Him their own tears; who couldn't guess that He who loved His father so, had nothing else but joy.

Like the holy angels / who behold Thy glory, / may I ceaselessly adore Thee, / and in all, great and small, / seek to do most nearly / what Thou lovest dearly.

The hymn was ended. There was shuffling and creaking of

benches as the congregation seated themselves.

Glenda wiped a tear from her eye. She had accustomed herself to the dim light and could discern a small gathering, perhaps fifty. At least a dozen empty pews separated her from the congregation. Four tapers were gleaming softly at the altar. The minister spoke to his parishioners now, invoking the memory of someone recently deceased.

Papa's arm steered her into the nearest pew, at the very back. He stationed himself behind, standing at her shoulder. Next she knew, she had the point of his dirk between her shoulderblades.

"Five minutes," whispered Papa in her ear. "And don't try to get up or else. I'll run you through and don't think I wouldn't do it. I never much liked you meddling with Leclair. I could slip out that door and let you bleed to death and no one'd be the wiser."

Glenda was watching the minister's kindly face, but all she could hear was Papa. His was a strange and terrifying logic. She was meddling. She had been grossly mistreated and abducted by a common pirate, yet *she* stood accused of meddling? Glenda had to fight the anger in her chest. She set herself to hearing the preacher's words for these few, precious minutes.

"From our neighbours in the Swedish Church, allow me to introduce the Reverend Pastor Snell."

The minister indicated a thin fellow who had risen from his pew, wearing three perfect rolls on either side of his wig. Pastor Snell helped a short, elderly woman to her feet and, in her dark dress and veil, she followed him to the front of the congregation. Pastor Snell looked around at the attentive faces. The widow smiled wanly.

"I'm happy to meet you," began the Pastor, somewhat diffidently. "And proud to say the magistrate was my countryman. His loving widow, Mrs. Agnes Cederhök, is here with me. We look forward to meeting many of you afterwards, as does my dear wife." Pastor Snell pointed into the congregation and Mrs. Snell rose to her feet at the pew where he had been sitting. She glanced about briefly, nodding right and left to strangers who returned the greeting cordially.

"On behalf of Mrs. Cederhök, I have an announcement to make. In her husband's loving memory, God rest his soul, she and I have made submission to His Excellency the Governor who will ask approbation from the Crown of Sweden to make certain changes. His Majesty willing, the Swedish church will add another room in the sacristy; a room for all other clerics who may wish to use the church."

A murmur of appreciation rose among the parishioners. The widow's spirits seemed to rally somewhat at this warm response.

"Yea, and if it please His Majesty the King," continued Snell, "I shall preach to you in English at our church, and also in the French tongue one Sunday of the month."

Glenda understood, from the response of the congregation, that this was no trifling announcement. She was, herself, surprised at these liberal offerings from one church to another, unheard of in Europe.

Papa hadn't budged. Was there no salvation for her, even in the house of the Lord? What if she were to give a great, sudden cry? Would Papa stab her and run into the street, or would the congregation be so suddenly alerted that they could be of help to her?

"The Right Honourable Magnus Cederhök was a most loyal servant to his sovereign. A man of great learning and indomitable spirit who had friends everywhere and enemies nowhere. His was the gift of bringing people closer, Anglican to Catholic, the Frenchman to the Swede and, I might add, even white men to negroes. Such a man was he, as will be remembered by all. Not by one congregation alone, but by all whose lives are bounded by the shores of St. Barth."

Papa's dirk jabbed her in the back. "Time to go," he snarled.

Glenda felt as though her heart could break in two. Here they were, these orderly rows of decent people, so near to her and yet so far. A panic seized her heart, a boldness that could lead her past all prudence. Before she knew it, however, Papa had grabbed her arm and hauled her roughly from the church.

They walked back the way they had come, the old pirate with his scraggly, ashen head of hair and the young governess in her tattered dress. Papa didn't seem to know where he was going. Maybe he didn't know what to do with her. Emilio wouldn't be back until sundown at the earliest.

The street was quiet now. The townsfolk had retired to their homes or the billiard halls to escape the worst of the heat.

"You don't like me very much."

Papa didn't acknowledge her statement in the slightest.

"Whatever you may think I'm doing to hurt Leclair, you're wrong," she went on. "I didn't ask to meet him. I don't care if I never see him again. And I certainly would've been happier to know nothing of his miserable soul."

Papa had stopped, indecisive. His eye was roving aimlessly along the margins of the Carénage, his thoughts obviously somewhere else.

"So I don't like taking the blame for whatever it is," added Glenda.

Papa turned from her and hobbled off. Glenda followed a few steps after.

"Why do you have to do this for him?" she inquired at length. "Shouldn't Leclair be doing this?"

But there was no point at all in trying to get Papa to open his mouth when he wasn't thus inclined.

"He gave you a job to do," said Glenda, guessing. "Unless you find me something to wear, you'll be in lots of trouble."

Papa stopped again and turned to her. Glenda saw, by the look in his eye, that she had found her mark.

He gave a sly grin. "I'll find you some dresses."

So that was it, she thought. Papa was under the gun to deliver the goods.

"I won't contradict you again," promised Glenda.

Papa kept on walking. Glenda tagged along beside him. They passed the brick portal of the Wall House, where half the town seemed to have gathered. From each window came songs and laughter and slamming of chairs.

"I'm getting hungry," said Glenda quickly, sensing another avenue for escape.

Papa kept walking.

"But I'm hungry," insisted Glenda.

"The crowd in there isn't for a lady like yourself," said Papa, leaving the Wall House quickly behind.

He was looking straight ahead, but Glenda could see that Papa knew what she was up to.

"Funck's Billiards is where we meet Emilio. Nice and quiet."

Glenda tried very hard now to hold her tongue, but alas. "They have a dressmaker?" she inquired gingerly.

He looked at her, again, with a grimace. "You were hungry, so we'll eat."

Glenda found that she had run out of words. And come to think of it, she could do with some lunch. And there'd still be ample time for the dressmaker.

They were marching past a large factory building from whence came a steady whirring of spindles and slamming of shuttles, reminding Glenda of other cotton mills she had visited with cousin Devon and his father. The mere thought of this served to redouble her own sense of entrapment, of utter remoteness, of unreality. She walked along quietly, making no effort to hide nor wipe the tears streaming down her face.

Before long, they arrived at Funck's Billiards and a small poster on the door which read: *"Afzelius & Funck - Music Conservatory - a Touch of Europe - Enquire Within"*. Papa had been right. This was a smaller, quiet alehouse where she was not likely to find a hiding place. Nevertheless, she was glad to escape the pelting sun. Papa walked close behind her, as in the church, threatening dire consequences if she disobeyed.

They took a table by the wall.

"The meat pies are good," said Papa, fishing some coins from his purse.

"Fine," she said. "And lemon water, if you please."

Papa limped over to the tapster to order his tankard of stout.

Glenda drew a deep breath. She looked around. It was divine solace to be thirty feet removed from the old man. In the far corner was a wooden staircase leading to the upper rooms. She had heard about the women who worked in some of those rooms.

Along the far wall were two large billiard tables, both of them in use. The place would have been in utter darkness except for shafts of light seeping from the narrow vent-holes along the top of the wall. The dust was forever blowing across the fingers of light, fading and vanishing and re-appearing again.

Glenda observed the players strolling at their leisure, their arms illumined as they plied their billiard cues, while their wigs and faces remained, phantom-like, in shadow. One would lean to the other, dishing out some news or gossip, and protestations or bursts of merriment would ensue. One of these phantom faces leaned briefly into the light and Glenda's jaw dropped.

"Fenwick," she gasped, her heart pounding.

It was the man himself. His vest was undone, his wig slovenly as ever, his pudgy fingers caressing the billiard cue.

"Mr. Fenwick!"

In the general noise, her voice may not have reached him. Glenda couldn't be sure whether, in the half-light, Fenwick had shot her a glance and hastened to look away. At any rate, he gave no other acknowledgement of her presence.

Glenda rose to her feet and headed across the floor. Her hands were clenched into fists. He was going to hear her this time. At the billiard table she stopped, placing her fists on the polished wood. Glenda fixed her eyes on him and let the words come. "Mr. Fenwick!"

There was no denying her presence now. Three or four of the gentlemen turned their heads, including Fenwick himself.

"Do you remember me, Mr. Fenwick?"

Of course he did. Cousin Devon had explained his plans as a cotton merchant and Fenwick, on the very morning of his great treachery, had pledged to Devon his willing assistance in any or all of these ventures.

This was the man who now looked Glenda in the eye with the air of an absolute stranger. The other gentlemen glanced at Fenwick, a smile playing upon their lips. On seeing Fenwick's expression, their eyes came back to Glenda with the most terrible disdain.

"Fenwick, my fellow, have you been a bad boy?" said one.

Fenwick broke into a bloated grin, shaking his head merrily.

"Have you been poking your poker in the wrong pot again?" said the man on his other side.

This ribaldry was spoken in a high, jesting tone of voice. It drew a good laugh from his wench and the other two players.

Glenda's eye lingered on the wench, realizing with a chill that her own appearance didn't differ much from this one's.

"Mr. Fenwick, you're a liar and a cheat!" hissed Glenda, trembling with anger.

Fenwick's fellow players were highly amused, pursing their lips in little ooo's of astonishment. One of them nudged Fenwick, speaking loudly. "Had you promised her your purse, you wicked man?"

And another joined in, using the billiard cue in a vulgar pose. "And did she get your man-gold instead of your money-gold?"

Hiccuping with delight, they peered inquisitively at Glenda's belly. She saw her own knuckles turning white on the dark wood.

But they hadn't finished. "You'll need more purses than you've got, Fenwick, to answer every wench who drags her little brat about the island, crying, 'Where's Mr. Fenwick?'" On these last words, the man cupped his hands at his mouth, the way one might shout over a distance.

Another round of laughter passed among them.

Glenda slammed her fist on the edge of the table. "You're an impostor and a damnéd traitor," she snarled, "giving us over to the rule of pirates!"

The smile vanished from Fenwick's face. His eyes widened with alarm. In the same instant, Glenda gave a gasp as her ribcage was stung, once again, by the point of a dirk. Papa was breathing in her ear. "Another word and you'll die."

Glenda hadn't had a better offer all day. She gave Papa a good jab with her elbow, quite expecting to feel the blade go through to her heart.

"Kill me if you will," she went on. "Go ahead, kill me before all these fine witnesses. Is there one among you who cares about the truth?"

The billiard players chuckled, coughing somewhat excessively. Out of nowhere, the memory of Leclair's words came to her, of him explaining that many pirates also had some respectable vocation in Gustavia. She gazed on these flushed, contemptuous faces and felt a chill to the very bone. Perchance each of them had a secret like Fenwick's.

A voice came from the stairs. "Mr. Fenwick, sir!"

Papa had Glenda in a tight clinch, pinning her arms to her side. She saw Fenwick glancing towards the man on the stair, a pasty-looking fellow in a tricorn hat. Fenwick gave a flustered smile, appearing suddenly quite pale. Without another word, he rushed into the street and was gone. The bystanders witnessed his sudden departure with bafflement.

While Papa was wrestling Glenda towards the door, she called out to the fellow on the stair. "Do you know that man?"

The fellow stepped off the stair, removing the tricorn from atop his wig. "Did he think I had a warrant for him?" he smiled.

Papa was still edging Glenda towards the door, showing the other fellow his missing teeth in a most ingenuous grin.

"Yes, I suppose I've known him," said the newcomer. "Mainly through the magistrate. He was our mutual friend."

Recognizing the gentleman's accent, Glenda drew a quick conclusion. "The Swedish magistrate. Has he passed on?"

The stranger nodded, offering Glenda his hand. Papa saw no choice but to let her be, while she laid her hand upon the man's curled index finger.

"I meant to ask Fenwick if he'd heard," said the fellow. He gave a solemn bow. "The name is Hansson."

For half a moment, she had forgotten hers. "Miss Burchill," she said, feeling a flutter of fresh hope. "We attended his memorial today."

"The old man died of a broken heart. I know, because he told me as much. Some years ago, his only child sailed for Boston and was never seen nor heard from again. That was it. Day by day, he began to die."

Hansson's tale had Glenda quite riveted, but she was jolted by a tug at her arm. Papa had, cunningly, stowed his dirk away and was simply insisting that they leave.

"He's a pirate, sir," said Glenda in a steady voice. "Fenwick is a pirate and this man too."

Papa had released Glenda's arm; he was wearing a coy little grin. Hansson replaced his tricorn hat, smiling. "No doubt Fenwick's quite the pirate. Some there are who rob with a mere pistol. Others rob under privilege and charter of a trading company. It's all quite philosophical."

"No," cried Glenda, "he robbed us at gunpoint!"

Hansson shifted his gaze to Papa, then back to Glenda. "I can't speak for this fellow; as for Fenwick, he's not your man," said Hansson, heading for the door. "My wife will be waiting and so I must bid you a good day."

Hansson disappeared into the street and, once again, Glenda's hopes had been dashed.

"We're going upstairs," growled Papa under his breath.

The old man proceeded to drag her towards the far corner. Glenda resisted at first, but was so taken aback by the strength in his arms that she relented. Other guests looked up glancingly from their billiard game or their tankard of ale. Plainly, her predicament was a common sight. As they clambered up the noisy stairway, Glenda feared the worst. What manner of punishment did Papa have in mind? Would he be capable, still, of assaulting her chastity? What would he perform on her in those bleak rooms?

"Kill me!" she heard herself sobbing. "Kill me and may God Almighty have mercy on my soul!"

They reached the top landing and a short hallway with several doors. Glenda launched herself at Papa, knocking him off balance. He fell to his knees, yet his hand was like a vise on her lower arm. She couldn't have fled without dragging him, anchor-like, in her wake.

"What do you want with me?" she hissed, like a cornered animal.

"Your dresses," gasped Papa, pausing for breath after every few syllables. "I need to... I'm going to... look for... the dresses."

This was, at least, some slight comfort to Glenda. Papa was not about to punish her. Not yet, anyway. Maybe he would leave that to Leclair. Glenda began to imagine new horrors back on La Fourchue, but banished such thoughts. After all, she was going to have something fresh to wear.

As she turned down the hall to follow Papa, a dog-eared placard caught her eye. It was nailed to the flat post at the top of the stairs. Across the top were large block letters spelling the word "Reward"; underneath, the promised amount was shown as "Twenty thousand pieces of eight". But the first thing she had noticed was the name "Captain Leclair". Above it was a drawing; a crude, incomplete rendering with no resemblance to speak of. But the black bandana was shown the way she'd seen him wear it, rolled into a headband on his brow. In a flash, it was quite clear to Glenda why Leclair couldn't be the one to escort her.

There came a sudden yelp and a stranger's voice swearing a blaze of obscenities. Papa was inspecting the rooms; he slammed the door on whatever he'd seen and moved on.

Glenda followed behind. How could there be a dressmaker's shop tucked away in the drab attic of this alehouse? Papa was waving for her to hurry. Glenda hastened her step and followed him through one of the doors. They were standing in a smallish room with a three-drawer commode, a dishevelled divan and a straightback chair.

"There's a placard out there," said Glenda, "with Leclair's name on it."

Papa's eye met hers. "Now do you understand why he couldn't be here?"

He hobbled around the foot of the bed and picked a crumpled silk dress off the back of the chair. The bodice was of a garish pink with feathery, sable trim, reinforced to hoist the bosom high above the bustline.

"That takes care of that," he mumbled and tossed the dress at Glenda.

She shrunk away, loath to touch any particle of this tainted room, this lair of sinful appetites and vice.

"Your meat pie is waiting," said Papa, showing her the door.

Glenda looked at the old man's wizened features, the dark eyes hiding beneath his brow. She stooped to the floor, forcing her fingers into the sheer silk, picking up the dress. It was perhaps the final degradation of soiling her hands with this vile dress that gave her another rush of strength.

In a flash, her fists had a firm grip on the fabric and she rushed Papa, wrapping the dress across his face. With a loud grunt he stumbled and fell against the bed, catching the sharp edge in his back. The breath went out of him and he stayed seated, blinded and gasping for air.

While Papa was thrashing around with the dress, Glenda had

a moment to reach into the old man's shirt. She found the dirk. As she pulled it out, Papa was deft enough to clamp his hand around the blade. Had she been of a more ruthless disposition, she could've ripped the dirk away, slashing his vein wide open. Instead she let go of it and was free of him, throwing herself at the door, racing down the hallway.

She imagined herself to be quite a sight as she came bolting down the creaky stairs, her hair tumbling every which way, eyes darting madly for any sign of danger. But the customers downstairs didn't seem to take much notice. Perhaps they knew that Funck would climb the stairs, by and by, to clean up whatever was waiting to be cleaned up.

Her heart in her throat, Glenda made for the door. The dark outline of a man stepped through the sunlit doorway. She was ready to knock him over but he stopped her short, his two hands jabbing each of her shoulders.

"Time to go home," she heard him say.

It was the smooth, guileless face of Emilio.

ငဒ သ

OF THE ARCHIPELAGO

ଌ ଓ

GOD'S HEART

℘ ℃

Olof starts towards the gunwale. From behind, Raoul's hand rides his shoulder like a cast-iron anchor, impelling him to continue even when nothing is left in his knees to hold him up.

The northeasterly has deserted them. More nauseous than before, the infections of the swamp have risen on the fetid air, filling his nostrils. Not a breath steals across the sandbar to puff the vapours inland. He cannot get his breath, lurches sideways, his body slipping away from his mind. Strong arms plunge in from everywhere. His lip is smeared with sweat from someone's muscled forearm, as they hoist him once more to his feet.

"Them's good boots," hollers the fellow with a cleft upper lip.

The half-grown boy steps forward, hair across his eyes. His trousers are back on, but the sight of his lean torso fills Olof with a sinking, crunching ache. The boy gets a grip on Olof's boot and wrenches it off his leg.

Big Raoul clamps a hand on him again. Like a mongrel in the back alley, the boy tugs at the other boot. In bare feet, Olof stands on the dank timbers, his dull gaze sweeping the deck. A baffling lot, they are. Polite, ceremonious, almost reverential now. Wiping the brandy from their breath, even while it is dancing like a dervish in the glazed crystal of their eyes. The boy, looking flushed and greatly overwhelmed, bends his head to his armpit to stifle a belch, but ends up coughing.

Even on this deck that reeks from spilling of rum, a hush descends at the approach of death. The insolent peep show of the living, watching for a soul to arise from perished flesh. The execution. The flesh which has been his body.

A roll of thunder passes slowly overhead, smothered in the cloak of unyielding cloud. Above the mute assembly of pirates,

Olof squints at the sky. Drab and solemn, glowering with pesti-lence. All along the swampy curvature of the anchorage, not a single lick against the shore. Even from the open sea beyond the low sandspit, not the faintest boom of breakers. It occurs to him that every last thing, flesh or wind or water, is smitten with silence. Only the broad mirror of the anchorage is still rippling, still busy with the surge that will suck his body into the deeps.

His cheek is brushed by a memory, a sudden presence of a warmth that wasn't cruel, wasn't poxy like this one, but issuing gently from the grey stone that he used to embrace. When he had endured a thrashing from his father or when his playmates would hide themselves from him because his papa was a captain of the Royal Suédois and not a farmer like theirs, that's when he would walk away, walk up from the village to the great moraine. With his heart so low that it could've poured out of his boot, he would wander the windswept hillside until he came to his rock, a lone boulder of grey granite three times his own height. This giant had been rumbled along by the ancient ice, marooned when the glacier turned back. He would kneel before it, spreading wide his little arms. Thus he attempted to hold it close, embrace it while touching his cheek to the rugged granite.

Nothing could soothe his spirit like the warm lull of the granite with its tufts of scratchy lichen. His ear snug to the rock, he could hear the ancient heart beating within. It was his secret all those years. He never told a soul that he had found the rock with God's heart in it. It was his greatest, fondest mystery. A decade later, while training in Berlin, it occurred to him that it was himself he had listened to, his own pulse he had marvelled at.

"Step up," says Big Raoul in a Spaniard's English.

Rippling water, brooding sky, all vanishes when Olof's forehead is jerked back by the sling of a taut bandana, stretched between Raoul's two fists. It plunges him into darkness, wrenching his neck as Big Raoul ties it behind the ears. The musty rag on his face, his hands bound behind his back, he braces himself for the end.

"Step up."

He brings his left foot forward to where he saw the crates piled beneath the gangplank. His toe encounters wooden slats and, stepping onto the crate, Raoul's hand releases him. By this, he knows how little is left. His naked foot seeks a second step and finds the higher crate, the slats giving a sharp cry beneath his weight.

From behind comes the brazen click of Raoul's pistol being cocked. With a faint sense of surprise, he experiences his own calmness. A warm lull of granite. Parrot beneath a shroud. In the dark of his blindfold, this picture fills his mind, prodding him to a new verge of giddiness. A caged parrot reduced to serenity by the dropping of a shroud. His soul has come to rest; the parrot snoozing in its false nocturne.

Only the body is still stirring, climbing at last onto the plank. His left knee is stopped by a waist-high barrier. He remembers the grain barrels stacked for counter-weight at one end. Edging backward, he turns toward the water and uses the left foot along the side of the plank, guiding himself along the length of it. As the plank begins to toss under his feet, he knows he has crossed the mark where it straddles the gunwale. He is walking with nothing else between himself and the eddying waters.

All this while, the pirates have choked back the derision and profanity lurking behind their cock-eyed wonderment. As Big Raoul's arm rises, levelling the pistol at his solitary target, the men show signs of impatience.

"Now, captain. A ball in his head!"

The lone figure has stopped, knees bent and slightly stooped, using his toe to warn him of the end of the plank. With his arms pinned behind his back, he could be a crane or heron poised to snap its lunch from the teeming water.

"Your prayers, sir."

"And say them well," a comrade joins in. "Them that's dead should stay dead."

And another, spurred by the other two. "Aye, so they should! Don't you come back up with water in your veins."

There are shudders and shivers among the men. At the head of this jagged congregation of bandits, Big Raoul finds his aim and closes the other eye. In that moment when his lungs have paused in order to allow him full concentration, the grim sky splits from top to bottom.

A crack of thunder strikes the gangplank in a twist of cold fire.

It is an event of such blinding brevity as the eye of the beholder may only guess at. As Raoul's heart jumps, he pulls the trigger and the pistol booms across the lagoon. But he's too late. There is no one to receive his ball.

The plank is a smoking stump. Olof's body has vaulted through the air.

ॐ ৡ

CAPTAIN WOOLSLEY'S AFFECTIONS

☙ ❧

And so Glenda got her dress.

The story was heard again and again, first from Papa and then from those who had heard it from Papa. It grew in the telling, as any good yarn must, until Glenda had stabbed Papa in the neck with his own dirk, set fire to Funck's alehouse and run halfway up the mountain before Emilio could catch her. These elaborations were enough to keep the pirates occupied on the voyage home.

But Papa wanted to be alone with his chief. Leclair locked the door on Glenda, leaving her to sleep in the same cabin that had previously been hers.

He walked forward to the galley, where Matt and Whiskers and a couple of others had made themselves comfortable in their hammocks. Their hushed conversation ceased as Leclair went by. Pierre sat cross-legged with awl and twine. He had hauled an old canvas from the sail closet and was mending the jib.

Papa was seated on the stairs next to the foremast. He nursed a cup of rum, looking rather morose.

"She's safely stowed," said Leclair.

The old sea-cook gave him a lingering look, then got to his feet grumbling.

"What's on your mind, Papa?"

"In the cabin," he said.

Leclair paused at Papa's brick oven and reached into the hanging pot, scooping up a ladleful of warm rum for himself. Then he followed Papa to his little cubby alongside the foremast. The door shut behind them.

Papa eased himself down on the narrow berth, cradling the cup between bony fingers. Leclair leaned back against the door, his arms crossed. Their faces were no more than five feet apart, half of which was the height difference of their positions. Nothing was said for some time. The ship rolled gently side to side. Big Raoul had them coasting on a light southeasterly, sails nice and free, which would land them perfectly at the inlet on La Fourchue.

Papa looked Leclair flush in the eye. "The magistrate is dead."

Leclair didn't budge. In the silence between them, the ocean whispered something they both understood. Through the wall came a quick burst of Whiskers' laugh, followed by some sort of harmless, half-hearted scuffle.

Papa tipped the rum through his sieve of yellowed fangs. Leclair had set himself to perusing the wall above Papa's berth. The two of them had a way of existing in close proximity of each other without a need for words. Things were allowed to ripen, to grow from within.

"It doesn't change anything," whispered Papa.

Though Leclair wasn't looking at him, Papa could see that he was breathing deeply; that, perhaps, something *was* changing.

"We ran into Fenwick," he hastened to add. Then he spoke very low, choosing his words carefully. "I should've cut her throat."

Leclair's eye met Papa's. "What happened?"

"Fenwick got away just in time. This woman is trouble."

Their words were urgent, yet they slipped them to each other softly, in a low murmur that must never rise above the casual.

Leclair leaned forward from the waist, touching his hand to the other's shoulder. "You're getting old, Papa."

"And you're getting out of hand."

Leclair raised his chin for a long, slow draught of rum.

"We take no prisoners," explained Papa. "Remember? And since when do we send off some English lord in a rowboat, hale and hearty and full aware that his sweet coz is in our clutches? And if that weren't bad enough, you're keeping her all to yourself." Papa sat up on the berth. "That's not in the articles."

"Miss Burchill is none of their concern," said Leclair, licking the rum from his lips.

"That's what I mean," insisted the old man. "By the articles she is."

"Maybe you should stay on shore."

Papa looked at him for a moment, then lowered his gaze into the open palm of his hand. "Maybe I will."

A silence came back between them; any comfort had gone out of it.

"Chloe needs me," croaked Papa. "And the sheep too."

Leclair turned slowly to the door, ready to leave.

"There's a prize on your head," muttered Papa, avoiding Leclair's gaze. "Upstairs at Funck's. It'll be at the Wall House and everywhere else too."

Leclair spoke over his shoulder. "How much?"

"Twenty thousand."

Leclair stood for a moment looking down at his boots.

"By God's blood," he mused, "I've never known my true worth."

"It's not funny," said Papa, chastising. "You'd better move on. You've been too long on La Fourchue."

Leclair opened the door. "It was beginning to feel like home," he said and left.

⚜ ⚜

Hair tumbling about her shoulders, Glenda rushed directly at the door, concealing the dirk within a fold of her dress.

At that moment, the door swung open. Glenda knew she mustn't slow down or the alehouse would win her back, she would be drawn back into its dim bowels, her own will swallowed by the all-pervasive indifference within. The man in the doorway, darkly outlined against the sun, must not impede her.

She rushed him, full force, but was rudely jolted by his two arms braced on each of her shoulders. Through tears of panic, she looked up to see Emilio's youthful face. He was saying something to her but she had no time, nor desire, to listen. From the fold in her dress, she drew Papa's dirk and thrust it straight into his abdomen. She felt a moment's surprise at how easily the blade went in, vaguely sickened that he had no ribs, nothing to shield himself.

In a sudden convulsion, Emilio dug his fingers into her shoulder, his body reeling away from her. Glenda helped him along with a good, stout push and leapt through the door.

She was free. Blinded at first by the sun, she raced madly over the cobblestones. Before her, the town spread like a shimmering, secretive mirage. It felt unreal, almost sinister, unearthly, inhabited by sleepwalkers without eyes.

As she was running, Glenda tried to glance over her shoulder to see if she was being pursued. What she saw was Leclair, not fifty feet behind. He was standing on the esplanade, between her and Funck's Billiards, waving to her.

She looked ahead to see where she was going.

Then she looked quickly back, her heart pounding. Leclair was there, at half the distance now, still waving. Any closer and she would knife him too. She strained her legs to the utmost and threw another glance behind her. He wasn't waving as if to bring her back. He wasn't even coming after her. His arm was waving goodbye.

Was he saying goodbye? Did he want her to run? Was she supposed to escape? Was she performing his will? Was her will his will? Or was her will something other?

Before her eyes opened, it occurred to her that she had been dreaming.

Glenda heard Matt and Raoul shouting overhead. There was a

loud crash of water which could only be the dropping of the skiff, unless somebody's body was being dumped overboard.

Had she slept all this way? Glenda sat up on the narrow berth, shivering. He hadn't even given her a blanket. She rubbed her arms vigorously, trying to get some heat into her body.

Leclair. What was he doing in her dream? That's not how it had happened. Emilio had been sent ahead to check up on Papa. He said he had ridden from some bay or inlet on the far side of the island, arriving at Funck's Billiards at a very propitious moment. She had glowered at him without answering, as he led her back inside and managed to discover, from the tapster, where he might find Papa.

On the stairs they met him, still carrying the crimson dress in his fist. Contrary to what Glenda had feared, the old man did not mete out any punishment. He had looked Emilio in the eye and shaken his head, waving his arm as if to say he washed his hands of her. Once again, Glenda had to suppose that it would be up to Leclair to decide on the most fitting consequence for her intractable wilfulness.

She felt annoyed by the fanciful flimsy of her dream; annoyed and strangely agitated. Fanciful indeed. A sweet reprieve from the looming prospect of Leclair's wrath. And yet, why had he chosen Papa to be her custodian? Some compulsion kept prodding her with this same question, as though unsatisfied by her previous conjectures. If indeed he loved the old man, as it would certainly seem, then why willingly subject him to the burdens, and even perils, of this assignment? And moreover, since he had singled her out as the sole captive besides Woolsley, why would he send her on such a poorly guarded excursion? She searched for some method in his actions, no matter how reprehensible. Some solid, sensible underpinning. But none appeared to her.

The door opened and it was Emilio.

"The boat is ready."

Glenda felt a pang of guilt rush upon her as she recalled the dream of Papa's dirk sliding effortlessly into Emilio's chest. She composed herself and followed him to the deck.

With greater ease than before, she climbed into the skiff. Matt was at the oars while Whiskers sat in the bottom. In the bow was Leclair, looking at her all the while, evidently not compelled to utter a single word.

It was dark and the island looked harsh and forbidding. A slight chill swept across the water. The oars creaked on their pegs. Glenda glanced over her shoulder and noticed only six or seven others remaining on the schooner's deck. She wondered if the rest had gone ashore at Gustavia to lead, for a while, a pretense of an edified life.

"You're to blame for all this," she said at last.

Leclair was eyeing her again, his gaze flinty and remote. Matt rowed silently, gazing off towards the schooner.

"Wasn't it a bit ill-considered to send an old man as my only guard for the day?" she continued when, apparently, no response was forthcoming.

"That's why I sent Emilio after," said Leclair, unruffled.

Matt stopped the oars in mid-air, giving a forced little grin. "You never sent nothin'," he said in the silence of the oars. "Emilio went because Raoul was refusing to start the accounts until someone went."

Matt dropped his oars into the black water and continued to row. And then, almost as an afterthought, Leclair said, "Did *you* want to be away for the settling of the account, Matt?"

There wasn't a peep from Matt; only his set jaw and his fierce eye as he propelled them towards shore.

"Only Papa would trust me to get him his share," mumbled Leclair, almost to himself.

Not another word was spoken. The boat ran aground and unloaded Leclair, Whiskers and then Glenda. She was gratified to note that Leclair had stopped trying to offer her the courtesy of his arm. Matt headed back to take on the rest of the men.

There was no fire lit inside the house. It looked grim and haunted as they approached. Indeed, thought Glenda to herself, its present inhabitants were lost souls in an endless night of which she feared she might become a part. As Leclair had no further instructions for her, she hurried upstairs and shut the door thankfully, alone again in this peculiar room which was, for now, her shelter against the tempest.

Without undressing, she threw her weary body on the bed and rolled in under the covers.

CR SO

When Glenda awoke, she had no idea what time it was nor how long she'd been sleeping.

Something had roused her and, now, there it was again. A very light tapping came from the door. Glenda gave her head a shake.

Yes, she was awake.

She brushed the hair from her eyes and looked towards the door; again, a light knock.

"Who is it?" she whispered.

There was no answer. Glenda felt a tingle of dread coursing through her arms and into her fingertips. This wasn't Leclair. She certainly knew him well enough not to expect a knock on the door.

Maybe Papa. Had he decided to punish her after all? Or was it one of the others, unable to curb his appetite any longer? Watching the door for any clue, she got out of bed and tiptoed across the floor.

"Who's there?" she demanded in a loud whisper.

Without warning, the door swung open and a dark, stocky figure stepped inside. She halted, gasping, and was about to scream when she noticed the finger he was holding across his lips.

It was Captain Woolsley.

She was baffled. Such a possibility hadn't even occurred to her.

He shut the door behind him. "It's me," he whispered, somewhat redundantly.

Glenda came to him, tears stinging her eyes. He raised his arms to her shoulders and drew her, a little awkwardly, into an embrace.

"It's alright, m'dear. It's alright."

They stood in the faint moonlight, without moving.

"Where were you?" she sobbed against his shoulder.

"In the back room downstairs," he whispered.

"Have they hurt you?"

Woolsley shushed her gently. "I'm alright," he answered. "But what about you?"

The chin against his chest gave an affirmative nod. Woolsley led her to the bed and they sat side by side.

"God be praised," sighed Glenda. "I thought you were dead."

"As long as they've not..." Woolsley reached carefully for the words, "...not stained your virtue."

"I'm fine," said Glenda, thankful that Leclair had only gazed upon her.

"I couldn't forgive myself," hissed Woolsley, "if any harm had come to you. Your mother is a very dear soul. I promised her to bring you safely to St. Kitts."

Glenda held him closer, his portly belly in her ribs. "You've done all you can."

"She's such a dear soul," continued Woolsley. "When we return, I'm of a mind to..." Again he halted, struggling with his thoughts. "I'm only a sea captain but an honest one. And seeing as Mrs. Heywood might have use for a man around the house, a good honest man..."

Glenda looked up at him. The Captain showed his teeth in a coy grin. Glenda returned his smile.

Her mother a sea captain's wife. As far as Glenda was aware, they'd been introduced casually through Devon's shipping ventures and on two or three subsequent occasions. Glenda had known nothing of the Captain's budding affections.

"We're leaving tonight, m'lady."

She stared at him, incredulous.

"They're not drinking tonight," whispered Woolsley. "The downstairs is full of sleeping bodies. But we can use those doors," he said, pointing to the French windows.

Glenda shook her head. "There's nothing but water outside."

Woolsley nodded slyly, as much as to say he had taken this into account. He slunk across the room. Very slowly, he pushed the doors open and moonlight seeped over his feet and into the room. The night was very still, the bare rock bathed in silver. From the lush groves behind the house came an incessant, wavering shrillness of unseen night creatures.

Glenda was at his shoulder now. "But we'll never get off the island."

Woolsley was inspecting the reservoir below, which measured about three-quarters full. He saw, now, the protruding joists which remained from the erstwhile balcony.

"True, I can't sail the schooner by myself," he mumbled, "but the two of us can weigh anchor and cut her loose. While they're busy being stranded, we'll drift out to sea."

Glenda hadn't imagined such a thing in her wildest hopes. The Captain was making it sound somewhat sensible. He was now on his hands and knees, one elbow on the threshold, showing her his copious posterior. He reached below for a long plank which had remained, upright, against the side of the house. He clasped it with one hand and, passing his hands down either side, heaved it up to their level, the lower end dripping wet. It must be over a foot wide.

"There now," he mumbled, wheezing a little.

Still on his knees, Woolsley manoeuvered the long plank with both arms. Keeping it snugly to the wall, he pushed it along until the end was past the protruding joists. Now he was able to slide it sideways onto a joist, using the latter for a brace. He pushed the plank even farther, releasing his end so that it pivoted neatly down onto the stone-and-mortar rim of the reservoir.

Glenda looked on with anticipation. Woolsley waited now, to see if anyone had been roused by the minimal noise from his covert operation. All was calm; even the hidden serenaders in the dark had taken no notice.

Woolsley looked at Glenda. She looked at Woolsley. A faint smile passed between them. Woolsley grasped the end of the plank and pushed down, first on the left corner, then on the right. It was wobbling a bit, so he tipped the far end up off the reservoir's wall and swivelled it a few inches along the joist before he let it down again. This time, it lay more securely; there was an incline from the joist down to the reservoir, but steady nevertheless. The water had put a warp in the far end of the plank but it couldn't be helped. This was as good as it was going to get.

"I'll go first," whispered Woolsley.

Glenda gave his arm a quick squeeze. Clinging to the doorframe, his boot reached for the beginning of the plank. He began to shift his weight gingerly, testing the joist and the plank once again. Changing his hold on the doorframe, he brought his shoulders around to the outside and eased himself forward onto the plank, perched on the joist about four feet above water.

Glenda saw her portly Captain assaying the plank. She sent a silent prayer to God above. It occurred to her that there might be quite a wind at sea. She tiptoed back inside to fetch her make-shift shawl. As she swooped it up from the corner post on the bed, a pistol shot rang out. She jumped with fright, clasping the shawl to her chest.

Another shot followed and someone bellowing, *"Sancta Maria!"*

There came a third shot and, a moment later, a great crash of water.

Glenda felt all the colour drain from her cheeks. She dragged herself leadenly to the French windows and looked out. The plank was empty, as she knew it would be.

From the corner of the house burst a sudden commotion as the pirates arrived, Matt running about angrily while Whiskers and another man were picking Raoul off the ground. Raoul had a dazed look, still clutching the pistol and bleeding from his chest.

"Where did he get that goddamn pistol?" she heard him yelling.

Glenda's eyes had shunned the sight of the reservoir, but now she had to see for herself. Her Captain was stretched, face down, in the shallow water, swirls of black issuing from his head, swirls which, she knew, would prove to be a deep crimson in the morning sun.

"That's our hostage, right there," growled Matt. "What good is a dead hostage?"

Raoul glared at him darkly.

"Just look at him," mused Whiskers, unconcerned. "What a way to die. A captain on the high seas and he dies in the reservoir!"

Whiskers and a couple of the other men burst out laughing, but not for long.

Into their midst walked Leclair and the laughter died abruptly. In the wink of an eye, every man wore an expression of pained earnestness.

Glenda's legs wouldn't hold, so she had sunk down by the doorpost, staring blankly into space. Leclair surveyed the moonlit scene, examining the entire spectacle, glancing up at the huddled form of Glenda in the gaping doorway. A hush had come upon them all. Even the forest was silent.

Briefly, inadvertently, Woolsley was paid his last respects.

CR ЯD

INDIGO

ಐ ಅ

Each time he tries, the darkness begins to throb with a bluish crimson flame. The consumptive rawness burns in his lung, snares his breathing. Bright bursts of pain shoot through his head. His throat refuses to do it. There's no sound left in him. But his only way to endure is to scream again.

Olof remembers his own screaming later. It's not a sound. His voice is long dead. For him, screaming has no sound; it's merely a sustained spasm of the throat. He remembers these spasms, repeating themselves unto utter extinction, from which he wakes, still breathing, with prayers of thanksgiving. But he has no idea how long he's been dozing. Or where he is.

There is a hillside. Three stone-and-mortar reservoirs sit side by side, terraced like the steps of a giant's staircase misplaced in the bush.

At the bottom is a fourth reservoir, small and quite shallow. It stands out from the rest; it doesn't belong with the deep green arrows of grass and foliage or with the sparkling water in the higher reservoirs. It gapes at the sky like a rectangular eye of deep, deep blue; a mongrel gem, half sapphire and half amethyst, set among lesser colours. A blue deeper than nature. A blue wrung from nature by human hands.

She walks up the dusty slope beside the giant's staircase. Every day, in the quivering heat, Chloe walks between the reservoirs, inspecting the long, waxy leaves floating, since the day before, on the second highest level. She watches them yield up their form and colour to the warm water. It means fermentation has begun. She must open the sluice-gate to drain this active water into the next reservoir.

Before picking up the long staff, Chloe shades her eyes with her hand. Fifty yards downhill begins the field where she can see other slaves bending over the indigo bush, filling their baskets with precious leaf. Their singing fills the stifling heat, singing the vastness of their sorrow and the unbreakable crystal of their joy, the songs that link them, chain by chain, to the slave ship and the distant mother-mouth of Africa.

She lifts the staff and, with both arms, whirls it round and round in the water. Several minutes on end she must weave and wind, watching the inky dye settling like silt to the bottom.

Meanwhile, Akeeba has arrived with two baskets full, dumping them into another compartment of the second reservoir. From the high reservoir at the top, Akeeba fills his compartment with new water.

Chloe glances toward the tamarind tree. The white man is still leaning against the trunk, his wide-brimmed hat pulled low over the eyes, the heavy cane in his right hand. From under the hat, his gaze is sharp as a spear; it's never far from her, or from any of them.

When the water comes to rest, she'll stir it up again. In the silence after the song, she'll hear the water murmuring softly around her staff. After the fifth time, she lifts a tiny shutter. The clear waste water seeps slowly into the bushes. On the sloped bottom is the inky sludge she's been waiting for. She bends low to open the final valve. At the downhill side, the dark silt emerges into the fourth reservoir.

She trowels the grainy paste into the corners, like an eyelid lifting slowly to reveal again the sapphire's gaze. There are three of them, including her friend Winnie, who tend the fire and keep the pot boiling. Into the pot goes the inky paste, spooned with ladles or cupped hands. The boys will come around to pour the bubbling indigo into their little cones, straining out the blue pulp from the last of the steaming juice.

In the shade from a straw roof, they dump the hot pulp into boxes, using trowels to press the indigo into a solid block. There it will sit, cooling overnight. A few weeks later, it will re-appear on a wholesaler's shelf in Paris, or maybe Stockholm or Amsterdam.

It dawns on Olof that he isn't dreaming. He is listening. And Chloe has just told him the story of her life.

There are other voices too, though mostly Chloe's. Her words flow trippingly, but the voice is thin and meek as though she had moth's wings for lungs. He wishes he could see her. He has that wish. He's now capable of thoughts beyond mere dying. He would like to look at her. Even now that he wants to, he cannot. Because he can't see. He hasn't left the darkness where all he heard was himself screaming. He's still groping in that void, which throbs with crimson whenever the pain returns.

He touched his hand to his face, his fluttering eyelash. He found his eyes open. But he has no use of them.

"Lift his shoulder. Turn his face this way."

Once again, Olof is roused from a dreamless sleep. This is the other voice, not exactly ill-mannered but void of any striving, any urge to win favour or persuade, any grace notes of compassion or enthusiasm. Even when he's comparing Chloe's skin to dark molasses or her breast to a ripe mango, the old voice is flat and unsentimental. Chloe calls him Normand, stressing the second syllable.

They think no one is listening. Olof has heard them making love, quite sedately but with utter devotion in their breath. He was content, for those moments, to be blind.

Now they're pawing him again, shifting his neck and shoulder on the stiff fleece.

"I have coconut and manioc," she's saying. "Bring some aloe."

Olof is sprawled on his belly, a skin smelling like sheep tucked under his face and chest. He can't guess how long he's been like this. Something cool and wet trickles across his elbow, down his ribs.

Normand's boot scrapes the threshold but she stops him.

"And moco leaf. Some moco leaf too." Her voice is right next to Olof.

Normand's steps fade away in the stillness.

"Don't talk to Normand about the English," says Chloe for no apparent reason. "He come from up north. When he ready, he tell you."

If she thinks Olof is capable of a reply, she certainly doesn't wait for it. She talks to him as if to her cat. But he heard another voice once, one that she saves for private moments with her Father in heaven. At first he thought they had a visitor. After lying awake half the night, he was beginning to drift off when a voice reached him, moving about on the other side of the wall, asking her Father's blessing on Normand and Winnie and on her blind guest, her voice soaring to such resonance as he has never heard again.

Olof winces when another cold dribble slips along the neck and collarbone. It must be Chloe's doing. It occurs to him that she's spreading something on his back. It frightens him, only because he can feel nothing at all.

CR SO

COUNTERFEIT

℘ ℜ

She made Leclair promise that Captain Woolsley would be buried in the deeper soil of the forest.

It was done accordingly, the following afternoon, but Glenda didn't move from her settee all day or the day after. Papa had some food for her - a bowl of crab chowder and, at dusk, some skillet-fried fish with calaloo leaves - but she was indifferent to it all. Her eyes kept straying to the reservoir; she had been mistaken. The morning sun had shown no trace of pink in the water, yet in her mind it would never go away. Their only water supply was contaminated with Woolsley, like Jehovah's curse upon the Sodomites.

The searing sun climbed to its zenith, yet she was cold to the bone. The day slipped into the west. A sea breeze stole softly through the broken glass and fanned her face; she felt like nothing more than a sieve or a broken window.

That's how Leclair found her at twilight. He had poked his head in the door a few times, but she seemed so oddly strained and preoccupied that he'd gone back downstairs. Raoul and Matt, in particular, had been badgering him all afternoon about the riotousness and discontent among the men. Leclair had turned to Raoul, at last, and asked him who, in his opinion, should be blamed for the shooting of their precious hostage. When no reply was immediately forthcoming, Leclair strode up the stairs to check on their controversial guest.

She was on the settee again, slumped with both arms in her lap, her head bowed. Leclair closed the door behind him and flung himself on one of the chairs. He felt no rush to speak.

As the light was waning, Glenda receded from him even further, becoming a mere outline in the dim window. Behind her came the flickering glow from the cooking fire downstairs.

Leclair opened his mouth to speak, but her thin, remote voice interceded. "Are you happy now?"

His jaw closed again, as he waited to hear more.

He didn't have to wait long. "This wound you spoke of. The world is bleeding, you said, or something. All the world is wounded, except me." A subtle shift in the outline of her head told Leclair that she had turned to look at him. "You've certainly rectified that little oversight. Am I hurting enough now? Have you done enough to break me? My cousin's dead on the ocean. Me trapped in this rat's den with no hope of deliverance. Captain Woolsley was most wilfully murdered and my mother bereft of..." Glenda's shadow rocked to and fro. "He would've been her friend. A dear, dear friend to her."

Leclair waited for her to finish. He felt the old fire mounting inside his ribs. Once she was silent, he waited a while longer before speaking.

"The violation of the body is not the worst," he said. "It's nothing like the violation of soul."

"What are you saying?" Her voice rose impatiently. "Woolsley is gone! His dear, blessed soul is gone."

"It was not my intention he should die. He would've fetched me ten thousand pieces-of-eight."

"But it was your intention he should be kidnapped and kept in this pit of adders."

By now, Leclair's tongue was cleaving to his throat. His chest was burning. He had to get up from the chair.

"Miss Burchill," he said, breathing deeply. "Woolsley's soul is in heaven. The body is nothing. But fear you him that can destroy body and soul together."

Leclair saw Glenda's dark figure rise from the settee, facing him squarely now. Her left eye glinted with the fire's faint glow.

"Again you say this. I heard it from you once before." She stepped towards him. "What does it mean?"

"It's the same wound," said Leclair, trembling as from a fever. "Nothing can heal it. You'd know what I'm saying if you were hurting enough."

Without warning, Glenda lunged at him like a dark fury, beating him about the head with both arms.

"Stop lecturing me!" she screamed. "I know what this is. I know what I'm feeling! I'm hurting enough! I've had enough of it! I've had enough!"

Leclair took her blows without shielding himself.

At length, Glenda slumped with exhaustion and he held her, lightly, against his shoulder.

"I may have to let you go," murmured Leclair.

Glenda was so taken aback, she could give no reply. All she wanted to do was ask why, but it would've given him altogether the wrong impression. Her body had never weighed so much. She would've fallen if it weren't for his arm.

"I hadn't expected so honorable a notion from you," was all she said.

"It wasn't my plan," said Leclair. "It's my men. We have an article."

"No women?" she assumed.

"No, not quite. But we say no wench or *everyone's* wench."

Another silence ensued. Downstairs, the men were heard calling to each other and heavy steps left the house.

"And your men chose not to have me along?" said Glenda frostily.

"On the contrary," he answered.

In other words, thought Glenda to herself, he would release her if it was the only way to preserve her from the other pirates. She walked away from him, shaking her head, her feet dragging.

From below came Whiskers' voice. "All's well. It's Fenwick."

Glenda drew a quick breath. Leclair came to her, reaching for her hand. Glenda was too weary to resist him now, as he pulled her along to the door and down the stairs.

Only Emilio was still indoors. He was sound asleep, his spiky black hair crushed into the genteel fleurs-de-lis on the wall. A general hubbub issued from the little fire in the yard.

Leclair stepped out with Glenda. By now, it was dark. The firelight danced across the faces. Papa was ladling some soup out of the pot. Matt had made himself comfortable on the ground across from Papa. Big Raoul and Whiskers stood near the edge of the fire's glow, welcoming three men who came walking up from the dark shore.

In front was Fenwick. One of the other two was Bruno.

"You're late," grumbled Raoul, extending his hand.

But Fenwick took no notice of Raoul's hand. His eyes were entirely on Glenda.

"What's she doing here?" exclaimed Fenwick, staring at Glenda with not a trace of amusement.

"Ask the boss," huffed Raoul behind his shoulder.

Papa came up to Fenwick and handed him the bowl of soup. Bruno and his companion moved to the fire to help themselves.

"I can't seem to be rid of this woman," said Fenwick with distaste. "Will you be holding her here?"

"Damned if I know," mumbled Matt from his comfortable recline by the fire.

Fenwick held the bowl up to his chin. While slurping the soup with greedy lips, he looked Leclair frankly in the eye.

"You met Miss Burchill in Gustavia," said Leclair.

Fenwick lowered the bowl, licking the soup off his chin. "Who did you say?"

Glenda pressed her eyes shut.

"This is Miss Burchill," explained Leclair.

"Like hell it is," answered Fenwick.

Glenda opened her eyes just in time to catch his contemptuous gaze.

"She's a Heywood," continued Fenwick. "And her cousin is a man of influence and very little patience. If you wanted the little

lady for yourself, you should've shot him without further ado."
As he spoke, Fenwick walked to the fire and handed his bowl to
Papa for a refill. "You know, Leclair, I don't much care what
prisoners you take or how they're used. The ship is mine, the men
are yours, the gold is ours. It's that simple."

He took a full bowl from Papa and squatted on a little rock at
the edge of the darkness, using a spoon this time. "I've nothing to
do with your band of robbers. I don't want to know anything
about them. But when I'm playing billiards in Gustavia, I don't
wish to be accosted by someone who knows about me and is
ready to tell the world."

There was a silence as the men traded glances with each other.
Some of them were glaring at Glenda; some glances went
furtively to Leclair. He seemed unruffled by Fenwick's litany.

"She's been my personal charge," he said. "So I'm the one to
blame."

"And I do," replied Fenwick directly. "I do."

The stout little man looked across at Leclair with unabashed
hostility.

"We've tried tellin' him," said Matt.

Fenwick did not acknowledge Matt's existence. "I have news
from St. Kitts."

The men looked up in anticipation.

"The Governor has our offer regarding Woolsley. After some
hesitation, he agrees to ten thousand pieces-of-eight." Fenwick
looked around with a triumphant smirk but, curiously, his good
tidings left no imprint on the faces of his listeners.

Again, they were glancing apprehensively at each other. No
one was looking at Big Raoul.

"Well?" croaked Fenwick. "Is it feast or funeral?"

Leclair stepped away from Glenda, walking into the middle of
their circle. "Funeral, sir. Very precisely."

Fenwick's spoon halted in mid-air. He gazed at the downcast
faces, each pleading utter ignorance in the matter.

114

"Raoul couldn't stay his finger from the trigger," said Leclair. "The Captain was buried yesterday."

Fenwick saw no remorse in Raoul's piercing eye. Papa shifted nervously from foot to foot. Matt was sitting up, glancing from Leclair to Fenwick to Big Raoul and back to Fenwick.

Raoul stood his ground, a towering hulk of a man against the black wall of night.

"So we have no hostage," said Fenwick flatly. "Charming. And in order to find Woolsley, the Governor will now bribe my messenger to find out who sent him."

"The devil take Woolsley," growled Raoul. "These are good men, sir, excellent gentlemen. But the likes of you always put the fear of God in 'em, so they can't say what's on their mind. I have no fear of you, sir, struttin' about like a peacock just on account of it being your ship."

Raoul took a breath. Leclair was listening calmly. In the silence, Fenwick slurped his soup loudly, seemingly unaffected by Raoul's words.

Glenda, also, took a deep breath, realizing she hadn't breathed all this while.

"We had a ship before," continued Raoul in his rumbling monotone. "She was old and small but, by God, we carried off some good gold in her. I, for one, want my own ship without the likes of you telling me my business."

"Wait now," said Matt, sitting with his arms clasped across his knee and calves, "we needed a new ship. She was old and leaky, no two ways about it. We all had a vote. Leclair knew where he could get us a ship. Right there, we took the vote."

Fenwick laid his spoon in the bowl and placed them, punctiliously, in the dirt. Everyone waited for him to speak, but he pulled a white kerchief from his shirt sleeve and merely proceeded to wipe the perspiration from his bloated face.

Leclair stood in the centre, his eyes downcast.

"So we had a new ship," roared Big Raoul and pointed at

Fenwick, "but look at the worm that's in it. That's no honest robber. He's an eel, that's what, slippery as an eel. He's got his own gold in St. Maarten, his own factory and his own office. He'll sit in his leather chair all day, tellin' people their business and taking their money. And now he's here, telling us our business because he wants a piece of our money. But I don't need that. I don't need a fence takin' our booty back to market and keeping a third on every dollar. You're not gettin' mine. And I'll sleep under hatches tonight, till we get some fresh air around here."

Big Raoul turned on his heel and stalked off towards the shore, his broad shoulders fading in the night.

The threshold gave a sudden creak and Leclair turned around to discover Emilio hanging about the doorway, his eyes drunk with sleep, looking altogether clueless. Matt had laid his head back into his hands and was peering up at the stars.

"Fetch me some rum, would you, boy?" said Fenwick.

Emilio went back inside. Bruno and Whiskers and another man settled on a log, their backs to the fire. The other two pirates met Emilio returning in the doorway and stepped inside the house.

"Do you know about Cederhök?" asked Leclair.

Emilio was dangling a full jug in one hand and two mugs in the other.

"I was at the funeral," said Fenwick, nodding. "Didn't understand a bloody word, but very affecting. Everyone was touched."

Leclair took his rum from Emilio and brought it to his lips directly.

"He was a grand old man, he was," mused Fenwick, taking a careful sip of his rum. "Better than most."

Fenwick and Leclair looked each other in the eye. The Englishman raised his mug. "Here's to the old man. May he rest in peace."

He had a toast for everything.

Leclair raised his mug. "Better than most," he echoed.

They drank a silent toast. The fire was dying, flickering in the cool breeze.

Glenda was overwhelmed and silent. She had stepped back against the house, bracing her drained body on the clapboard wall.

"Right," said Fenwick, getting back to business. "Well, all is not lost."

Leclair looked at him, perplexed.

Fenwick beckoned him to approach. "What I mean to say is," he went on in a lower voice, "do you still want that ten thousand?"

Leclair stopped about five feet from Fenwick, observing his round, animated face. "What are you proposing?"

"A counterfeit," chuckled Fenwick gleefully. "That is, I mean, if you want your money. Give them a counterfeit of Woolsley." He nodded towards the fire. "That fellow Whiskers will do fine. Make your arrangements carefully, so that you'll be gone with the prize before they discover their mistake."

Leclair was clearly amused, the corners of his mouth lifting.

"The worst that would happen is they might come chasing after," said Fenwick, leaning forward and looking Leclair earnestly in the eye. "But then, they're chasing you already, did you know that? There's a prize on your head."

Leclair nodded. "And I never knew my true worth."

Fenwick gave a quiet, wheezy laugh. "There you go. We never know our own worth in this life. Our epitaph will have nicer things to say than anything we heard in our lifetime." Fenwick took a deep draft of the rum now.

Leclair gazed towards the anchorage but there was no moon and nothing much except darkness.

"Be serious now," resumed Fenwick, ever attributing his own banter to the other person. "'Tis also true that we don't know the true worth of this life until we're about to depart it. The grim reaper is a master of nostalgia. So have a care to save yourself,

Leclair. Don't go too far in this."

"It could work," said he. "We'll dig up the captain and take back his uniform. It should fit Whiskers very well."

Glenda couldn't believe her ears. Pistolling Woolsley like a rabid dog hadn't been enough. They were now getting ready to desecrate his grave.

"Have you no shame!" she called out.

"Look," said Fenwick quite affably, "Woolsley won't mind, now will he?"

Glenda was speechless. She turned and rushed into the house.

But another voice came from the fireside log, a voice which, not surprisingly, belonged to Whiskers himself. "Begging your pardon, sir, I couldn't help overhearing..."

"Shame on you," said Fenwick. "for eavesdropping on a private meeting."

Whiskers hemmed and hawed, shifting nervously on his log. "I didn't mean to," he protested.

"Well, then," persisted Fenwick, "go to. About your own business."

Whiskers obeyed and turned back to Bruno.

From the far side of the fire came Matt's voice. "I believe you had somethin' more to say, didn't you, Whiskers?"

Fenwick turned his face again to the three men at the fire.

Whiskers found himself greatly embarrassed; a blush came to his cheeks. Bruno nudged him supportively. Whiskers glanced at Fenwick, then looked over to Matt who had lifted up his head long enough to wink encouragingly.

"I just... I was just sittin' here," stammered Whiskers, his eyes downcast, "havin' a good old conversation when I hear my name. You said Whiskers, didn't you? And something about wearing the Captain's uniform, didn't you?"

Leclair and Fenwick looked at each other. The cat, it seemed, was out of the bag.

"We're in a bit of a fix, you see," said Fenwick. "To foil the

Governor, we need someone with a touch of class. Someone with the Captain's manly, portly stature. Someone, I should say, with the stride of a lion. I haven't seen that in any of the men, excepting yourself."

"I ain't wearin' no dead man's uniform," insisted Whiskers.

"When you signed on the account," said Leclair, "you were told that sacrifices would be required for the greater good."

Whiskers was shaking his head vigorously. "Nothin' about wearing a dead man's uniform. See, that's something I would've remembered!"

"You'd be paid, of course," said Fenwick.

There was no immediate reply from Whiskers, which Fenwick interpreted as his cue to continue. "I should think a double share isn't enough."

Fenwick looked over at Leclair, who shook his head solemnly in agreement.

"I should say a triple share," suggested Fenwick.

Now Whiskers was looking straight at them.

"A triple share is yours," said Leclair.

"You'd give me three times the gold?" asked Whiskers.

Leclair was nodding.

"For doing a job beyond most men's capacity," added Fenwick. "As aforementioned, it requires a certain manliness and fortitude, both of which are evident in you."

There followed a solemn pause. Whiskers turned anxiously to Bruno and then Matt, but both of them looked nothing but pleased. So he looked at Leclair, straightening himself and puffing up his chest.

"Aye, aye, Captain. Let me have that stinkin' uniform."

CR SO

ROOTS

ℬ ℬ

At every step, a clutter of sea shells cuts into his bare foot. Olof shifts his weight gingerly to dodge the pinprick pain of coral edges. This relentless prodding underfoot is his only sensation, along with the old Frenchman's faithful grip on his forearm.

Olof's other hand traverses the numb, inanimate flesh up the length of his back and neck. The skin is no longer his, so he cannot desist from touching.

There is nothing else. The rest is darkness, a deep sphere inhabited solely by his own breathing.

"The moon. She's full tonight."

Olof's hearing is unaffected. Nevertheless, the old man insists on shouting, perhaps from a misplaced goodwill towards an apparition as grotesque as what he must now presume himself to be.

There is a softening underfoot. They must have crossed the high water mark and now the soft sand pampers his feet.

"Herrans plåster," he sighs with relief, knowing full well that each word perishes in his throat. Or if he were capable of speech, old Normand would not understand. Heavenly balm.

The sleepy surf is drawing close. It spills into the centre of his darkness, right alongside his breathing. The sand moistens between his toes. A seeping coolness tingles at his ankle, sending shivers through him.

He touches the deadness on his back. Only his fingers know the touching. His back is unaware that he is being touched.

"This little green slime," squawks Normand, "can grow in water."

Olof turns in the direction of the old man's voice. Sending his will into the eyelids, he strains to lift the shroud. Not even a glimmer beyond black. This has nothing to do with willing, nothing to do with eyelids.

Perhaps Normand is squatting now. The wizened old hand tugs downward, pulling him gently onto his knees in the moist sand. "This came first." Olof's fingers are guided by Normand's hand, closing around a wisp of cold velvet seaweed.

He lets go of it and Normand's hand swings him to one side, guiding his fingers into the sand. His fingertips are pinned beneath a taut cord.

"Roots, my friend. A world of roots. They keep their heads low, and hold the sand so fast that nothing can wash them away."

Olof follows the sound of Normand, crawling up the beach. Through the frayed cotton, his own knees encounter the web of creeping roots and leaves.

"Look what happened."

At Normand's words, he reaches out. Instead of a root for his fingers, Olof finds his face smothered in stiff, slippery leaves.

The old man chuckles in his ear. "*Coccóloban*, we call it. The flower is a great beauty."

Pulling his face back, Olof runs his finger along the arching stem. A long cluster of tiny, grape-like fruit fills his hand.

"And so it is," grunts Normand, satisfied now at the completion of a thought. His voice is hushed, as though confidentiality were an issue on these barren sands. "The little creepers always come first, binding up the sand, busy with the ground. Creepers is what makes the beach dry. That's when the coccóloban comes along. Nothing could grow without the creepers. But once the beach is dry, you'll see the bush everywhere, *mon Dieu*, nothing but coccóloban on the upper parts. They don't like getting their toes wet, see. The creepers and the bush don't mix. The creepers keep gettin' pushed into the water."

Olof can hear the old man's voice moving a little away. With the words still resonating in his dark orb, he listens for Normand's return. They think alike.

He remembers King Gustav. At break of dawn, Olof's duty had been to provide escort on His Majesty's stroll through the palace garden at Haga. Gardens made gorgeous by foreign blossoms, made sumptuous by foreign gardeners. And King Gustav sauntering in his languid, careless sort of way, freed from the rigours of palace walls, his idle gait at odds with the impetuous mind.

"The Queen of France shall go free. I have promises, you know. I have willing allies for a crusade upon Paris. Upon my word, we shall end the tyranny in the streets. And good taste shall prevail."

"Yes, Your Majesty."

Such a clamour of outrage because Marie Antoinette was in the dungeon, awaiting a speedy execution. The very pinnacle of empire had been struck and, of course, the new word was anarchy.

"Anarchy must not go unchecked," resumed King Gustav, plucking a hibiscus flower from the nearest bough. "Robespierre and all his *confrères* will hang."

Everyone was crying out in disgust but was there one among them who had looked *outside* of Paris, at the slain innocents, the trampled rights of other nations? The path to empire had been paved with pillage and terror. The throne of France had long since forgotten what it meant to be at the receiving end. But now the word was anarchy. A word to legitimize *her* imperial cause above all others.

"Indeed, Your Majesty."

But Monsieur Rousseau knew better, so Olof used to remind himself. The fire had been lit. Even Rousseau's initials were spreading like a bushfire. From Jean Jacques to Johan Jacob. And J. J. Anckarström was not to be stopped. Contrary to what this king might think. This Francophile. This *coccóloban*. This foreigner.

Olof listens for the old man's return, yet it comes without

warning. The wet rag slaps Olof's bare shoulder. He jumps with pain.

Old Normand is laughing. "Tell me your name," he repeats.

ROOM OF RIDDLES

෨ ଓଃ

Glenda lay awake in her bed, listening to the men downstairs. She heard Fenwick's voice and Leclair's and a couple of others from the night before. They were obviously about to make good on their gruesome scheme.

It was this thought that had roused her at the crack of dawn and kept her from even the briefest slumber until, now, the whole house was abuzz with shouts and intermittent clanging of metal, presumably their spades and picks.

Sunlight breaking in around the drawn burgundy drape told her it was late morning. Likely as not, they'd been up half the night guzzling their rum and madeira. Now, as she heard three or four of them stomping off into the woods, her racing thoughts turned to other things and Leclair's words came to her mind. He would set her free, he had said, before he'd give her over to abuse by his men. It was a peculiar breed of gallantry. It didn't exactly exonerate him from his several and sundry crimes against her. It didn't transform a knave into a knight. It was merely Leclair's way of saying that unless the task of tormenting her belonged to him exclusively, he'd just as soon be rid of her. He wanted sole access to her uncovered body, if only to gawk at. It should be his exclusive privilege to press broken glass against her skin and drag it ruthlessly along the length of her back.

This wasn't a gallantry to which she was either accustomed or disposed. But whatever Leclair's motives, he had now promised her freedom, like precious manna suddenly dripped from his tongue. As Glenda found herself alone again, left behind in the derelict serenity of the ruined house, her thoughts dwelt on Leclair's cast of mind, maddeningly obscure but also unlike anything she had imagined in a common bandit. Perhaps it was his intimation that she might soon go free that allowed her, now, to admit to her own curiosity about his person. This self-serving villain continued to baffle her.

On an impulse, Glenda got out of bed. She wriggled into the bright moll's dress; the hem of it didn't even reach the length of her calf while the bodice was too ample for her breasts. She had meant to take up some water from the reservoir and launder her own garment but Woolsley's blood had changed everything. Perhaps she'd ask Papa to walk her to the shore where she could soak her dress in the sea.

She tiptoed to the door and listened at the doorknob. All seemed quiet on the stairs and down below. Across the landing was that other door. When Woolsley had told her where he was quartered, her assumption was that the other half of the upper storey belonged to Leclair. Glenda made her mind up to find out if it was true.

She pulled the door open and inspected the stairs. No one in sight and not a sound to be heard, except the occasional shriek or chattering from the brooding woods. Glenda stepped softly across the landing and tried the other doorknob. It was unlocked. The door yielded and she stepped inside, closing it gently behind her.

The room gave a peculiar divided impression of tranquil calamity. There was a bed, though not as large as her own. A floating bough of rainforest hovered against the papered backdrop of olive trees. This was the side of the house where Glenda had seen, on her very first approach, a portion of the roof lifted and peeled back by some high wind. She was looking now at a large patch of sky, framed within a jagged circumference of broken laths and open rafters. From that jagged edge, a thick, charcoal-grey bough hung into the room, densely wrapped in a vine of dark, polished leaves. The sap had dripped on the floorboards along with rain, staining a portion of the floor in tones of ashen grey.

It was as though Glenda had stumbled upon some unimaginable plumed serpent smashing through the roof and spewing his poxy bile on the floor. Behind the bold, fibrous arc of the intruding bough was a pale papered landscape dotted with dainty olive trees. Lusty warriors chased naked nymphs from tree to painted tree and, in places, a resourceful nymph had grown branches in lieu of arms and legs, which led Glenda to suppose that these were themes from Ovid. Through the gaping roof, rain had lashed the wallpaper, imposing a rougher, more random stripe over the measured delicacy of those sylvan scenes. It appeared that the gods of the Indies had decreed perpetual rain on the papered land of Ovid. And to enforce it, they had stationed this silent sentinel who made no noise, drew no blood, yet was inexorable and terminal as any beast. A slow and silent predator; an invasion measured in months or years rather than moments.

Against this leafy green assault Leclair had done nothing. His bed was safely tucked in the opposite corner. The room, unlike hers, appeared to have been built as a bedroom. Beside his bed was a dresser and a window without drapes. An upholstered chair was boxed into the corner behind the rampant bough of green. On the same wall was an elegant, chest-high chiffonier and chair, much of its dark veneer flaking and peeling from harsh cycles of rain and sun. A Persian rug, which would have seemed less out of place in her own room, covered the middle of the floor. A good portion of it, though dry, was discoloured and disintegrating from rain.

Slowly, Glenda walked into the room. Across from the dresser, on the opposite side of the bed, was a night-commode with a basin of white porcelain lodged within the cut-out at the top. The basin was half full of water and Glenda found herself thinking that this was, perhaps, not merely ornamental. Perhaps Leclair actually practised cleanliness. Most of the men didn't; she had learned to give them the widest possible berth when they were upwind of her.

Once again, Glenda's eye went to the chiffonier. The fall-front was open. Some papers were strewn on it. Maintaining a respectful radius between herself and the renegade bough, Glenda made her way towards the chiffonier. The inkwell was almost full; next to it, a quill was wedged under a slim book.

Glenda felt her cheeks burning with the guilt of trespassing. In one sense, of course, it was a trespass. But when weighed in the scales with this man's several and sundry transgressions, her unannounced visit was surely a trifle. Righteous guilt was a quality instilled by her dear mother, for which she would be always thankful. But in this house it wasn't sufficient. That brazen bough had entered, no questions asked. So she, too, mustn't stand on ceremony when satisfying her curiosity.

Not that she knew what she was looking for. Glenda stood before a stranger's desk. Her hands sifted idly through a stranger's disarray of documents and personal objects, a conglomeration whose only meaning or significance was buried within the mind of a stranger.

Even as her thoughts were arguing the futility of this pursuit, Glenda's hands rifled more resolutely through the contents of the chiffonier. The narrow, vertical cubbyholes contained letters and a few scrolls of larger manuscript. Glenda picked her way through the bundles of sallow, rumpled paper. She didn't pause to untie the twine. She pinched a few sheets at the middle of each bundle and wriggled them free of the rest. But her efforts didn't yield much; only one was in English and it concerned some monies owed to officer Rydström in the port of Gustavia for special considerations.

The rest were penned in a language altogether unfamiliar to her, with added dots and curlicues and all sorts of extraneous notations. In one of the bundles, she pulled several sheets out of the centre and found the same signature on each letter. As she examined the remainder of the bundle, each and every letter ended the same way.

J. J. Anckarström.

There were fifteen or more epistles, ranging from a single paragraph to three pages, each signed J. J. Anckarström or simply J. J. Whatever affections or slander had been conveyed in these pages, thought Glenda, Leclair had not wanted to part withal; the date, added by Anckarström on only two or three of them, was six years past. Exasperated, Glenda pressed the bundle tight and, without the twine, forced it back into one of the cubbyholes.

She lifted the little book away from the quill. Brushing a few sheets of scribbled paper off the opened fall-front, Glenda laid the book down upon it. She leafed through the book. The pages contained no print, but had been well used for handwriting. Glenda eased herself down on the straight-back chair and began to read.

The paragraphs were short and each, or every two or three, were assigned a date. Her eye fell on the middle of the left page.

Two days in Marigot, just inside of La Tortue. We careened the ship. Matt is a hard worker. But Raoul hasn't forgiven me.

That was all. And then on to the next entry.

D. 14 Nov. About the blindness again. Although it's now behind me, I think of it daily. Now that I can see, a lot of things look different. The world is different. En annan värld. Papa anser mig vara fit as a fiddle. Där tager han miste. He's mistaken. This I know.

Glenda went back over the short paragraph, deciding where English ended and where it began again. She could make sense of it, though the other bits gave her no clue at all. The next entry was dated *D. 16 Nov.,* but Glenda flipped forward to the end.

The chiffonier held no other book and this appeared to be a diary, likely Leclair's. She noticed her hand trembling as it clasped the back cover. She began at the end now, thumbing her way backwards until she had found the last written page. She read the latest entry.

D. 9 Sept. Fenwick is a fox. A likeable fox, but a fox nonetheless. Dig up Woolsley and train Whiskers. Better sport than ever the army! Miss Burchill is not Miss Burchill. Headstrong and pleasing to any man's eye. Add to it that she has had me fooled.

Glenda went back over the last two sentences. She gazed at them, her eye reluctant to let go. She found herself trying to hear his sentiment behind the words. Was it anger or admiration? Or how much of each? If she could know the answer, she might better prepare for his coiled aloofness.

Glenda thumbed backwards again, looking for the peculiar reference to a blindness. She couldn't find it but, casting about in the vicinity, her eye paused at another entry.

I was dead, he says. At the high tide mark in the middle of night. He was harpooning turtles. He found me. Brought me back to life. He's like a father now. I've started saying Papa.

At that instant, just as her eye had lifted to begin the paragraph over again, a noise came from behind. The book went up inside her sleeve as she jumped to her feet. But a large hand clamped itself on her mouth, wrenching her violently from the chiffonier.

The shock was enough to throw Glenda into a helpless stupor. She felt herself being dragged across the floor and thrown, face down, onto the bed. At last, she thought, Leclair would exact his punishment. Her legs and arms had gone suddenly lame and useless.

Nevertheless, Glenda made an effort to hoist herself on one arm and look behind her. What she saw was even worse than she had imagined. Leclair was nowhere in sight. It was Bruno, having now dropped his breeches around his knees and climbing onto the bed with a very wild, reckless aspect between his legs and from his bulging eyes. Glenda endeavoured to swing her legs away from his side of the bed, but he caught her by the ankle and twisted it sharply. With a yelp, Glenda collapsed again on her stomach and Bruno threw his full weight upon her.

Overcome by his vile odour and the brutality of his assault,

Glenda tried to roll out from beneath him. His knees dug painfully into her thigh, pinning her to the mattress while he tugged and picked at her garments. She couldn't get a word out of her mouth, and little good it would've done. Glenda felt his hands reaching under her dress, dragging the knickers down to her knees. She was sobbing now, her sobs breaking into a soft wail.

Bruno's hairy belly came crushing down on her buttocks. She felt his erection between her legs, poking ever closer as he used his hand to open a path in the soft flesh betwixt her thighs. Glenda resisted his fingers with all her might, her body stiff as a plank. Pressing her eyes shut, she gasped a final word of prayer to her Lord Father and surrendered herself to His will alone. Her fate was sealed. By His grace, she'd find a way to rise again from her defilement.

She had reached this point of inward resolve when a sharp crack sounded in her ears. Though it made her start, the stronger reaction came from Bruno. He gave a shudder, a convulsion that shook the entire frame of his body. She might have mistaken it for a precipitous spilling of his seed if it weren't for the abject shriek that went with it. Bruno's head dropped like a boulder onto her shoulder blade.

Before Glenda could crane her face around for a peek, another loud crack had racked Bruno's body and, this time, he let go of her and toppled off the bed.

He ended up on his side, trying to get his breath while reaching awkwardly around to his back. His hand came back bloody. Bruno paid her no attention now; his eye was elsewhere.

Glenda sat up and discovered Leclair at the foot of the bed. He had a very pale, frightening expression about him, a cowhide whip trailing on the floor.

"Get away!" said Bruno. "No more!"

"Twenty-eight more," said Leclair, winding his whip into a roll. "For later."

Bruno struggled to his knees, still clutching his back. His shirt hung in tatters and blood was filling the raw gash.

"Share and share alike," he bleated. "Yours and ours, yes?"

Leclair shook his head, the whip now restored to his belt.

"But we have articles," stammered Bruno. "We have articles that say any prisoner of mine is yours and..." His breath was catching with pain. "And yours is mine."

Leclair answered with a single word, spat from between his teeth. "Trespass!"

Bruno met his captain's eye. "The articles are binding on everyone," he burst out.

Leclair stepped closer. "How about trespassing? Captain's cabin. That's an article, isn't it? Remember that article, Bruno? Thirty lashes and you'll never forget it."

Bruno shook his bald head, getting slowly to his feet. "*Sancta Maria*," he groaned, pulling his breeches back on. "It's not right. Keepin' her locked up like this! You're breaking the articles, as very well you know, so the only way I can get what's mine is by breaking 'em, same as you."

Leclair turned his back on Bruno and stepped from the shade into the brilliant sun that streamed down on the green bough.

Bruno eyed Glenda with unabated hunger.

Leclair lifted his eyes to the sky. "You're a trespasser. You've been where you shouldn't have gone. If you have more to say, I'll hear it later."

Bruno shifted from foot to foot, but his feet wouldn't let him leave. "Is this different?" he insisted sullenly. "This is something I don't know."

Leclair half turned, a striking figure in the flood of light. "Yes," he said, shooting Bruno a piercing gaze. "There's something you don't know."

Bruno lingered another moment but Leclair was impervious. The intruder turned angrily on his heel and left the room.

Glenda saw the dark welt forming across his back. She looked over at Leclair. His eyes were on her. From downstairs came the casual commotion of the men returning with Whiskers and his new suit of clothes. In a moment, Bruno would surely provide fresh fodder for their palaver.

"I owe you all my thanks," said Glenda.

Leclair approached her. Without breaking their eye contact, he came close. Instinctively, her hand straightened the dress, brushing it down towards her ankles.

From nowhere, Leclair dealt her a whopping blow to the side of the head. Her jaw seemed to drop off her face. Tumbling headlong, her eyes were wrenched with pain. Nothing could've prepared her. The floorboards tackled her hard, snatching away her breath. She lay in a heap, squinting up at Leclair.

Any sign she may have imagined of his better self was shattered now and evermore.

"If he'd had his way with you," said Leclair hoarsely, "that would have been good and proper according to what you deserve. You're no better. As much a trespasser as Bruno. You and that dress. A common wench. A slippery whore. You wilful piece of work! I should whip you. By God, I'll whip you like any man. I'll whip you till you're clean."

These words sprang forth with such rage, such a seething ferocity that Glenda could only cringe and gape at the man who thus pummelled her astonished ears. From their moment of utterance, his words did not frighten her by any persuasiveness in his argument but by the monstrousness of his invention. Such was her shock that she didn't see him leave.

She blinked away her tears and the room was empty. Inside her sleeve, the weight of his book. All she could see was the sprawling bough. A hideous beauty.

CR ℘

GASHES

ౙ ಐ

Glenda was in a great deal of pain. Her jaw didn't swell up, but the left side was throbbing and very tender. The flat of his hand had struck her in front of the ear. Had it been a fist, Glenda thought to herself, she might have been spared an hour or two of excruciating consciousness.

As it was, she'd been cured of any further curiosity regarding the contents of his chiffonier. Leclair was still a puzzle to her mind, but no longer a puzzle that she cared to concern herself with. Her ears full of the din downstairs, she had stumbled back across the landing into the relative comfort of the other room, the room that she must think of as being her own. Here she lay, limp and dishevelled, with her right eye buried against the mattress and the other side of her face burning and throbbing.

From a shallow slumber, Glenda awoke to the sound of the flogging. Through the window, closer to the shore, she heard the unhurried, unmitigated repetitions of Leclair's whip descending on Bruno's bare skin.

At first, it made her jump as if her own body had been slashed. At the fifth or sixth strike, she pulled her knees up towards her chin, hugging them tight to her chest. From Bruno came no sound, at least nothing audible to her. Another blow fell and then another.

Leclair had vowed to punish her like Bruno or any man but, for the moment, she was being spared. The reckoning was being postponed, or merely accumulating towards a grander aggregate of unimagined proportions.

Glenda let go of her knees and released her body. As the whip struck again, she felt nothing. She focused her attention on her flesh, releasing every thought through her fingers, legs and neck, feeling her weight settle deeper into the bed. The next crack from the whip did nothing to her. She was at peace, at rest in a crystal of numbness, deafened by the muteness of Bruno's pain.

At eighteen stripes, Leclair paused. The whip hung from his right hand, wet and glistening in the sun. Bruno had his hands tied in front of him, his arms around the trunk of a small, knotty juniper. He had gone down on one knee, resting his bald forehead against the onion-skin bark.

Leclair looked around at the men. In accordance with the articles of agreement, everyone who had remained at La Fourchue was there. Papa had tried to excuse himself by fussing with dinner preparations, but they dragged him along. A formal punishment was everyone's affair. It would remind each man of the conditional, exclusive membership he had in the group.

For this reason only, Matt had voted in favour. He had, however, expressed a personal disclaimer to Leclair. "You should be minding your own end of the bargain, sir."

Matt was perched on the sloping rock, eyes downcast with his reddish locks sprouting from the bandana. He was silent now, respectful of Bruno's predicament. A few paces in front of him, Whiskers observed Bruno with a nervous twitching at the mouth. Already he was wearing Woolsley's double-breasted jacket in order to, as Whiskers had put it, air out the ghost. He stood next to Pierre and Ripper, a part of the general huddle of others who witnessed Bruno's thrashing with uneasy fascination.

Among them was Big Raoul. He stood with legs apart and his broad arms crossed on his chest, a defiant and stony-faced gainsayer. The flogging went against his will and he was making sure that this was apparent to one and all. He didn't bat an eye when the whip racked Bruno once again.

Without pause, Leclair raised his arm and dealt him number twenty. But Bruno gave no sound; he had managed to block his breath at each new blow. Number twenty-one and the knotted leather tore away a strip of flesh from below Bruno's armpit. His other leg buckled.

Leclair snapped the whip lightly on the bare rock, leaving a spray of crimson speckles.

Her flaxen hair

As he drew back for the next blow, Leclair felt the churning fire inside his ribs. *Her flaxen hair is tangled now and dull. From behind, the boy has gathered his fist full of her hair* It was best forgotten. Leclair's arm aching with something other than fatigue.

The boy has gathered his fist full of her hair and gives a pull, forcing her head backwards. This folding at her neck pries her lips apart. From her throat escapes an intermittent sound of gasping or choking. Her torso is stretched forward across the coil of hawsers. Each arm is held and pulled almost from its socket by a dull-eyed bandit

The knotted leather hurtled to its target and Leclair felt his fire surging through the arm, bursting from his fingertips along the length of the snaking whip.

‹‹ ››

Her flaxen hair is tangled now and dull.

From behind, the boy has gathered his fist full of her hair and gives a pull, forcing her head backwards. This folding at her neck pries her lips apart. From her throat escapes an intermittent sound of gasping or choking.

Her torso is stretched forward across the coil of hawsers. Each arm is pinned and pulled almost from its socket by a dull-eyed bandit. The rose-coloured dress is snug about her neck, tapering along the torso and disappearing under its own skirt, draped in a heap of folds across her lower back. From the edge of the rose fabric, her smooth buttocks protrude, luminescent white in the dusky air. Her thighs are perpendicular to the torso, extending to the deck where her knees are wide apart on the jagged timbers. Her white calves lie parallel on the deck, still bound in a tangle of garters and pale muslin.

Between her calves, the boy is on his knees and his buttocks toiling incessantly. At every lunge, his force travels the length of her spine, thrusting her torso and shoulders forward, erupting in her sobbing gasp.

CR SO

Leclair winced, pressing his eyes shut. When he looked again, he could see better. The men were scattered round about, eating without much talk. Leclair sat by the fire with a generous helping of salt pork and yams on his lap.

Bruno's flogging was on everyone's mind, but so was the promise of an easy ransom for Whiskers, masquerading as Captain Woolsley.

After briefing Leclair on arrangements for the ransom, Fenwick had departed unceremoniously, sailing with two of the men in the little cutter with which he had landed after dark on the night before.

"We need to bring everyone," said Leclair, picking thoughtfully at the remains on his plate. "We'll stop over at Camaruche and L'Orient. That's another ten to twelve men."

"Don't do it." Raoul was seated on the bench by Papa's fire. "We need to be more careful now. There's money on your head."

Leclair considered Big Raoul's words. Matt was glancing from one to the other. Pierre belched noisily, a cup of rum in hand. Whiskers had also finished eating, cradling his rum in both hands.

"They're not signed on the account like the rest of us," continued Raoul. "If they're not all the way in, I say to hell with 'em. You don't know who they've been talking to. We have to know who's in and who's out."

A few of the men were nodding in agreement. Leclair recognized the good sense in Raoul's argument.

Papa was in the doorway now, having delivered a plate of dinner to Glenda and another to the downstairs back room where Bruno was recovering.

"I suppose so," said Leclair quietly. "Now is the test of true men. But how many of those have we got?"

After a moment or two, Matt had made a quick tally. "Seven and twenty, and that's counting Papa." He shot Papa a questioning look.

The old man gave a nod. "One more," mumbled Papa. "I said I would, so I will. After that, you can find a new cook."

"Aye, then," resumed Matt. "A day or two and Bruno will be good as new." And then, counting them off on his fingers, "We've got Angus, Loman, Snake, Twitcher, Rogers waitin' in Gustavia. That makes seven and twenty."

"It won't be a burn and plunder," said Leclair, speaking mainly for Papa's ears. "It's not like we're taking a ship. If we had Woolsley, half a dozen would do. But we've got Whiskers, so we need enough pistol fire to cover his escape and the retreat."

Leclair looked around at the men. They were listening. Every face bore the mark of battle or other extreme conditions. Leclair could look at each scar and name the ship or the town. Pierre lost his eye on board His Majesty's brigantine *Palisade*. A cutlass had slashed Raoul's eyebrow and plowed a deep furrow down his cheekbone to the jaw. Matt was an exception; his face had scars like the rest, but Leclair was not familiar with their history. Matt's nose was already broken when Leclair first laid eyes on him. Matt had always had the top part of his right ear missing and an upper lip cloven by a dirk or some such weapon. Whiskers' face was intact, except where Loman had slashed his nostril in a fit of rage.

Each man knew the price of carelessness. Each man had paid it at some time or other. No matter how great the division or the argument, there always came a moment to abandon all differences and pull as one.

Once again, it was that moment.

 CR SO

THE NEW LIGHT

๕๖ ๙๓

We got married in August. That was wedding season.

Yvette was sixteen. I had twelve years on her. She was a good woman, my Yvette. God-fearing, fun-loving. Good mother too.

Alphonse was always trouble but he was a good boy - and clever, *mon Dieu!* He'll be forty-four now, or forty-six or something. God bless him. It's been thirty-five years. *Oui*, yes, that's about right. He was eleven.

Olof is listening to Normand's voice, slow and nasal, serving up each new detail in a drone that allows no favourites, no rhetoric, as though each train of thought, no matter how revelatory, is merely water under the bridge. Olof's dark void fills with images, brushstrokes from Normand's private canvas, fitful and meandering.

They're sitting outside the cottage. As he listens to Normand, he can feel the old man's bony arm brushing his leg. The inside of the goatskin is still wet and giving off heat from the dead animal.

This is the secret, explained Normand, to making a good boot.

The old man has taken the skin fresh off the animal and molded it to Olof's foot, lacing it around the ankle and calf. The other hands are there too, whose lightness is like a bird, the long-fingered Chloe who spread each day a fresh poultice on the skinless oblivion of his back, weeks upon weeks until one day he winced from the heat and Chloe laughed and he could hear her half-whispering a profusion of thanks to her heavenly Father.

"Sit in the sun and they'll dry," says Normand. "Two days and they'll take the shape of your foot. Best pair of buskins you ever had."

But for him who lives and breathes in a dark void, Normand's canvas of words has been interrupted. It's patchy still, but more compelling than the new boots.

"Thirty-five years since you saw them?" asks Olof.

He gets only a grunt from Normand. The old man eschews a reply because it would pain him or because he's too indolent to bother repeating himself. There's no telling which.

"Where are they?"

"I don't know." Old Normand blurts it out, as though his soul were a slingshot drawn and loaded with those words alone.

"But where did you leave them?"

A silence follows, while the four hands finish the lacing of his boots. A rustle in the nearby brush gives away the fitful stirrings of the goats.

"Our home was Acadie. A long way north, straight to the other side of America and then some. The villages were burned by the English. We got in their way, you see. So here were these transport ships, a dozen or more, waiting to take us away. They knew about our families. They'd seen the strength of a family, eh. So what they did was take the wife away from her man. They wanted us weak, see, too weak to come back. They had orders to do it, the English bastards. Jackals! You know jackals?"

Normand waited for a nod from Olof, then continued. "I call them jackals. They had me on the ground, four soldiers standing on my arms and Yvette and the boy were taken to another ship. God knows where..."

The hands are winding the twine up Olof's leg.

And they are blue.

As he listens to Normand's story, he studies the long, delicate fingers of indigo. They tie the twine in a knot and fold the goatskin over it. Arms of midnight brown tapering seamlessly into picture-book blue.

"Chloe," he says.

"Yes?" asks Normand.

"Your hand," continues Olof, shifting his eye to Chloe's face.

"The blue on your hand."

Their eyes meet. A reply from Chloe becomes unnecessary, as her hands of indigo ascend shimmering toward the pale heavens. "Praise to the Holy Father," she whispers.

It dawns on Olof what has occurred. Unannounced, the bright hillside has flooded his eye, the deep, green luxuriance of the valley and the ashen face of the mountain dotted with shrub and thistle. He has been released from the folds of darkness.

"Jesus, look at you!" croaks Normand.

Olof looks over at the chestnut-brown, leathered features of the old man, girded round with a grizzled beard. So this is Normand, his bony fingers stretching the twine and tying it off behind the knee.

Chloe edges backward, as though the fact of his seeing makes her more negro, more fully disclosed, more endangered.

Olof smiles and she returns the smile. Across this new distance, an aging woman who inhabits her dark, furrowed skin with ease and honesty. The arms are thin and stretched from the burdens of long life. Even physically, she and Normand are well matched.

"My eyes," repeats Olof, almost to himself. "My eyes."

He rises from the bench. Gingerly, he puts his weight on the moist buskins. Taking a few steps towards the road, he studies the silent, wind-swept landscape.

From town, he used to see the road climb to Fort Gustavia and vanish. He had only the foggiest of notions about where it might lead. This is where, he realizes now. This is the rest of St. Barth.

"You're as good as new," croaks Normand gleefully. "We'll get you back into town by week's end."

"No."

Normand and Chloe trade a quick glance. Their young visitor is momentarily oblivious to them, his gaze lost in the deep tangle of green across the valley.

"Of course you'll go back," insists Normand. "You're good as new, Olof. Your friends will lend you enough for the passage to America. You'll see, all is well."

The young man turns to face them again. It's obvious, from his expression, that he has given no heed to Normand's reassurances.

"Your hands," he says. "They're beautiful."

Chloe withdraws her hands, hiding them behind her back. Hers is not a little girl's coyness; but it's just too much fuss.

"Beautiful," says Normand, coming to her with a quick embrace. "No one has hands like my old girl."

"You quiet," says Chloe, making a blue fist, "or maybe you'll have an eye this colour."

Normand snorts with laughter. The three of them laugh together, affectionately.

"Winnie," calls Chloe.

Another black woman comes shuffling up the road. She's no taller than Chloe but more heavy-set, and panting now from the steep climb. Winnie comes to Chloe's side, greeting the men with a nod.

"Show him your hands," says Chloe, nudging the woman beside her.

Sure enough, Winnie raises her hands, fingers spread like blue branches. Chloe adds hers to Winnie's, making a pretty little grove of blue.

Laughter gets the best of Olof now, wrenching him from the pit of his stomach in a most comforting, salutary way. His first laugh in weeks.

"But no more," explains Chloe. "She cuttin' the sugar cane now. After work, she come up to see if you still breathin'."

Winnie smiles.

"These people saved my life," says Olof.

"See, fit as a fiddle," croaks Normand.

"Here, Normand," calls Chloe suddenly. "Do my nails."

The old man hobbles off to look for something. "Let's give you a trim before it gets dark."

Much to their young patient's delight, Normand crawls backwards from under the little bench, sheep shears in hand. It's Chloe's turn to sit on the bench, while Normand gets down at her feet, crosslegged like a tailor. With meticulous care, he takes her toe between his bony fingers and slowly guides the shears along the margin of her untrimmed nail. Chloe's head settles against the clapboard wall, her eyes closed with contentment.

Olof watches them fondly. Winnie steps inside to fetch herself some lemonade.

"You're good for each other," he says at length.

Chloe's eyes open and look at him. Her head hasn't even lifted away from the wall.

Normand is occupied with the shears. "Chloe got her blue hands in Guadeloupe. Then her owner died. She was given a choice. Tell him your choice."

"I could stay," she says. "Be a slave in Guadeloupe. Or leave it all and go."

"That's my girl," croaks Normand. "Left it all and went. Winnie and Chloe. They got off the boat in Gustavia."

"And Normand, too, he leave it all," continues Chloe. "His wife, the boy, the farm. All of it he lose."

"We left something but we found something," smiles Normand, winking at her. "We deserve a few good years, *oui*?"

Olof nods solemnly. "You should move into town. You're too old to be alone up here."

Normand looks up from the shears, laughing mirthlessly. "Into town, eh? You want to see us dead, maybe?"

Chloe gives a quick shriek, pulling her foot away. Normand takes it back, fondly, putting it to his lips and kissing the toe where he's nicked her skin.

"Don't get so hot," scolds Chloe, "or you not cuttin' no nail of mine."

"In Gustavia," continues Normand, more sedately, "she's

nothin' but a nigger and slave. The mountain is a safer place when you're coloured and white together. Here's good for us."

Normand is back at his shearing, more conscientious than ever. Right beside him, Winnie emerges from the low doorway with a cup of lemonade, squinting at the low sun. She takes a long, indulgent sip.

"It's all here, what we need," says Normand, as Chloe's eye catches his. "All except a wee little one."

Chloe touches her hand to the hairy lobe of his ear. The old man is lost for words.

"You have me."

They both turn their heads.

Olof is sharply outlined against the green chasm. "Well? I owe my life to you."

Chloe glances at Normand. He shakes his head, lifting the shears away from her toe, for fear he might take a bigger gouge out of her.

"*Père*," says Olof, hearing the word roll off his tongue. "How do you say it?"

Normand looks at him, smiling. "*Père*, yes. Or papa is fine. More like papa."

"Papa."

The word comes eagerly to Olof's tongue, rekindling a flash of winters long past, in the snowy woods. They could hear the moose crashing heavily through the crusted snow. A feeble sun sloping through the white forest. He wasn't far behind his papa. His skiing had improved, enough to qualify him for the hunt.

Alongside them were his uncle and a few men from the local regiment, the crisp air charged with silence. Only their forced breath and the thump and whoosh of the skis. The crust held their weight while the moose was breaking through at every step. The musket dangled from his papa's shoulder, the tails of his midnight blue Karolin infantry coat twisting with each new stride. Not a big man but tough as nails, a hardline partisan who had dispatched the foreign tutors, sent them packing back to France. Prince Gustav must learn the native virtues of Sweden. The human race wasn't created so that twenty royal houses might play musical chairs with the thrones of Europe, so he used to preach.

And before him, his father had been a footsoldier with the great King Karl in the killing fields at Poltava. The last grenadier. He had earned this nickname because he never carried a musket, too old or set in his ways to bother with the new breed of musketeers. Rotted away in a Russian dungeon. The last grenadier, Olof's grandfather.

"*Ici!*" Normand's hand slices the air before him. "Can you still see?"

Olof gives a laugh. "Papa. Yes, my Papa."

Normand shows his gums in a wide grin and turns to Chloe again. "You're done, old girl."

She gets to her feet, stretching arthritic limbs.

"He lookin' much better," says Winnie.

"Yes," agrees Olof, turning to Normand, "and I need to find this Raoul."

The old man tucks the shears under the bench, shaking his ashen hair. "After what they done to you, I wouldn't."

"Where do I find them?"

Normand is still on his knees, bracing himself with a hand on each thigh, as he stares up at the young man. There can be no doubt about the earnestness of this question. "Are you crazed?" whispers Normand.

"You told me you're a sea-cook. You said you cooked for them. You've been on their ship."

Normand puckers his lips in a tight scowl.

"Eh, Papa? Take me to them."

"Go on, leave St. Barth," hisses Chloe.

Olof can hear her, but his eyes are on the old Frenchman.

"Now you can go to America," she insists.

But he has turned his back on them. All he can see is the green, impenetrable ripeness of the hillside.

ଓଃ ଏୠ

THE BLEEDING

ഔ ൠ

She had never imagined that the solitary house on La Fourchue might feel like home. And it didn't, not really. Yet, as the *Clifton* gathered some speed and the little inlet closed behind them, Glenda felt a twinge in her stomach.

Leclair had given orders to strike camp. Since the break of dawn, the men had been shuttling between the house and the ship, wrestling their provisions into the two skiffs, spreading their bales of silk and cotton on top and rowing out to the anchorage to load.

It was the way of the unrighteous, she supposed. To stay alive they must be always on the move, always a step ahead of what they had coming to them. Leclair would slip every noose before it began to close. With sheets groaning in their blocks and foresail cracking in the wind, they were finally on their way.

Glenda turned carefully onto her side. From the hammock, she reached into a sack which Leclair had tossed at her before they boarded ship. From the jumbled contents, she retrieved the black tome which had been her companion each day of this godforsaken journey. She leafed distractedly through Philippians and Ephesians, where she had found much solace of late. The apostle Paul had borne his foul internment with such serenity and faith; Glenda would bear her own cross like a true believer. In the end God's will, whatsoever it might be, would prevail.

In fact, there were moments when her travails appeared merely as a crucible for her spirit, an opportunity to attain that higher commitment to her heavenly Father which, perhaps, she had resisted in her younger years at home. In those moments, Glenda's worst torment was not her own welfare, but that of her afflicted family, of her old mother and her little sister and, Lord preserve him, cousin Devon. What was to be done? What would they be thinking this very moment? Had the news reached England? Did Squire Heywood even know that something was amiss with his sea-faring niece? Would she still be alive and breathing by the time they learned the terrible news?

And was poor Devon breathing even now? Her mind's eye couldn't rid itself of Devon's pale image, his face a bluish grey and his lips, formerly so resolute and composed, now parted wide in a last, incoherent gasp. About his head the unrelenting surf continues, each time stealing into the channel of his ear; only a sandy dune for his pillow and gulls whose cry he would never hear. Thus lived Glenda's cousin in her worst imaginings.

Now her eyes darted irritably around the narrow cabin, where creaking timbers and the hissing sea pulled her ever away from her more pious ruminations. Once again, the Bible was before her. While in her thoughts, she had let go of her page and now it was opened to the gospel of Matthew. The text was not one she was accustomed to, yet she had read it before, long ago it must have been, perhaps at school.

Some stirring of recognition compelled her to read on, then pause and flip forwards and back. Nay, this recognition was of more recent date, though she couldn't recall what. As her eye traversed the page, the words jumped at her. *Fear not him who can destroy the body; fear him who can destroy the body and soul in hell.* She glanced at the top corner of the page. Yes, chapter ten, verse twenty-eight in Matthew. Fear him who can destroy the body and soul in hell.

Twice, now, she'd heard her captor repeat those words, or some paraphrase thereof. Clearly he was no man of God, despite the masquerade of black robe and crucifix at their first encounter. She doubted whether he had ever read a word of Scripture, yet he had spoken of the English philosophers and Rousseau's new influence with startling assurance, or even with passion. It would seem he possessed some worldly learning, but surely none pertaining to Holy Spirit. Leclair's scriptural phrase was, without a doubt, a mere catchphrase heard and remembered from some preacher's pulpit in his past.

What was it in these present circumstances that had warranted his harsh evocation of the Adversary? Was he, in fact, likening himself to Satan? If so, why would such a knave think it necessary to use this high rhetoric with her? And after Woolsley's death, had he not seemed to console her by extolling the captain's righteous soul when compared with those less fortunate who must suffer the perdition even of their soul? His words had felt like a condolence, not a threat.

Absorbed by this train of thought, Glenda looked up from her Bible. Through the porthole, the sun shone warmly. She craned her neck until the brightness spilled on her face. With eyes closed, she strained to feel the sunlight in her hair. It soothed her scalp and curbed those careening thoughts, touching her cheek with merciful peace.

She remained thus for a brief eternity. Then she looked again towards the wide horizon. Barely within scope of the porthole, she caught a final glimpse of La Fourchue.

The cabin door opened. She paid it no heed, for she wasn't about to break her precious reverie.

"Are you bidding the house farewell?" she heard Leclair asking.

"No," she answered distantly. "Not the house."

"Ah," he replied, musing for a moment. "The Captain, then?"

She didn't give a nod nor turned to him. "*My* Captain."

Glenda heard him step in and close the door.

At the horizon, on the far side of that little pock of an island, the house would remain. After sundown, when a chill had settled on the water and shadows enfolded the earth, the house would remain. No ship, no homecoming, no returning voices, no fire in the hearth, nevermore the fall of feet on the rotted carpet, nothing but a weightless, sultry gleam of stars. And a stone's throw away, the remains of Captain Woolsley. An old man, with not even his uniform to grace him, abandoned to the whimsy of wind and worm.

Again, Glenda felt tears burning behind her eyes. "Was the house yours?" she asked at length. She knew full well that it wasn't, but hoped to stem her emotions by engaging her thoughts elsewhere. "It was a sorry mess."

Leclair observed the back of her neck. The pretty ringlets had come out of her hair; instead, she had braided it and pinned it up, a braid above each ear.

A smile came to his lips. "Yes, a sorry mess but not mine. Aaron Åhman built it for his wife."

All the while reclining in the hammock, she had drawn her legs away from him, towards her chin. One elbow rested on the ropes that held her to the wall; the arm supported her head, which had not turned or in any way acknowledged his presence. Nonetheless, it pleased him to look upon her.

He had done much more and much worse to women whose mere aspect had been indifferent to him. But if beauty was more than science, more than a prescription for well-wrought limbs and a pleasing hue, then this woman was possessed of such a beauty. The slender firmness of her shoulders, guarding the proud, prominent collarbone which had thrilled his eye time and time again, this configuration of bone and flesh might mean nothing more than womanly comeliness to another man. To Leclair, however, it brought a beacon of recognition, a sense of redemption and wholeness. And with it came the hideous ache, that old familiar ague in his very bones.

"They've been gone about four years," continued Leclair. "I've never seen a man made so wretched by love. You see, his wife wasn't Swedish. She was among the most decrepit of the French, an actress both onstage and off. She was the soul of aristocracy, false and cruel. Many is the man who was invited to her boudoir and would've gone, were it not for Aaron who was, at first, too well-liked to be made a cuckold and, eventually, too frightful to dally with."

Glenda was listening. She turned to face him. Leclair kept his distance, though the cabin didn't permit much over six feet of separation.

"So Aaron vowed to get away from the temptations of Gustavia. He built them a house on the island. But that wasn't enough. He demanded that the Governor declare La Fourchue a free and sovereign colony of Sweden. The Council in Gustavia, of course, had a good laugh and dismissed his application. But Aaron grew angry and very, very nasty. He lost his friends, one by one. He wasn't welcome even at the magistrate's house. When the doors to high society closed on Aaron Åhman, so did the door to his wife's bed. She sailed home to the salons of Paris and he turned his back on their house and vanished, Lord only knows where."

In her mind's eye, Glenda imagined this strange man driven to distraction by his wife. What words of contempt and sorrow had been uttered within those four walls on La Fourchue? How had they strained and struggled to outwit each other? Maybe Glenda's old bed in the parlour had been placed there long before pirates landed.

"You said the magistrate in Gustavia," answered Glenda eventually. "Was this the same who was buried a fortnight past?"

Leclair arched his eyebrow. "As a matter of fact, yes, the same."

Glenda was laying a puzzle, piece by slippery piece. "His name begins with cedar."

Leclair nodded, smiling oddly.

"And a daughter lost at sea," she went on. "Another tale of woe."

Glenda had almost turned back to the porthole when she noted a change on Leclair's face. He looked ill. His lips moved as though searching for a sound.

"Are you not well?"

Mustering another smile, Leclair grimaced. "I hadn't heard about a daughter. How long since?"

"He didn't say."

Leclair eyed her intently. "Who was it said this?"

Glenda shifted restlessly in the hammock. "A Swedish gentleman. He put the fear of God into Fenwick. And then he said the daughter was what did it."

Leclair crossed his arms on his chest, holding himself with both hands lest he should give in to his rising tremors. "His daughter did what?"

Glenda lay flat on her back in the hammock. She observed Leclair shrewdly. "Losing her is what finished him. That's what the man said."

CR ℘

A GHOST FOR CAPTAIN

℘ ℂ

As he begins his walk down the mountain, he can see them.

About a mile above the festering swamp, they have made a bonfire. They have dragged some deadwood out of the forest and piled it four feet high, out in the open, on the barren hillside above the trees.

In the anchorage below, the moon has dropped a net of silver, holding their ship by the masts. He can hear the capricious rise and fall of their shrieks and whoops. They must have an endless store of rum.

Olof is walking better now. His new goatskin buskins are well worn-in and moulded to his feet. Chloe's goat cheese and plantain pies have restored some strength. His neck and shoulder are still absent, unconnected and unreal to him but there is, at least, no pain. No ache to drain what little strength is left. His feet tread confidently through the brush and across the pock-marked rock bearded with sparse, blondish lichen.

By the fire, Raoul lounges. Across from him, the boy and two others are jumping and circling in a kind of heedless frenzy. Several bodies are stretched on the ground; impossible to tell whether merely resting or truly incapacitated.

Away from the fire, four of the men are gathered around a log. They are using sticks to beat out a shrill rhythm from the hollow wood, a rattling cadence surging and stretching, breaking away and lost and then found again. Hoarse howls and snatches of song burst from the three dancers and from some of those stretched on the ground, urging the drummers ever on and on.

Raoul's burly frame is resting on one side, supported on his

elbow. A stocky, bald-headed fellow squats in front of him.
Without taking the pipe from his mouth, Raoul throws his head
back with a snort of muted laughter. "You're too greedy," he
mumbles with teeth locked around the pipe.

Bruno waits patiently for Raoul's chortling to come to an end.

"We'll all be rich," says Bruno at last. "Everyone is happy.
Silver in bars and plates, silk and indigo, fresh cable and sheets
of sail. Enough for everyone."

Raoul is watching him, amused.

Bruno slaps his hand on the rock between his feet. "Divide it
tonight."

Bruno has had too much of the rum to know when enough is
enough. But tonight Raoul is laughing, tonight he is indulgent
and willing to be entertained. So he laughs again, pointing his
beard at the immensity of night sky.

Again Bruno observes him, awaiting a chance to speak.

"You know the articles," says Big Raoul at last, removing the
pipe. "Look at these men. If you put them all together, would you
have enough brain for a monkey? They have more rum in 'em
than blood. That's what the articles are for. The giving of loot is
business. A man needs to have a clear mind or he could lose an
arm or maybe his head. Greed is a grievous sin and, Bruno,
you're among the worst. If it weren't for the articles, boatswain,
you'd be quick into the grave."

Bruno turns his head and peers into the fire. A shudder
wracks his body. He knows that when Raoul speaks, it is not idle
talk. Without taking his eye from the swirling flames, he makes
his next bid.

"Raoul, I don't fight with you. I know my captain. When all
these others forget, you'll see. Long as you need a boatswain, I'm
your man. Maybe something will happen, maybe an accident,
maybe I'll get to be master on your ship." His small, round face
turns to Raoul. "Now lookit, Whiskers and Matt been gettin' a
full quarter on top of their share. Now, with you taking a good

share-and-a-half for yourself and giving 'em each a share-and-a-quarter besides, why isn't there a quarter on top for me?"

Raoul observes Bruno, the way a python would study a lamb. As his sense of the ludicrous begins to overflow, his head rocks back onto one shoulder as he fires another riproaring laugh into the night.

Bruno doesn't move, but a shudder courses down his spine. By this, his own anger is made known to him and, with a silent plea, he prays for strength to hide it from the other.

Raoul hiccups, shaking his mane of black matted hair as he looks back to the boatswain. His eye catches a stranger. Right behind the mustard-yellow bandana on Bruno's head. A newcomer. A moment before, Raoul closed his eyes on a view of the boatswain and those straggling dancers in the background. His eyes open to a new sight. A tattered figure looms behind Bruno. Tattered like his men, but not one of his.

Responding to Raoul's stare, Bruno scuttles sideways to get out of harm's way. He looks at the intruder and knows who it is.

"It's him," comes another's voice. "Last of the prisoners."

Some of the others are stirring, getting onto their feet. As they draw closer, the fire's glow plays on their greased, puffy faces.

"Can you talk?" says Big Raoul.

"Aye," comes the answer.

Old Normand, the ship's cook, appears through the fire's smoke. "A talking ghost," says he.

"That one is dead," says another. "We had him at the end of a plank."

"Your ball was too late, Raoul. It was lightning that got him. And that's him, dead sure," says the fellow with the cleft upper lip.

"He's dead," whispers someone else. "That one is dead."

The dark hillside is silent. Raoul rises to his feet. The drummers have dropped their sticks. The flushed, sweating boy cringes behind Raoul's shoulder, unsteady on his feet.

"We told him to say his prayers proper, we did," croaks someone.

"A spirit," repeats the boy hoarsely. "Mother of Christ, a real live spirit!"

Raoul stands broad-legged, arms folded on his chest. These men have never seen him cower and nothing is going to change that. Only the muscles in his jaw give a hint of the fierceness of his turmoil at this moment. His deep, hooded gaze remains on the intruder.

"You call yourselves pirates?" he says loudly. "Are these my rovers, my hearties, my gentlemen of fortune? A pack of lily-livered cowards? Then God rid me of the whole bunch!"

He pauses, allowing a deathly silence to settle. There is not a movement among them now except the fitful flames. Not a sound is heard above the hissing fire and a cool brush of wind from the moonlit sea.

The uninvited guest has not moved, nor spoken past a single word.

"Now then, is your noggin clearing yet, Bruno? And Pierre, what about yours? And yours, Matt?" says Raoul, pointing at the fellow of the cleft upper lip. And then at the ship's cook, saying, "And you, Normand? Is it a ghost? Well yes, to be sure! And what do you know about spirits? Not a damn thing! You've all seen them, except this boy here, but which of you was ever harmed by one? Tell me, which?"

Again Raoul waits in silence, his eyes probing darkly from face to face, right around the circle.

"He that knows anything about spirits knows this. They can do you no harm. They'll flap about in the night and make your blood run cold or make your skin crawl with all their howling and hissing and make your dreams dark as the grave, but that's all the power a spirit has. It cannot hurt a living soul."

The pirates are listening. Among them comes a flutter of fresh courage.

"And gentlemen, there's more a spirit cannot do," says Big Raoul with rising confidence. He draws the cutlass from his belt. "A spirit cannot bleed."

The stranger makes no move to shield himself.

Raoul steps closer. "I'm about putting it to the test," he rumbles.

"My business is with you."

Raoul halts at the stranger's words, not quite a warning, almost an invitation.

Now drawing a dirk from his buskin, the intruder sets the point to his own neck and, without flinching, drives it through the skin. He observes his own blood tainting the cotton on his shoulder, as though issuing from another's body. Only when it spills onto his chest can he feel, at last, the warmth from his own wound. He looks around at the pirates.

The effect of his deed has been riveting. A scowl is etched on every face.

"What kind of ghost is that?" whines Bruno, retreating behind his comrades.

"That ain't no ghost," says another. "Not with all that blood in 'em."

But Raoul hasn't finished. He turns back to his men. "You're afeard that ghosts will harm you, which they cannot. Why aren't you fretting double worse about what they *can*, which is to fool you? I'll tell you, now, what fooling is. He'll put a spell on you, right inside of the eye. He'll twist your eye to seeing what ain't there. He can open up his vein and let you see blood where there ain't none. So long as he's the one makin' the cut, it's in his power."

Big Raoul lifts his cutlass to strike at the apparition.

Old Normand steps in front. "I have a good blade that's cut many a side o' beef. Let me be the one."

Raoul lowers his weapon.

Normand stops in front of the visitor. Nothing is spoken

except in their eyes. Olof looks at Papa. The old sea-cook steps around to one side, studying the stranger with a moment's deliberation. Placing one hand on the shoulder, the old man raises his other and sets the dirk against the rumpled cotton between the shoulder blades. With a smooth stroke, he slits through the shirt and the scorched flesh.

Olof can feel his skin parting but only the slightest prickle of pain. The dirk goes back into the old man's belt and, with two hands, he rips the rest of the shirt off Olof's back. The rock at their feet is sprinkled with blood.

Turning the stranger's wound for all to see, old Normand hobbles back to his comrades. "Mercy, Raoul," says he, "did you ever see so much blood from a spirit?"

Olof stands where the old man left him, displaying the scarred, disfigured tissue on his back.

He can hear someone whispering. "Look where he was scorched!"

"I saw it," adds Bruno. "Mother of God, he took the firebolt right between the shoulders."

"I saw it," says the boy, looking very pale.

"Me too," says another.

Olof turns to face Raoul, the blood still dripping between his boots. "Give me charge of your men."

Big Raoul is rooted to his spot. The pirates watch for his next move, their eyes trained on his mighty neck and shoulders.

"What?"

"Put me in charge," repeats Olof.

"A man like any other." Raoul speaks slowly, dangerously. "And you want what's mine?"

"His flesh may be mortal," croaks Normand, "but what about the inside?"

Raoul's head tilts back in another burst of derision.

"He was struck by a thunderbolt," adds the old man quickly. "So how is he still here among us?"

Raoul turns slowly, dreadfully to face old Normand. The pirates are wavering now, awash with doubts and imaginings.

"It's dark at night," says Raoul. "Little tots and old men don't like the dark. They should stay indoors. The night is for real gentlemen. The night is for the strong of heart, for booty and prizes enough to make lords and gentry of us all. Go home to your goats, old Frenchie."

No one speaks at first. Raoul looks around at his men. Many heads are bowed, in subservience or confusion or drunkenness. He cannot tell which.

A sudden scratch of metal turns his head. The stranger's cutlass is drawn.

"I will settle with you," says Olof.

Raoul is content. He has had enough. The cutlass is in his hand.

"Any man that says lightning can pass through a man and live, he's a liar," growls Bruno in a drunken daze.

Big Raoul swipes the air between them slowly, stepping in for the kill. His adversary makes no move to protect himself.

"God's truth," shouts Normand, grasping for words. "No bolt of fire would pass through a man and him still walking and bleedin' like this one. But you saw him thrown from the plank, you did!"

"The bolt must've stopped inside of him!" stutters Bruno.

Now a gasp comes from the men. A soft whistle from some. Olof can see Papa biting his lip.

All eyes shift toward the stranger. The pirates look him up and down, as if seeking a sign of this fire coiled inside.

Maybe Raoul is more shaken by these words than he lets on. For whatever reason, he is unable to anticipate Olof's move. It is a clean forward thrust with a twisting whip of the wrist which, in the wink of an eye, has Raoul's cutlass clattering on the rock beyond his reach. The chief is disarmed.

Papa's mouth is dry, his eyes narrowing.

Big Raoul shoots his adversary a baleful look, then turns to his men with a smirk. He reaches out to Matt for another cutlass. The fellow looks down, shifting his weight from leg to leg.

"Matt!" demands Raoul.

Still the pirate makes no response. Raoul gives a contemptuous snort, stretching his palm instead towards Bruno's mustard-yellow bandana. But he, too, avoids Raoul's gaze, his short neck wracked suddenly by violent coughing.

"Is this a mutiny?" asks Raoul hoarsely.

The men glance anxiously at each other.

"This here is council, sir," says Bruno, his coughing finished all at once. "We always had the rights of council. To each man his vote."

"You bunch o' ninnies." Raoul growls like a caged animal. "Council is for matters of great import."

"We're sayin', sir," replies Matt, "that there's import enough in this here matter."

Big Raoul looks around. At a glance, he knows which way the scales are tipping.

"Honour your captain," croaks Papa. "Honour him because he knows his business. Raoul is a master of the trade." A twinkle plays in the old man's eye. "But this new one comes with a fire in his belly. One day, the lightning may pass from him. That'll be his time to die. But for now, we're his men."

A low murmur rises on the air. The pirates are talking each to each. No one bothers about Raoul.

CR SO

MORNE ROUGE

හ ශ

Near the top of Morne Rouge, Leclair called a halt. They were following a footpath that scaled the precipitous heights above Anse de Grande Saline.

Glenda eased herself down beside a craggy boulder and leaned her back against it, breathing hard. A multitude of axes and cutlasses thundered like metal rain into the short grass, as the pirates flopped down on the hillside to catch their breath. They were armed to the teeth now, more frightening than Glenda had ever seen them. Every man had added at least one pistol in his belt and a dirk in each boot.

Below them was the sea, lazy and lackadaisical in the noonday sun. She was a crafty one, thought Leclair of the blue water, his eye drifting into the distance. On a day like this, no one could suspect her dark moods or sudden tantrums. On a day like this, she could be mistaken for a friend.

The *Clifton* was hidden from their view. Leclair had not sailed her into the Anse de Grande Saline. Inspired by Fenwick's scrupulous planning on La Fourchue, Leclair had gone one step further by avoiding the enclosed harbour of the Anse. On a calm day such as this, the open water would serve for anchorage. Off the point of Morne Rouge, he had sheeted home the sails; Glenda had followed his twenty-seven men into the skiffs and rowed to the mouth of the Anse, where they waded ashore amidst rocks and starfish.

"Matt."

Matt opened his eyes, without bothering to turn.

"You're taking your fifteen across the gulley and round the outside," continued Leclair, pointing a short way uphill to the crest of Morne Rouge.

This assignment was no news to Matt. He simply nodded and gazed into the blue yonder.

"We're meeting them at the marsh. Whiskers, you'll walk halfway across."

Among the lounging bodies, Whiskers alone was sitting upright. Purporting to be Captain Woolsley, his proud posture was perfectly in keeping. In truth, however, this particular uprightness had much more to do with an insufficiency of volume in Woolsley's jacket than with any talent for mimicry.

"Watch you don't pop those buttons," smiled Leclair. "Now, Fenwick has already explained all particulars to the Englishmen. Three of them will come forward to meet you. Don't be looking up the hill, d'ye hear, because you'll see us behind their back. They're not going to see us but, by God, they'll hear us. These English will have their hands full, I warrant you. We're not firing anywhere near the halfway, so there's your cover. Their backs will be turned. Just run like a goat, my hearty, and the day is yours."

Whiskers was smiling now, his eyes aglow with inklings of great purpose and glory. A glimmer of merriment passed among the men. It was the prospect of seeing their rotund comrade, his considerable belly well nigh rending even Woolsley's ample jacket, and this man to be bounding downhill like a goat!

From her perch beneath the tall boulder, Glenda could observe Leclair, noting to herself the quiet assurance of his voice. His was not the sway of grand gestures or fiery invective, but rather of a formidable sense of resolve and inexorable purpose. Gone was his sullenness and his puzzling half-utterances to her. Here was a man who had others listening without so much as raising his voice.

"There'll be soldiers." Pierre had his hand up to shield his eyes. "They wouldn't send such a pile of gold without soldiers," he said.

A few heads stirred, turning to Leclair with a querying squint beneath their brow.

"Soldiers," said Leclair. "Yes, to be sure. Fenwick said on land, not at sea. To this the Governor said yes. Fenwick said on St. Barth, not on St. Kitts, and the Governor said yes. Fenwick even asked for a mule to carry the gold. To all this, the Governor gave his consent. But to ask him for a count of his troops would've been to give away the plan. So we don't know their numbers. We must be on the ready."

The chief looked around at his men. "Remember now, we're not here to do battle. We've got to cover Whiskers, that's all. But if they're not willing to part with their gold, well that's a different story."

The pirates were smiling, chuckling, grimacing among themselves.

"Three of the redcoats will come to halfway. So therefore, we're allowed Loman and Twitcher and Matt to go with Whiskers. Soon as your hand is on those sacks, we'll open fire. First thing you'll do is dispatch the three of them. Matt and Loman, grab that mule and off you go. If any among the troops bother with you, he'll have my ball in the back of his head, so help me God."

The pirates were already stirring, stretching their limbs and gathering their axes and cutlasses from the ground. The sun shrouded Morne Rouge in a stifling haze.

Glenda got to her feet, her cheeks throbbing and her mouth dry. In the blazing heat, the bruise on her jaw was still smarting.

"Rogers and Angus, you're with me," said Leclair as the men came trudging up the hillside. "Pierre, you can go with Matt and I'll take the rest."

Matt went off with his vanguard of Whiskers, Loman and Twitcher followed by another eight men. They took the footpath that sashayed into the gulley and across to the plateau where the great salt marsh would begin.

As Glenda was watching them leave, Leclair gave her a nudge with his pistol. "If you please."

Glenda didn't let Leclair bother her. She accepted her lot, unsavoury though it was, and set out with his half of the men. Leclair strode to the head of the pack. Over her shoulder, Glenda saw Raoul and Papa walking behind. Rather than descend to the marshes, Leclair led them unhurriedly around the other side of Morne Rouge. He knew his terrain. The dense shrubbery and dwarfed junipers would give them good cover on the way down. The pirates crawled on all fours, their cutlasses trailing through tufts of grass. Raoul had advanced to the left flank of their group, while Glenda scuttled close behind Papa. Each man trained his eye on Leclair and Raoul. When either of them halted, the rest were still too, waiting, listening, trying to peer through the greenery to the salt marsh below. But there wasn't much to worry about. By the climbing of the sun, they must be a good two hours early for their noonday rendezvous.

Leclair called a halt about two-thirds of the way down, where they commanded a good view of the dusty road and the peculiar intricacy of the marsh.

Glenda couldn't take her eyes off the swampy black water beyond the road. It was a grotesquely oversized bed of spikes. Nearly half of the basin was riddled with what was, in actual fact, a vast throng of upright, fibrous spikes thrust towards the sky. They measured anywhere from three to maybe six or seven feet above water.

Glenda wanted to ask how they had gotten there but only Papa was nearby, so she chose to leave well enough alone. She glanced up the dirt road towards the mountain. Everything was calm. Matt's team was nowhere to be seen. All was still, succumbing to the heat, except for the shrill, penetrating cacophony of crickets. The men settled languidly on the ground and Glenda rested herself against a twisted juniper.

Somewhere in the gulley, she mused darkly, the Captain's proud apparel was walking with the rest, merely a travesty of life. It had risen from the dead, bereft of soul or conscience, an insensible poltergeist corrupted and possessed by him whose loutishness it was now meant to conceal. Thus it would stumble onward through the Indies, a perpetual mockery of England's name.

At the sound of Leclair's voice, Glenda's heart jumped. She turned and found him squatting before her, his sunbleached hair made secure by the bandana.

Glenda looked about. No one had stirred. All was as before, except Leclair who had come to her side.

"The swelling has gone down," he repeated.

Her hand came quickly to her face, shielding the jaw, hiding it from her tormentor.

"Don't be afraid," said Leclair.

Without removing her hand, Glenda looked down at her feet. "I assure you I'm not," she said softly. "I'm not half the craven that *you* are."

Leclair gave no reply at first. Again, their minds were locked in peevish combat.

"I hadn't touched you," he said. "You struck the first blow."

"I struck you, it's true. On the Captain's ship, when you had a score of men to uphold you and I had none. Then who's lily-livered and who's not?"

Leclair peered over at his men.

Glenda's gaze brushed across the grim set of his jaw.

He got up as if to leave, then hesitated. "It may appear that might is on my side," he said. "It may appear thus. Because you're a woman and lack the highest power of learning, and because you've not bothered to understand how the world bleeds through every woman, you'll see things as they appear, not as they truly are. You struck the first blow and yes, it's true, it was after I had first made you my captive. But what is the might of men against a woman's nature?"

He had stepped closer.

Tears burned behind Glenda's eyes, but she didn't want him

to see this in her. "A woman's nature?" she said hoarsely. "What is it that has so offended you?"

"In a word, the whorishness. That's as much as to say, the weakness. Your failure to will it otherwise."

ೞ ೲ

The slender boy is finishing now, his pelvis flailing fast against her buttocks.

The slapping of his flesh upon hers is picked up by the bystanders. In their hoarse drunkenness, they mimic the sound or cheer him on, or grunt gleefully in time with the boy.

Eyes closed, his face lifts toward the sky and his hips come to a sudden stop, his hairy thighs joined snugly to her white buttocks. His hand lets go of her flaxen hair. Her head droops between the shoulders, hair like tangled sunbeams against the coils of shiny hemp rope. The boy flops forward, crushing her rose-coloured dress beneath his torso. He rolls off her, scuttling away on all fours until he's out of sight.

The fellow with the cleft upper lip steps forward again. He's ready to have another turn. His knee-length breeches are back up to his waist. With a sopping belch, he shoves the jug of rum at his neighbour. He steps up to her crumpled body.

But this time he is brushed aside by another robber. This one stands a head taller than the rest, and the arm that stops his comrade has the thickness of a cross-tree. He nods to the two robbers. They back away, releasing her arms.

Her eyes turn to him, dull and confused. With his boot on her rose-coloured dress, the man rolls her gently off the coiled rope. She ends up on the ship's deck, flat on her back.

"Now here's somethin'," he hollers. "You call yourselves men, do you? You want a piece of wench and all you know how to do is take. You cretins. Asses! Untaught puppies!"

Some faces glower at him darkly. Others are grinning, thrilled to be his puppy. Everyone is poised for his next word. He peels the shirt off his back. As he bends over the young woman, every movement ripples through the muscled ridges of his torso. He drops to his knees, her white legs on either side of him.

ൠ ൡ

A loud hiss drew Leclair's attention back to the hillside. He winced, pressing his eyes shut. When he looked again, he could see better.

Rogers was signalling from his perch behind a small boulder. On the serpentine road, the soldiers were approaching. Numbering a score or more, the redcoats rode at their leisure, their animals plodding listlessly through the dust.

From another direction, along the verge of the salt marsh, Matt and his men had appeared. Whiskers paraded in front, mustering every ounce of courage to deport himself as behooved the captain of an English merchantman. They came to a halt and stood close together, awaiting the Governor's deputies.

Glenda was speechless from Leclair's charges. Whorishness. This is how he had railed against her on La Fourchue.

But Leclair left her side to take up his post again. Several minutes passed, while the gap was closing between redcoats and pirates. Glenda debated what to do. She had been left to her own devices; no one was keeping an eye on her. She was back on St. Barth with nothing but dry land between herself and Gustavia. On the other hand, Glenda recalled fireside conversations in dreary November, when her uncle had warned cousin Devon of their destination, speaking of the Indies as a realm of savagery and cannibalism.

What was there in the brooding bush that frightened her so? The more serene the face of that intricate jungle, the more readily and vividly her thoughts seemed to conjure up all manner of mischief lurking within its entrails. The walk to Gustavia would be more than a matter of hours, perhaps of days. The prospect of facing the livelong night alone in the pitchy bowels of that forest was sufficient to make her abandon such rebelliousness.

At the foot of the hill, the English soldiers had come to a halt. The Governor was as good as his word; only three of the redcoats rode forward, bayonets mounted and a mule trudging behind, his saddlebags looking suitably plump. At the halfway, they stopped again.

Matt gave Loman a nudge; they grabbed Whiskers roughly by the coatsleeve and shoved him ahead of them, walking one on each side. Twitcher followed close behind, his pistol drawn. Whiskers' face underwent the strangest contortions, as he realized that his life now depended upon a most earnest and suitable demeanour, but uncertain of how to achieve the same. Matt was not in a mood to reflect on the humour of Whiskers' predicament, but he did feel a stitch of remorse for allowing this guileless johnny to suffer such anguish.

On their left was the steaming marsh, like a floating plantation of stripped, blighted tree-trunks. On their right, the run-off from the marsh seeped over a low escarpment into the small cove below, furrowing through the sand until it emptied into the high tide.

To a man, the pirates had loaded their pistols, each with a hand on the hilt of his cutlass. The sweat was pouring off their foreheads.

Matt and Loman were only moments away from the gold. Matt stole a quick glance up the hill. By his reckoning, Leclair had already given his signal to take aim. The hillside was green with hidden pistol barrels.

The three redcoats gave a stiff greeting. Matt was holding Whiskers back, at a few paces, while Loman drew his pistol and stepped forward to peek into the saddlebags. With his free hand he reached inside and craned his neck to get a better look. Satisfied, he stepped away from the mule and nodded to Matt.

The three redcoats were waiting with bayonets *en garde*. The short one with a red mustache approached Whiskers. He kept the musket trained on Twitcher and Matt.

"Woolsley?"

"The same, sir," replied Whiskers adroitly.

The soldier halted, glancing at Matt, then back to Whiskers. He didn't seem altogether satisfied. However, it was of no consequence for, on the instant, a pounding barrage of pistol fire erupted from the hillside.

The red mustache turned to look behind him and came face to face with the flame from Loman's pistol. He took Loman's ball directly in the stomach and fell against Captain Woolsley's worsted trouser leg. Whiskers pulled the leg away squeamishly and fired his own pistol, knocking number two to the ground.

In the main troop, four had fallen from their saddles and, inevitably, the remainder wheeled their horses about in order to discharge their muskets at random up the hillside. Within a minute, the torrid air was thick with the stench of gunpowder.

Loman had the prize mule by a rope and was racing towards the gulley. Twitcher ran off after Loman, laughing to high heaven. The third soldier had shot Whiskers in the chest but Matt felled him with a ball to the head.

"Get the hell out of here!" yelled Matt. "Go on, for Christ's sake!"

But Whiskers wasn't going anywhere. He was on his knees, teetering to and fro. He looked down upon his punctured chest and his clothes seemed less his own than ever they had.

Matt was about to run for it when a second round of pistol fire rang out from the hillside. He knew instantly that something was wrong. The jumbled volley of loud cracks came from a higher location and did no damage among the troops. Matt trained his eye on the hillside but couldn't detect any movement, either high or low. Leclair had mentioned nothing of splitting his team. It must be a double-cross. The English had set their own trap.

Matt was too intent on this horror to take note of a movement nearby. A mere eight feet away, one of the fallen soldiers was stirring. Too weak to re-charge his musket, the man had drawn a pistol from his belt. Suppressing a groan, the redcoat extended his pistol at arm's length, his elbow to the ground. The red mustache scrunched into his shoulder as he pulled back the hammer and took careful aim.

The blast knocked Matt off his feet. His jaw struck the ground and he lay there wheezing, staring in disbelief.

What he saw was Whiskers tearing at the buttons of his jacket for a breath of air. But try as he might, no breath would come, and from his mouth nothing but blood. Whiskers keeled forward and collapsed, his nostrils jammed with grass.

Glenda lay face down. Her hands shielded her ears from the howling ricochet of pistol balls. There was no way out, no thought of escape now. She was in the midst of Leclair's nightmare. They had been ambushed.

As Raoul turned to fire his brace of pistols up the hill, she had heard him yell a name and, right away, she knew it had to be so. Fenwick. Fenwick who had weaseled his way into Devon's and her own company, only to turn them over to Leclair. Fenwick who had masterminded the counterfeit release of Woolsley, labouring over each and every stipulation in the best interest of his pirates. In effect he had duped them all, stipulating only enough detail for an effective ambush. He had double-crossed their double-cross.

Her skittering thoughts were shattered by the thump of a body crashing almost on top of her. It was a pratfall, buttocks followed by shoulders, arms slammed to the ground and the head crunched on the bald rock of the hillside. He lay there so limp and free, his eye untroubled by the blinding sun. Glenda might've looked at the boyish hair on his chin and imagined Emilio to be daydreaming under a summer sky, except for the round, black hole into his forehead. Young Emilio had nothing left, not even a daydream.

Glenda looked up with dread, a frightful tingling at the roots of her hair. The hillside was thick with smoke and everywhere the brutal incoherence of men yelling and grunting and scrambling for cover. Glenda didn't need to be told twice, nor even once. She kept herself flat to the ground. Hastening to turn away from Emilio's body, she peeked over her shoulder to gain a view up the hill.

Between blades of grass, she could glimpse the uniformed troops advancing even as they fired their muskets. Glenda had no way of knowing their numbers, but even from her awkward vantage point she could count two dozen or more. Their ammunition came screeching through the brush, rebounding every which way.

Angus was already grappling hand to hand with one of the redcoats. He had struck the soldier a crushing blow with his boarding axe. Bleeding from the shoulder, the redcoat dropped his musket and Angus came at him again, pummeling him with the axe. At his back, another soldier was set to spear him on a bayonet, but the Englishman dropped from a ball fired at close range by Papa. Angus found no time to show Papa his appreciation; he had two more redcoats to contend with.

Glenda was looking for Leclair, but to no avail. The soldiers had come too close for musket fire, so they rushed the pirates with bayonets and pistols. Big Raoul stepped into their path, smashing his cutlass across an oncoming bayonet. Raoul's blade proved itself worthy of his ferocious arm, while the English bayonet was wrenched from its socket and crashed into the trunk of a dwarfed gum tree. The soldier attempted to wield his musket like a cudgel, but Raoul clamped his iron fist over the barrel and wrested it away in a single jolt. Before the redcoat could reach for his pistol, Raoul had spun on his heel and struck him across the windpipe with the musket's butt. The Englishman dropped without a sound.

Another soldier leveled his pistol at Raoul's face. Before his finger could squeeze the trigger, his arm was lopped at the elbow by a mighty slash from Leclair's cutlass.

Glenda saw him at last, brandishing two cutlasses at once and with a skill that left her breathless. She had seen the pirates fight, slashing and chopping and swearing, but Leclair had a different way. He appeared more at his ease, more fluid than his men. His movements were measured, precise and minimal and his face showed no sign of strain. At last she was witnessing Leclair the pirate, the dreaded renegade, instead of all those foibles and doubts which she had never imagined from a common rogue.

It was apparent, now, that Leclair was becoming a prime target; Rogers and a few more jumped in to form a shield of defence. The odd pistol shot rang out but, with no time to reload, firearms were not nearly so useful as the axes, swords or cutlasses that flashed everywhere in the sun.

Leclair swiped the air vigorously with one cutlass, while the other, serpent-like, was ready to thrust on the instant. To his left, Pierre and Snake and a couple more came scrambling up from the salt marsh with musket fire whistling about their ears. Leclair had to duck a vile blow from another redcoat. He bounced back with a thrust to the throat. With his other arm, he slashed high to the left and knocked the tricorn hat off a soldier whose snowy periwig sprouted a gash of crimson. His right arm raised for a parry, Leclair turned back and found the first soldier now on his knees with both hands to his neck and blood bubbling between the fingers.

Emerging from a little thicket, a rumpled figure caught Leclair's eye. It was Papa, looking no worse than usual, his cutlass in hand and a pistol in the other. He was motioning to

Leclair, his mouth gaping.

Leclair strained to hear the old man's words but nothing was said. His teeth were bared, but not for speaking. Leclair was rooted to the spot. He was within ten paces of the old man, yet he was powerless. Papa keeled forward and fell on his face in the dirt, the back of his shirt soaked in blood. A shot from behind, perchance a stray ball from the foot of the hill.

No sooner had this thought flashed through Leclair's head than he felt the point of a dirk digging into his back. The shock was not of pain but, more profoundly, of the sheer mechanics of laceration as the blade tore into the numb tissue of his old scar. In a daze, Leclair stumbled forward. Slashing to his rear, he screamed: "Retreat! Retreat!"

Looking around for Glenda, he kept shouting. "The ship! Retreat! All back to the ship!"

Leclair raced downhill at a diagonal, skirting above the half dozen redcoats that remained of the English delegation below. Stumbling on the rough terrain, he struggled to draw the load of his pistol. Pierre and Angus and Raoul were running at his side, discharging their weapons down the hill. Another soldier fell from his saddle.

CR SO

PANDEMONIUM

෨ ෬

The settling calm was shattered by one last scream. It came from Glenda, standing alone on the hill. Such was her anger that she had to open her mouth at last and let it out.

Far below, the English troops had disappeared into the cove, hot on the heels of the bandits.

She had kept her face to the ground while, only a few yards away, boots kept thundering past in eddies of dust and smoke. She hadn't looked up again until the worst of the madness subsided. Her heart still pounding, Glenda had risen to her feet and realized that she was alone. She was left behind now. Alone among the litter of bodies strewn on the hillside. She had seen the last redcoats racing to the shore and it occurred to her, too late, that they weren't the enemy. Not *her* enemy. She had been thinking of them as Fenwick's men, rather than the Governor's vengeance upon the wicked. They could've been her *salvation*. But she'd been too terrified to use reason. And now she was paying the price.

Emilio hadn't moved. All these bodies crumpled and twisted, and only one or two still moving. Everywhere she looked was oozing of blood, from raw gashes gleaming in the sun or from wounds so hideous that God in His mercy had left the bloodied shirt to shield her eye from such a sight.

Glenda began to walk. Her feet bore her slowly downhill.

From the shore came a few scattered pistol shots.

Then the ghostly calm descended once more. It was the presence of so many warlike bodies, all sentenced to eternal calm, that chilled Glenda most especially. As she walked, tears rolled down her cheeks. The wind tugged at her hair, blowing it across her face.

She almost stepped on Pierre, curled up on his side with his head tucked to his knees. Further along, she recognized two more of Leclair's men, familiar faces without a name.

A movement caught her eye. This single and sole sign of life came from a large black condor who had lighted on one of the English cadavers, his beak tugging vigorously at some part of the soldier's face. Glenda felt her gorge rise and, with a shudder, she stumbled on.

Where the ground levelled off towards the soft verge of the salt marsh, she found Captain Woolsley's uniform splayed in the grass. Glenda stooped for a last look, but Whiskers' lifeless hulk so annoyed and offended her that she was obliged to turn quickly away.

Had she taken another step, she would've had Matt's body underfoot. He was right under her nose, sprawled on his back with those shrewd eyes fixed on the sky. A pang of sadness came over her, for she had thought of Matt favorably, as being perhaps a better sort than the rest.

A tremor wracked his body.

She stared at Matt. His eyes shifted to her, his lips moving. He was still breathing. Astonished, she squatted beside him to hear his words. Another convulsion coursed through him and his jaw tightened with pain or fear or whatever demons had a hold on his mind.

"Lord Almighty."

These were the only words audible to Glenda, but his lips had moved before and after, so she asked him to say again.

He looked at her with eyes dull from exhaustion. "Pray for my soul."

Glenda stared at his harrowed face, lost for words.

"Pity on my soul." He drew a new breath. "You ask the Lord Almighty to have pity."

Matt's words were taking hold. A dying man spent his last breaths asking forgiveness. He was running out of time, she realized. To Matt, life was no matter of days or hours, but of a few lousy breaths.

Glenda reached for his hand and held it between hers, as she spoke softly, aimlessly, piecing together whatever shards of goodwill she could draw from her bruised heart. He must've heard her, for his eyes closed and he lay very still, as if readying himself for the passage.

She prayed for his soul, asking her good Father to forgive Matt his sins and, through Jesus Christ the redeemer, to take Matt even unto His bosom and deliver him from the fiery pit. When she could think of nothing further to add, she said amen and sat silent at his side.

Then she noticed that his eyes had opened.

"Pat O'Connor was indentured to an English lord, you know."

Glenda didn't know how to reply. She had to presume that he was growing delirious, though in fact she had heard of indentures. It was something the English did to the Irish. According to cousin Devon, it had been ever thus.

"Milo was indentured, because his old man was Pat."

Matt was looking her square in the eye, struggling at each breath. Glenda held his gaze, though she couldn't see any sense to his words.

"And Seamus same thing, because his old man was Milo. As good as slaves, they were. Not a stick of furniture to call their own."

Glenda bowed her head. "I've protested this in my own family," she said softly. "But a woman's voice is not loud enough."

Matt stared at her without speaking. She couldn't guess what he was thinking, or if he'd even heard her. A froth was forming on his lips. At length, he coughed some blood.

"And Matt had Seamus for a father." His words fell hard and empty. "The rich robbing the poor and callin' it the power of law."

He succumbed to another coughing fit, worse this time, and

blood bubbling freely from the corner of his mouth.

"I had to get out. I left Ireland," he went on feebly, "or they would've had me too, same as my old man. They robbed us to the bone. And here's me a robber, same as them. So if I burn in hell, I want to see them there. The bailiff and the jailer and the lords of the manor, all their bloody arses on fire."

He had no voice left, just a faint rustle on his breath. When Glenda didn't move, Matt's fingers stirred between her hands as if to beckon her.

"Come."

Glenda could easily resist his feeble effort, but lowered her head towards his lips. Out of nowhere, her back received a crushing blow which pressed her down upon Matt's body, her nose flat against his, her chin in the prickly hollow of his jaw. His hand slipped from her grasp and reached behind to join the attacker whom, she realized, was none other than his free arm, locked around her ribs like a vise of iron. The sudden strength of his arms was enough to squeeze all air from her lungs. She couldn't get her breath long enough to scream. A cold terror washed over her and throttled her so that, gasping pathetically, all she could manage was to flail with her arms against Matt's leg.

So this is it, a voice was saying in her head; this is how you will perish at the hands of these men. Matt has made a fool of you and, duped into compassion, this nameless hillside will see you satisfying his every desire. Glenda was choking on her own panic, close to vomiting, but nothing seemed to matter to Matt. He had one purpose only, which was to permit no air between her body and his.

As Glenda tried to crane her head away from his jaw, she became aware that he wasn't fondling her. His mouth was nowhere near hers. Matt lay underneath with arms locked around her; she felt herself riding upon his heaving chest, rising and falling to the wheezing cadence of his breath. His eyes were open but unconcerned with her.

Glenda tried to steady herself and get her wind. Trapped in his embrace, beyond any hope of escape, she waited to discover what was wanted of her. Matt was holding her as though his life depended upon it. Maybe it did. Perchance a warm body against death was all he wanted. Or was it his vengeance upon the English? Or had he lusted after her all along and resolved to have his prize before life was done, only to find himself without the strength to mount her? Or else she was nothing to him, a mere blanket against the black frost advancing from within.

Still she waited and Matt made no further move. Her neck ached from trying to dodge his sour breath. Glenda's eye lingered on the rugged set of his face. Whatever was afoot with Matt's soul, it was not apparent to her. He had gone inside of himself now, into the mystery, his eyes dull and distant. He held her only as a drowning man clings to a plank. She could breathe again; his arms had not moved, but their strength was leaving.

Had he meant to ravish her or had he sought to steady himself against the final plummet? The longer he held her, the more uncertain she became. Carnal heat and the hope of immortality. Maybe they're one and the same, thought Glenda. Maybe it's all the same. Beneath her, all was still. His chest had ceased to rock her up or down. The warm, odorous breath upon her cheek had faded. The dull crystal of his eye was empty. Around the corners of his mouth, the brown skin still held those deep curving lines which, alone, testified to the mirth and boldness which had, for all time, passed from Matt's body.

Glenda allowed her head to settle on his cheek. All the fear and foreboding had passed from her. She could've pushed his arm off her back and been rid of him. But she was tired. It was a comfort to feel her limbs relaxing over his massive frame, as if settling deeper, almost sinking into his warmth. In a few hours, he would be cold as the rock. Glenda lay motionless with a distant strain of the ocean in her ears, that faint, hypnotic murmur that persists when all else has ceased.

Out of the corner of her eye, she was aware of the condors, several of them now. Their unhurried diligence was shocking in this ghastly stillness. Glenda could glimpse one of them circling directly overhead.

But something else was there. She knew, in a flash, that she was being watched and not only by that pair of hungry, airborne eyes. Twisting her neck slightly, she discovered Leclair. He stood a few paces back. Slung across his shoulder was Papa, bony legs like a pair of pendulums across Leclair's chest. Leclair was wearing that same smirk again, the odd grimace of amusement which had come over him while Big Raoul fondled her on Woolsley's ship.

What in the name of Hecuba! Had she made herself too comfortable? With both arms, Glenda thrust herself away from the body. The limp arms slithered off her back and she was free.

"Are you amused?" she said, getting to her feet. "He's dead."

Leclair nodded slowly, the smirk still pasted on his face as though her remark had no bearing on his glee.

"He was a good man," said Glenda. "The only one among you."

Leclair gazed upon Matt's square jaw.

"Here's such another," he murmured, using the arm that cradled Papa's body to give the old man a light squeeze. "He's still got some life in 'em but not for long, unless I can get him a surgeon. Come this way."

Leclair turned and began to walk up the road, clutching his precious burden. Before she knew it, Glenda was walking after.

"Where are we going?"

"There's a doctor in Gustavia. He'll do his best for Papa."

Glenda glanced over her shoulder. "How about Matt?"

Leclair took no notice of her.

"Will you not give him a burial?"

The pirate stopped and slowly swung Papa half circle. Their

eyes met.

"Have a look," was all he said, his free arm making a sweep across the hideous display of the hillside.

Glenda apprehended his meaning and lowered her eyes in gloomy surrender. He trudged on, she following a few paces behind.

Once the salt marsh was behind them, Leclair veered off the road into a thicket of cactus and thistle. Glenda kept to the road, begging her Holy Father that He might fill Leclair so full of cares about the old man that he wouldn't miss her until she was out of sight. But her Holy Father was of no help. Within fifteen paces, Leclair had reached for his pistol. He didn't even waste his breath on words of menace but, without bothering to turn, waved his weapon as if to say, don't do anything you'd regret.

Glenda gave a sigh of desolation and followed, not without dismay but lacking the energy to act upon it. She had a hold of her skirt in each hand, lifting and sashaying between the thorns and spikes that threatened to tear it to shreds.

She was startled to find Leclair doing her the courtesy of anticipating her next request. "The soldiers will be using the road," he said, panting. "Soon as it gets dark, we can come out."

They were still walking uphill, making their way through a dense tangle of vines and shrubbery. Clouds had overtaken the sun and cast a sombre pall among the trees. Yet, Leclair's face was beaded with sweat. Glenda could hear him struggling for breath. She, too, was feeling the strain but could barely imagine the added burden of another's body.

CR ЯО

Barrels and crates are stacked up everywhere. Olof's nostrils are numbed by the foulness of bilge-water; he can hear it lapping softly underneath the crates. From above comes the occasional laugh or holler, but no more screams or pistol shots. The carnage must have come to an end. He has no idea how long he's been huddled behind the sugar crates. Now he must find a way to learn what has happened up above.

As Olof gropes along in the dark crawlspace, he tries to imagine what he's going to find. A warm drip catches him on the cheek and he jumps back. He wipes it off with his index finger, then rubs his thumb against it. There's no smell of oil or tar, but it's smoother and more viscous than water. He puts it to the tip of his tongue, then spits quickly. Someone's blood.

He can hear it dripping now, and almost trickling, onto the barrels. Again, the nausea wells up in his throat and he has to gasp for air. He hastens his step, not knowing what he'll do once he gets there. He had scrambled on hands and knees across these same trunks and caskets, bruising his arms on iron girths and hinges. His hiding place must be well forward of the main mast, somewhere below the galley. He is retracing his steps, treading carefully to avoid any tell-tale noise.

From far above comes a muffled crash of something heavy, followed by faint rounds of laughter. Amidships, he recognizes the black oblique of the stairs and, holding his breath, creeps up through the hatchway.

Ascending through the hatch, the first thing that meets Olof's eye is the round gaze of the ship's doctor. The doctor's stare is fixed at the deck from an elevation of a few inches, his ruddy cheek flat against the boards. The man is prostrate in his own blood, his throat slashed and still throbbing.

Olof glances quickly down the low corridor of the berth deck, charging and priming his pistol. He doesn't want to fire it, thus drawing untimely attention. He's standing somewhat aft of the main hatch. It hasn't been opened, though the pirates can be heard shuffling to and fro overhead. They'll be climbing down for booty any minute. About fifteen feet away, one of the ship's crew has fallen back against the main mast, pistolled right between the eyes. The man is mostly on the floor, only his head and shoulders propped upright, his arms limp and toes turned out.

Olof steps off the stairs and goes to the dead man, stooping to pick his cutlass from the floor. As he straightens up, he finds himself looking down the barrel of a pirate's pistol.

He has no idea where this bearded fellow was hiding; in fact, the pirate looks just as surprised. If the man's pistol goes off, Olof will be dead or, at the least, all others will be alerted. It may be his saving grace that the fellow has already tasted too much rum. With a spin of the wrist, Olof delivers a perfect butcher's stroke of the cutlass, severing most of the pirate's hand from his arm. The pistol lands with a thud, still attached to the man's fingers. The pirate has found no sound for his amazement and, before he does, the same cutlass runs him through. The broad blade enters the pirate's chest but gets stuck.

Olof rushes the pirate now, knocking him off balance. The man gives a howl for help, reeling backwards, stumbling and mincing his steps. They lunge across the deck in a macabre *pas-de-deux*, the prodding cutlass ever outpacing the pirate, who is given no chance to recover his balance. With a slam, he runs the pirate against a bulkhead. The cutlass breaks through to the wood behind. The pirate goes limp, collapsing on the floor.

Olof stands awhile, breathing hard. All is quiet. Crouching, he walks through the shadowy waist of the ship, stepping over another sailor whose head is nowhere to be seen.

At the companionway, Olof checks his pistol once again. Then he climbs the stairs to gun deck. His entire body is possessed of the darkest dread. At every step and every twitch of the eye, he expects a pistol's flame. But none appears. On gun deck, the corridor is quiet. All the noise and clamouring comes from outdoors, at mid-deck.

He runs to the second door on the left and swings it open. But Cecilia is nowhere to be seen. The oak chest hasn't been touched.

For a moment, he cannot move. The narrow chamber closes in around him. Only the knocking of his heart. Through several bulkheads the clamour reaches him, builds to a deafening drone in his ears, twisting his entrails.

Stepping back into the corridor, Olof walks as in a dream, magnetized by the pandemonious sounds from mid-deck. A ladder carries him through the hatchway to quarter-deck. He has abandoned caution, forgotten all but one thought. Without further ado, he climbs into the open air and, as providence would have it, there's no cutlass to crack him on the head.

The quarter-deck is empty aside from a few slain mariners. The air is balmy and steeped in twilight. A low sandbar runs in a crescent on their stern. He drops to his knees and crawls forward. He can look across to the forecastle and now mid-deck begins to emerge.

He drops flat on his face, pressing his eyes shut against what he just saw. All other thoughts have fled. His mind is no longer a vessel for thought, but only for seeing, for drinking of this poison.

He worms his way to a fallen mariner whose body teeters at the forward edge of the quarter-deck. From behind the corpse, he rears his head just far enough to give himself a view of the spectacle below. No turning back, no turning aside. It is plain to him now.

CR SO

FROM MEMORY

ೞ ೮ঽ

From where they sat, Glenda could see the moon meandering in and out of clouds. Their legs dangled from the back of a sturdy two-wheeled wain, rattling and bumping along as the farmer guided his crop of sugar cane up the hill. Leclair sat beside her, with Papa's head propped on his thigh. Behind her back, the old man's body lay knee-deep in husks and straw. The bundles had been stacked snugly between built-up side panels.

Glenda was gazing down between her feet, mesmerized by the stones and potholes fleeing into the darkness behind them. She was shivering now, hugging herself to keep warm though at times she needed her arm to stay herself from being thrown into the road.

"How is he?"

Leclair had his hand on Papa's sunken shoulder. "Still breathing."

She nodded, mostly to herself. The old sea-cook was as stubborn as they come. She had grappled with him once in Gustavia; she knew what mettle he was made of. The skin might be shrivelled as a fig, but there was no stopping the pump within. A half-smile tugged at the corner of her mouth as she listened to the merry tune of the farmer, singing to his ox in the still of night.

With both arms, Leclair reached under Papa to shift him gently, ever so lightly into a better position. A wind was rising in the trees and the dark was full of whisperings.

"And how are *you*?" asked Leclair after a silence.

She was lost for words. He hadn't asked her such a question. Not ever. Her impulse was to reply mockingly, but she stayed her tongue.

"I am broken inside and out."

Leclair let out an indeterminate grunt. "Be patient. Gustavia is over this hill. Another half of an hour."

In the corner of her eye, Glenda felt him observing her. Naturally, her words had had nothing to do with the helter-skelter of cartwheels. The longer he kept eyeing her, the more certain she became that he, too, knew better.

"How's the old man?" hollered the farmer from behind his sugar cane.

"Still breathing!" repeated Leclair loudly over the crunching of the wheels.

"I don't ask questions," came the farmer's voice. "I don't know if it's a surgeon or a priest he wants but, whatever it is, is none of my concern so long as you have a fear of God."

Glenda glanced towards Leclair, whose face was hidden in deep shadow.

"We fear God," he replied, "and in His name we thank you."

There was no further word from beyond the sugar cane. Maybe the farmer was content with this acknowledgement. The singing did not resume; his thoughts must've shifted to something else.

Glenda shuddered in the wind.

"If you'll release me, I shall never tell a living soul," she said.

"Release you?"

Leclair seemed genuinely startled.

"Release me, yes. Allow me to return to good society."

"Good society?" He echoed her like a parrot.

Glenda said nothing. The cartwheels rumbled on as they neared the summit.

"Why should you cleave to my company when you despise our very nature? You frown upon my faults and yet you've spared me from degradation? Why is it thus? You've foregone such advantage as you could, by your own admission, expect to have of me."

"I'm at the end of my patience. Do you understand? Women

have made me weary."

"Then give me leave to go," said Glenda.

Leclair jumped in almost before she had finished. "Mark this, how our institutions, our seats of office and government and every manner of leadership and enterprise gives preference to men. To be sure, men rule in affairs of the world. But in the affairs of nature, it's not so. In womankind, nature has triumphed over reason. Herein lies Monsieur Rousseau's mistake, for he claims that nature is incapable of folly. Yet what folly is there, greater than a woman's?"

Glenda stared at the dark oval of his face as she began to speak.

"I was raised, sir, in a small hamlet of England. I learned to say my prayers every day of the week. When my father died, Mother asked my uncle what he thought should become of me. He's not a scholar, yet of such a mind as had freely embraced the new philosophy. From my third birthday, he had spoke of me as the serious one, his serious niece. I suppose that's why he took charge of my schooling and had me tutored beyond the scope of my peers. I've known but a single suitor in my life and he has all my affections."

"You mean he *had*, before he sailed to the bottom."

"I've never desired another," she said, her voice trembling. "Had I been forced, by you or another of your vagrants, to forfeit my chastity, it should've mattered less than nothing in my heart. I'm a woman well-versed in letters, arithmetic, botany, and music and I'm possessed of a perfect heart. What, then, is this folly you speak of? Can you show me my folly?"

Glenda caught her breath, cheeks burning with passion. In the silence, the cartwheels groaned and rumbled. The dark forest had receded and, rising between the treetops, the lights of Gustavia gleamed like a dainty jewel on the coast below.

"You've not been put to trial," said Leclair, his voice now brittle with scorn. "You've not been tried. I knew someone that was. But you live in the world of reason. It's the smaller world, within a larger one that cannot be rightly accounted for. Didn't I tell you so? You're not bleeding yet. Therefore be assured, you're not what you seem."

Glenda was so furious that only her teeth clamped into the lower lip could stifle a reckless reply. There was nothing she wanted so much as to tell him off, to knock him off his high horse, to meet Leclair's trial head to head and cast off his mystic pose of self-importance. But she turned her head away.

She was shaking uncontrollably, not from tears nor from the bitter wind but from an ache that would not leave until she knew who that someone was.

ⓒⱨ ⱷⓓ

For the moment, the terrace was bright with moonlight.

Leclair stopped at the settee. He removed Papa's arm from around his neck and stooped low, releasing the old man onto the wooden seat.

"Papa, wake up," he said softly. "Normand. Ho, Normand."

The wizened old face was lost in slumbers, his breath feverish and shallow.

Leclair straightened his back, wiping the sweat from his eyebrows. From below his shoulder-blade came a stitch of pain. It had plagued him the whole way, even on the oxcart when he was free of Papa's weight. That's how he knew it was deep. He had drawn a few long breaths to test his lung for injury; it seemed to be unaffected. He took a few steps, unaccustomed to the lightness.

The house was empty now, drapes drawn across each window and nothing but darkness within. The good widow had moved out, he was sure of it. She had likely sailed for Sweden. After all, what was left for her in Gustavia? This smattering of odd expatriates who had gravitated to each other in hopes of simulating what they had left behind. The polite, inquisitive teas and conversations to fend off an inexorable intrusion of climate and latitude which, in the end, had left no one intact. Mrs. Cederhök would do far better back in old Linköping, with someone to shovel out her front steps and stoke her fire in the cold months.

For himself it was different. There was no going back, certainly not under Gustav IV Adolphus. A fourteen-year old on the throne of Sweden, surrounded by a clutch of over-zealous ministers. King Gustav's ghost still presided.

He contemplated the shimmering view beyond the terrace. It was as though the ocean took wing at night, rising from her natural bed and sleepwalking across the island, leaving the tiled rooftops and the steep alleyways soaked in sea water. Greasy amber lanterns gleamed from doorpost and archway, reflected in the wet stone.

On the hillside, between the harbour and the heights, palm trees swayed and bowed like black phantoms in the wind, intercepting the light in subtle, twinkling charades. The wind carried a faint clamour from the Wall House. He wondered who might be there tonight. Maybe Fenwick would be celebrating. Or would he keep himself offshore for a while?

Leclair glanced across to the adjoining hillside, where Fort Gustav presided above the inky black of the forest. That's how it had begun, with the Englishman inquiring about his rank and discovering the Swedish flag at half-mast. They had sipped their rum toddy and found a spot near the white balustrade, a few steps from where he was now standing, possibly on the same stone now occupied by Glenda. She had her back to him, savouring the view of a civilized community.

He found himself wanting to know her thoughts. He had pictured her chastity as a chalice of finest crystal. With a single swipe of the hand, he would smash it beyond repair as, indeed, he had done with countless others. After each successful sea caper, he had drowned himself in lust and liquor, rivalled only by Matt and Raoul. Time and time again, he had revelled in sweet amnesiacs of the flesh. Again and again, he had proven the end of innocence.

But here, across from him on the pale terrace, was a crystal unbroken. He couldn't quite account for it. He remembered an eerie recognition, from the first day, of Glenda's neck and collarbone, of her bearing, perhaps the particular disposition of her shoulders and physical proportion.

She turned and looked anxiously towards him. Leaning against the balustrade, the moonlight played tricks with her hair, with his eyes, with the years. Shadows rose and fell across her cheeks and her bosom. Had it been her standing there, how sweet the sight! How sweet and inimitable! Blessed and reconciled at last!

"Are you not well?"

The voice that broke upon his ear was another. Hers was not the flaxen hair. He squinted at her awkwardly.

"You look like a ghost," she went on, her voice trembling.

How fitting, he mused to himself. He gave his head a slow shake. Glenda came away from the balustrade. "Three times I've called to you."

Leclair had to hold it far enough inside. It was the vault with a lock, the vault that must not open. He gave a dismissive shrug of the shoulders.

"For the last time," insisted Glenda, "are you rested? I'm getting cold."

"Yes, we'd best be going," murmured Leclair. "It's not far."

They walked back up the slight incline of the terrace. Papa hadn't moved. Leclair dropped on one knee and yoked himself once again to the old man.

"So this was the magistrate's house," said Glenda, passing her fingertips across the well-preserved paint.

Here they had strolled, bathed in gold, among the after-dinner parasols and conversations. Her head on his shoulder. Her hair at his ear.

But his thoughts crumbled. His eye returned to the barren, desolate moonlight. Leclair found himself shaking from the cold. The old man's body gave him some warmth and shelter.

They followed the boarded veranda alongside the house. Leclair took a long look up and down the dark street but not a soul was stirring. By this hour, it seemed, the townsfolk had either retired for the night or gone down to the docks.

Not far, Glenda recalled him saying. She prayed that it was so.

C03 80

NATURE'S VACUUM

℘ ℂ

This one stands a head taller than the rest, and the arm that stops his comrade has the thickness of a cross-tree. He nods to the two robbers. They back away, releasing her arms.

Her eyes turn to him, dull and confused. With his boot on her rose-coloured dress, the man rolls her slowly off the coiled rope. She ends up on the ship's deck, flat on her back.

"Now here's somethin'," he hollers. "You call yourselves men, do you? You want a piece of wench and all you know how to do is take. You cretins. Asses! Untaught puppies!"

Some faces glower at him darkly. Others are grinning, thrilled to be his puppy. Everyone is poised for his next word. He peels the shirt off his back. As he bends over the young woman, every movement ripples through the muscled ridges of his torso. He drops to his knees, her white legs on either side of him.

"Give us a bit of a show," blurts someone, with a loud hiccup.

The men murmur excitedly in each other's ear.

"Alright now," yells he of the cleft upper lip, "you've been talkin', Raoul, but can you do it? Are you a man for it, Raoul?"

Big Raoul drops his breeches around his knee. A hush descends on everyone. Though his shoulders cast a shadow across the groin, there's no mistaking the silhouette pointing from his thigh, heavy as the unsheathed erection of a stallion.

ℂ ℘

Leclair winced, pressing his eyes shut. When he looked again, he could see better.

The brass plate spelled "Tobias Henckell, Medicus".

He nodded to Glenda, so she reached for the knocker and rapped three times.

They waited. Leclair had rolled Papa off his shoulder and was holding him by the waist, propping his own weight against the doorpost. Neither of them spoke. Leclair was in too much pain and Glenda was too cold.

Leclair tugged at Papa, jolting him back to life. The old sea-cook hadn't opened his eyes or uttered a word since Leclair came back up to fetch him on the hillside. Leclair's torment rolled inwards in waves from the gash at his back and outwards from the smouldering grief at his core.

Papa's face had always been a riddle; the flat indifference of his lean, leathery features was not a measure of his thoughts, but of his skill in keeping those thoughts to himself. But tonight, Leclair was seeing the same inscrutable face and looking right through it. Only Chloe could've seen, as he did, that there was nothing now to hide, that behind the mask was nothing left.

The door swung open. Glenda stepped back as a massive figure darkened the doorway. The good doctor peered at them with spectacles askew on his nose.

Leclair looked him in the eye, poised for whatever was to follow. Henckell observed them calmly but still made no reply, so Leclair said, "May we come inside?"

Doctor Henckell had noted the limp body at Leclair's shoulder. Huffing all the while, he backed away from the threshold and Leclair dragged Papa inside. Glenda followed after, squeezing politely past the heave and huff of Henckell's voluminous shirt-front.

His was a commodious and well-appointed sitting-room. The colours were austere, with dark wainscoting half way up the wall and armchairs of polished mahogany. From on top of the chiffonier came a feeble lantern's glow. A small wood stove gave the only other light, the reflected flames skittering phantasmally upon the darkened wall.

"The Lord be praised," cheered Glenda and hurried to the stove to warm herself.

Henckell shuffled off after her.

He, too, had grown old, noted Leclair. His unconscionable weight was finally getting the best of him. The doctor had always been remarkable for the great hulk of his mortal frame, but never pitiable. At last, it had defeated him. As he waddled about, his body seemed not so imposing as grotesque. And escaping the inclemencies of Swedish winter had evidently not been sufficient to rid him of his rheumatism. His ankles had worsened.

"I'll have a look at him," said Henckell, drawing the brown velvet from a doorway.

Leclair stepped through and hoisted Papa's body onto a table that bore an eerie resemblance to a chopping block. He turned Papa onto his stomach, tucking the old man's arm under his cheek for cushion.

Meanwhile, the doctor had rolled up his sleeves.

"He's been shot," said Leclair. "The ball must out."

Henckell's eye went to Leclair. He felt the doctor's unabashed scrutiny upon his face. Then, breathing loudly through his nose, Henckell set about removing Papa's shirt.

"Your accent is Swedish," said he.

Leclair clasped the corner of the table, steadying himself. He kept his eye on Papa, whose back was encrusted with black blood. Two inches from the spine, the English pistol shot had entered his right lung.

"Is he going to live?" asked Leclair.

Henckell had brought his instruments from a low cabinet by the door.

"Först en tvagning. Herrn får vara god och hälla lite vatten på såret."

Henckell was indicating a bucket beneath the table.

Leclair stepped around to the far side and picked the bucket off the floor. He felt a dizziness come over him but proceeded to drain the bucket slowly over Papa's ribs, while Henckell loosened the crusted blood with his towel.

Papa made no sound or movement but, mercifully, his ribs still signalled a faint rhythm from the lungs. The doctor dabbed the wound until the skin showed a clean, raw edge around the little hole. He had uncorked a bottle of ether and sprinkled a small amount over the wound.

Something must've come to him at that moment. When he set the bottle down, his hands remained idle on the edge of the table. For several moments, Henckell gazed solemnly at Papa while the blood began to unclot and seep.

Then he turned his spectacles back on Leclair. "Begging your pardon," he continued in Swedish, "I surely know that voice. Are you not Lieutenant-Major Crohnstedt?"

The doctor sounded calm, almost amused.

Leclair had prepared no disguise. He had anticipated that he might not go unrecognized, but nothing had prepared him for this. To hear his native name again, after three years. A hidden vein of fire began to throb behind his ribs.

He had chosen Henckell not only because the doctor was likely the best that the island had to offer, but because Henckell's loyalty was certain. So Henckell knew his old name. More to the point, did he know about his *new* name?

The doctor's question still hovered between them while they eyed one another. Behind Henckell, the brown velvet moved and Glenda appeared in the doorway. She looked somewhat restored.

"Olof was my name," answered Leclair, unaccustomed to speaking Swedish. And training his eye on Papa, "The young lady is not to know."

Henckell flashed him a half smile and, shaking his grey locks, took the scalpel in hand. He tested the edge on Papa's skin. The old man gave no response. Henckell pushed the point just barely through the skin, still keeping his eye on Papa's face. Reassured, the doctor began to probe the wound. The depth at which the pistol's ball had lodged would determine the nature of his incision.

Heeding Leclair's request, he continued in Swedish. "Olof, is it possible?"

"I didn't perish," said Leclair simply.

Glenda noticed a stool and settled upon it, releasing her weary back against the wall. She was intrigued by the foreign conversation. It must be Swedish. Leclair was speaking Swedish.

The doctor had spread his broad fingers across Papa's skin, to steady himself as he manoeuvered the scalpel between thumb and forefinger.

"We had heard you were dead."

Leclair was observing Henckell's handiwork. "I would've been, except for this old man."

The words made no sense to Glenda, mere conglomerations of sound. She found herself interpreting their voices, their intonations to each other. They weren't strangers, that much was clear. A pregnancy of thought and deliberation played, in turn, upon their faces.

"I did perish," resumed Leclair, "but it was different. It was Olof that died."

A groan burst from Papa. Leclair's heart jumped with hope. Henckell withdrew his blade. Papa's mouth was twitching at the corners. From the cabinet, Henckell brought a fresh towel to wipe the seeping blood. The used one was tossed into a large enamelled basin. Then a quick rub of ether along the knife's edge and his work went on. Papa moaned pitiably and, more than once, a scowl creased his forehead or the corner of his eye.

Leclair had to steel himself against the sight.

"You're bleeding," said Henckell calmly.

Leclair was tempted to smile. This was Henckell at his best. His attention didn't stray from Papa. But from some earlier moment of their meeting, Henckell had determined that the stains on Leclair's shirt were also Leclair's. And above all, what Henckell thought was not always what Henckell said; not until

he was ready, not until now, and without urgency or even inquisitiveness. In view of the fact that Leclair's shirt had been sopping
up Papa's blood all day, the doctor's observation was miraculous.

"There now," said Henckell, holding the little lead ball in his
cupped hand. And then he switched to broken English, "Take
your shirt off."

The doctor picked another towel off the cabinet. It was
discoloured from old blood forever boiled into the cloth.
Henckell folded it into a small, thick pad which he pressed over
the laceration on Papa's back.

From a peg on the wall, he fetched a leather girdle. Huffing
loudly with the effort, he slipped it under Papa's belly and
centered it over the cotton pad, pulling the buckle tight. Already
the cloth showed some fresh blood, but pressure would help stem
the flow.

"We'll sit by the fire," said Henckell, giving Glenda a cordial
nod.

She answered his attention with a smile, thankful for his
courtesy, his expertise, his capable hands. Apparently this made
no impression on the doctor for he reverted to Swedish again and
left her, once more, to her own surmises.

"Who is she?" asked Henckell as they stepped into the sitting-
room.

With some effort, Leclair was pulling the shirt over his head.
He had no easy answer for the doctor nor, he realized now, for
himself.

"I'm very tired," he said, dropping onto his knees.

He eased himself down on his stomach in front of the stove.

Glenda came into the room and stopped, her hand to her
mouth. A lustrous bluish scar reached like a leprosy from
Leclair's left shoulder and covered one-third of his back. At the
extreme fingers of the scar, a new gash had been opened. All day,
realized Glenda, he'd been toiling with the weight of Papa while
ignoring an injury of his own.

She wanted to say it to him, not as a reprimand but to commend him, though by now Glenda felt so much the intruder that the words stuck in her throat. So she flopped listlessly into an armchair by the front door.

"Nothing to fret about," mumbled Henckell while sprinkling some ether on a fresh towel. "I'm more interested in your burn."

Leclair's chin jumped off the floor as the doctor dabbed his stab wound. There was the sting of the ether and then the other sting, of realizing that he had thoughtlessly exposed his old scar. He forced his eyes shut, groaning through clenched teeth. Then he opened his eye a crack to check on Glenda's whereabouts. She had her head back against the chair, eyes shut.

"I didn't see it coming," said Leclair. "They told me it was lightning."

He could hear the doctor breathing above his head. Henckell's hands explored the wasted tissue. To Leclair it was, at most, a remote sense of pressure, a dull nudging, nothing more.

But the good doctor had become inquisitive. His fingers worked more intricately. "We have here," said he, still maintaining the privacy afforded by their Swedish, "something which is known in medicine by the name of fistula."

Henckell paused. Leclair had let his head down on the floorboards.

Glenda rose from her chair and began to amble aimlessly. Leclair guarded her from under half-closed eyelids.

"After a laceration, the flesh begins to heal. So also, in your instance, the body began to manufacture new tissue."

"They had a poultice for my back," remembered Leclair. "Old Papa and his wife. Day and night, they attended to me."

"You owe them your life, my son, or the use of your arm perhaps. But they didn't understand your fistula."

The conversation had proceeded without Glenda, so she resolved to make herself useful. She pushed the brown velvet aside and walked through to see if there was anything she could do for Papa.

Meanwhile, Leclair's eyes had opened. He was listening. "What is a fistula?"

Henckell had some ointment on his fingers and was rubbing it over the dead tissue.

"As we say, nature abhors a vacuum. Therefore, where the skin is broken, she'll mend it. Where the flesh has been sundered, it will come together as one. But when the laceration goes deeper, nature may fail. Infection may linger unseen in the recesses of the flesh. So, you see, the natural course of physic is obstructed. Nature is disabled. Instead of filling the recess with new blood and flesh, it remains a hollow. Yours is at the shoulderblade, under the edge of bone."

Leclair could feel nothing at all.

"Do you have any sensation?"

Leclair shook his head.

"Skin began to grow on the inside," Henckell went on. "It means you'll be safe. It's become a skin-clad tunnel beneath the surface. That's a fistula. You have nothing to fear, no pain, no infection. But it has no means of closing."

"What should I do?" asked Leclair suddenly.

"Nothing at all. Nothing to fret about." Henckell sounded confident.

Without warning, a great sob burst from the other room.

Leclair wriggled out from under the doctor's hands and crashed through the brown velvet to find Glenda standing by Papa's table, white as a sheet.

He didn't have to ask her. He knew what he would find when he looked over at the old man. He didn't even check his ribs for breathing.

The face had told him all.

CR SO

RITES OF PASSAGE

৩০ ৫৪

"I'll fetch you a ride," said Henckell a long while later, after they had rolled Papa's body into a blanket and laid it to rest inside the door.

It was raining outside, a driving rain that rattled the window panes.

"Be my guests tonight. I have a boy who brings my shopping in the morning. He'll find you a carriage."

Leclair hadn't stirred from the chopping-block table, upon which he was perched with legs dangling. He needed to decide what to make of the doctor. The pelting rain pounded in his ears; it kept growing louder and louder. His mind seemed incapable of anything but an eternity of rain.

"But first, tell me what happened." The doctor's voice came from behind the brown drapes. He was being sociable now, speaking in English and stirring a toddy on the stove.

"It's a long story," said Leclair evasively. "I'm not sure I'm up to it."

"Come and join us," said Henckell. "A cupful will do you good."

Leclair walked back into the sitting-room. Glenda had made herself cozy on the settee, cradling a cup of steaming toddy between her hands.

Henckell handed Leclair his cup. "What about Cecilia?"

Leclair filled his mouth with the warm beverage, allowing it to pass slowly into his gullet. Henckell's question wasn't going to ruffle him, especially not in English and in the presence of this woman.

"Doctor, you've been very kind," said Leclair, mustering a smile.

"Who is Cecilia?" asked Glenda suddenly. It was obvious to her what Leclair was up to. She needed to know why.

His eyes shifted to her and, once again, a brittle glint of contempt had turned him into a different person.

Henckell gulped back the last of his toddy. "Do you recall a Mrs. Fridell?" he asked, apparently wishing to forestall further tension. "Well," said he, squeezing into an armchair, "she married Hansson."

Leclair couldn't resist a smile.

"Wonders never cease," mused the doctor. "A year ago, Hansson offered his apology for that damned business with Ribbing. Cupid's arrow overtook them directly."

"Was Ribbing a rival?" inquired Glenda.

Henckell gave a laugh that rocked his huge frame and the chair along with it. "Not a rival, no." He glanced at Leclair. "Ribbing had been her father's pupil, remember? And next thing, he was on the list with Anckarström."

Glenda would've enjoyed the doctor's gossip, except that she felt her eyelids getting heavy. "Pray, what had he done?"

"He helped murder the King of Sweden, the king who gave his name to Gustavia."

Glenda felt a shiver down her spine.

"Anckarström fired the fatal shot, you see, but Ribbing was nearby. To this day, their names are dirt. Theirs and many more."

Glenda lolled her head against the wall. It had to be long past midnight. She was distracted by that other name, the longer name. At the doctor's second mention, it had tweaked something in her memory. Anckarström. Where had she met an Anckarström? Try as she might, Glenda couldn't picture him. Nor would her eyes open. Words kept humming in her ear but made no sense.

Leclair rose from his chair. "Look," he said, reverting to Swedish, "how you've put her to sleep."

The doctor shrugged his shoulders jovially, as much as to say *touché.* "You've not yet introduced me to the young lady."

"She's my captive. Nothing more to know."

Henckell arched his eyebrow, much impressed. Again he eyed Glenda, whose head hung forward, lifting slightly at each breath of her bosom.

"But if Olof died, who is he that still breathes?"

Leclair met the doctor's gaze. What Henckell thought was not always what Henckell said.

So, Leclair drew the pistol from his belt. "You shall hear more when I return."

Henckell shook his head, a rueful smile about his lips. He gestured for them to follow and started up the wooden stairs.

But Leclair knew that Henckell would not hear the rest, that there could be no returning. It was too dangerous already. He would bury Papa on the mountain and set out for Anse Paschal. They were going to wait for him until sundown. Such had been his parting words with Big Raoul.

Leclair took the cup from Glenda's hand and set it on the window sill. He reached around her and, with some pain from his wound, hoisted her in his arms. Henckell waddled ahead as they made their way to the upstairs.

Glenda dreamt she was being carried. In her dream, it was Leclair who carried her. He must never find out that she could dream like this.

CR SO

When in his cups, Fenwick was wont to chatter. This time was no exception. Even at the Wall House the revelry had subsided, the hour being a full watch past midnight. But Fenwick was nowhere near subsiding.

He had begun his ascent of those winding stairs to the private chambers, ably assisted by Madeleine. It was merely the prelude to an hour or more of conveying Fenwick from his table to the upstairs chamber where Madeleine would remove his garments - to his general delight and approbation - whereupon she would tuck him into bed, fondle the forlorn appendage between his legs and give him the fullness of her breast for a pillow.

Once he was snoring, she could claim her customary three ducats from his purse and go home to Antoine, rinse her hands and make love to him until he went off on the fishing boats at crack of dawn. But that was still an hour away and, for the moment, Fenwick's gleeful cackle would spill along the corridor and through the walls into each darkened chamber.

He was being particularly unmanageable on the stairs. "It's well past your bedtime," said he, holding her firmly by the buttock. "I'm afraid I've ruined you altogether."

Madeleine smiled as she strained to hoist his unruly frame one step higher.

Fenwick gazed over the banister, trying to comprehend what was going on below. The proprietor, whatever his name, had instructed his boys to clean tables and stack benches against the wall. Fenwick gave a beneficent smile.

He had no idea what the time was. He couldn't begin to guess how long ago Hansson had bid him a good night, that dreadful, upright, earnest bore of a man who could never stop gnattering about his little wife and how their love had overcome even Swedish politics. These Swedes really were a breed unto themselves. These long-legged, obliging do-gooders. Their presence here was a blemish on the West Indies, mused Fenwick, an accident of European statesmanship which would surely right itself before long.

"You've got the smile of an angel," he told Madeleine. "Did you know that?"

She shook her head demurely, though she knew right well that she did. Antoine told her as much almost every day.

"In my considered opinion," huffed Fenwick, hauling himself

up by the banister. And then again, "In my considered opinion… oh my God but that's a good arm you've got there, girl." He giggled as Madeleine did her utmost to coax him along. "As I was saying, they're an odd sort, those Swedes. They've had pretensions of empire, you see. Pretensions, I say, because there's no more substance to it. Greatness is not in their destiny and well they know it. But there's the rub, for it's made them bitter. If they cannot play, they'll sit in judgement. And spite is the cruellest judge. Oh yes he is, my little hussy, you'll see. One day you'll see for yourself. So they have their revenge on the rest of us. What Sweden lacks in gumption or wealth, she'll skewer on the horns of her judgment. Her self-satisfied mediocrity spares no nation, looks with equal contempt upon the greed of England, the unruliness of America or even the depravity of bloody France!"

Madeleine was content to let him ramble. She had learned a lot of what she knew on these stairs, with Fenwick slavering at her shoulder. He was always full of opinion, progressively less intelligible as they reached the upper landing.

The hallway was dim, with only a single lamp lighting the way. The fifth door on the left would be theirs.

"They got away with my ship," pouted Fenwick half to himself. "But I'll get 'em yet."

"Yes, you will," she cooed, comforting him softly. "I know you will, sir."

In the shadowy passage, Fenwick's body tossed suddenly. "God's sake, girl, use my name. Can't have you calling me sir. You're going to get on top of me and ride the beast all the way to hell and I don't want to hear 'sir' and 'is it good, sir?' and 'poke me again, sir'."

This was the only difficulty for Madeleine. "Sir" would've made it easy.

"You're going to look at me and say Edgar. Poke me again, Edgar."

Staggering side to side, they had passed the languishing

flame of the lamp and the corridor lay dark and silent before them.

Fenwick was being peevish. "I've told you it's Edgar," he insisted. "I don't tell everyone, you know. I tell you because you're my angel. Downstairs you can say sir but once we're alone it's Edgar, d'ye hear?"

"Yes, Edgar."

The lamp went out behind them.

Madeleine caught her breath and clasped Fenwick's arm. He turned around and saw nothing but black. Only at the top of the stairs was there a sliver of light.

Fenwick snarled, suddenly in a choler. He reached for their door knob, but something bumped him on the forehead. With his other hand, he reached up to brush it aside. His fingers found a pistol's barrel, levelled at his skull.

The light from the stairs had vanished. Madeleine gave a quick sob. The pistol went off in a blaze of thunder, but Fenwick never heard it.

Neither did Glenda, half a mile up the hill and fast asleep.

CR SO

By early afternoon, Papa was in the ground.

The wind was constant up here, blasting up the side of the mountain, teasing out the tangles of the forest, bellysliding on the flattened grass and tugging petulantly at the highest shrubs and thistle.

A little wooden cross marked the spot. It stood only two feet high but reached another two feet underground. The wind would get nowhere with it. Leclair was satisfied.

Without a tear, he turned his back and walked to the cabin. The wind kept buffeting him from behind, ripping the bloodied shirt almost off his back. The hair in his eyes reminded him that he should make good use of the shears before they left.

In the village, he had sent the coachman back to Gustavia with five pieces of silver. He had spent another four and fifty pieces on a pair of mules, which carried them up the hill. The ride to Anse Paschal would be two hours.

He was going to pay his men handsomely for their losses, five hundred pieces for a leg or an arm or an eye, two hundred and twenty for a finger or an ear, and personal stores of rum or port for lesser damages. But when would he ever make restitution to Papa? It would've been the sea-cook's last caper. And so, indeed, it was.

Even today, Chloe was serene and self-composed. Once again, her fathomless obedience to God's will had fortified her against the more desperate protestations of lesser souls. She was sitting calmly now, blue hands folded on her lap, looking at nothing in particular. A bright bandana covered her grizzled hair. The mosquitoes had all come inside to flee the wind. Even when they lighted on her arm or forehead, her hand brushed them gently, almost considerately.

Glenda, on the other hand, gave herself a hard smack across the jugular, where one of the little critters was preparing to feast. They looked up to find Leclair in the doorway.

"Didn't he tell you to leave?" said Chloe weakly. "You should've left St. Barth."

The door clanged shut behind Leclair. The wind was playing the roof like a reed pipe.

He looked at her darkly. "There were things he didn't know."

"But you should've listened."

Leclair leaned his spade in the corner. He knew he couldn't contradict someone who was speaking from so deep within. He just accepted the blame and set his thoughts on tomorrow.

"You can't stay here now," said he. "The weather's changing. You can't be alone up here."

Chloe made no protest, but neither did she allow any enthusiasm.

"You can move down with Winnie. You won't be with a white man, so they wouldn't bother you."

Chloe looked down at her blue feet.

"Maybe in Gustavia they would," he added, "but not in the village. And all the fish and vegetables come in from Corossol. You won't have to walk up and down this hill."

Chloe looked up. The long, moist eyes were as brown as midnight. He knew, of course, that she blamed him. But there was something more. It reminded him of that day when his sight came back. Chloe had been his nurse and confidante. She had listened to him dying. She had heard him howl and sob. She had told him her stories, including the slavery. Before he could see, her portrait had painted itself in his mind's eye.

Then had come the day when he could see for himself. He had looked at Chloe and she had felt like a swatch of colour, nothing more. All the rest didn't matter. She knew that the eye's judgment is the most dangerous. Of a sudden, she had grown wary, almost formal. Only a week later, they had laughed together as before but now, again, Chloe retreated.

Though she was only a few feet away, she was observing him from a far greater distance. Her eyelid fluttered as mosquitoes swarmed about her. Papa had been the mortar between them, Leclair knew that now. Without Papa, his own skin was still too fair.

Leclair crossed the room. At the back corner he knelt down. Thrusting his finger between the floorboards, he expertly lifted one, then another, and then a third.

Beneath the floor, Glenda saw a shallow cellar from which Leclair pulled a sackcloth bag, the size of three or four coconuts.

"I'll take three bags of gold," he said to Chloe. "The other twelve are for you."

Glenda watched with admiration. Who would ever think of looking for Leclair's treasure under an old cabin on the mountain!

"It's for hurricanes," he told her. "Papa dug it out ten years ago."

After the gold came a deep leather satchel and a pile of books and papers bound with heavy twine. Leclair was stowing everything inside the satchel, securing it with leather straps.

"So I dug some more." Leclair pointed to the centre of the room. "Now half the house is sitting on gold." He winked at Chloe. "Tell her what it's like down there."

A smile came to Chloe's face. Each memory had grown fonder now. "You can't sit up, you know," she said. "It come so fast, there was no gettin' away. Two days we lyin' on our back." She shook her head with silent mirth. "Just the two of us and nothin' else to look at. Just the bottom of those boards, and prayin' to sweet Lord Jesus."

"Did the house blow down?" asked Glenda.

Chloe shook her head, still smiling.

"When Winnie comes by, go down with her," resumed Leclair. "I'll come again to help you move your things. But first I need a fresh gown for Glenda."

Chloe glanced over at Glenda, who freely showed her astonishment.

"My gown too short," said the old woman. "You better take a kirtle instead."

Chloe hobbled off into the back room.

Through the low doorway, Glenda could see a spinning wheel and one end of Chloe's hammock.

Leclair had used her first name, realized Glenda.

She avoided his gaze. "I take this kindly." The words jumped from her lips quickly, as though they might get shut inside.

Leclair had set the satchel at the front door. He looked around. "Are the shears outside?"

From the other room came Chloe's voice. "Look under the pots."

Leclair turned to the long, rough-hewn shelf, sagging with iron pots. He pulled the shears off their peg.

"In return, you might trim my hair."

He handed the shears to Glenda and pulled up a stool. She grasped the well-worn wood, holding them gingerly. He was facing her, with knees wide apart. He had doubled over, his matted hair thrown forward in a lush cascade.

Glenda was at a loss. "Where do I begin?"

"Wheresoever you wish," said he.

Chloe returned with arms full.

Glenda was dithering with the shears. "But how much should I leave?"

He gave a soft chuckle. "Leave me at least half."

Chloe had laid out her garments on the bench below the window. "Here, child, I help you," she said, coming to Glenda's side.

She reached for the shears and Glenda was quick to surrender them. The long, blue fingers poked the shears into Leclair's tangled tresses. With a quick scratch of metal, a sheet of his fair locks tumbled to the floor.

"You go and look," said Chloe kindly.

Glenda did as she had been told, making sure not to leave her eyes behind. She could only surmise that Chloe might be distracting herself from her new sorrow, or perhaps rebounding from the initial shock to redeem herself as mistress of the manor, or even seeking to relieve her guest of a drudgery better suited to hands like hers.

Glenda examined the pretty, rust-red kirtle, cut from a buckram cloth. There were three shirts as well, one tawny and two white, all of the finest calico. Each in turn, she held them up to her shoulder but, try though she might, Glenda couldn't rid herself of a sudden fluster. She had quaked with apprehension when she was given the shears; yet the moment they were taken from her, Glenda felt she had been robbed. It was annoying, indeed, to be thus affected by a trifle. Leclair's unruly mane of hair lingered before her mind's eye. He had petitioned her. She knew now that it wasn't inconsequential to her. It was a bewildering thought.

"Don't bother choosin'," said Chloe, breaking into Glenda's thoughts. "Take everything."

Glenda peeked back at the rounded hump of Leclair's curled body and the thin negro woman leaning forward on her chair. The floor was sprouting hair everywhere. They were an odd match, mused Glenda. Papa was not forgotten. Together, those two would remember. Theirs was a bond of unlikely and indelible meanings, unknown to her. She must be content. Why should it be of consequence to her? When had these bold thoughts first begun, this cruel prodding in her heart?

"My room in there," said Chloe, continuing to officiate. "You can dress in there."

There was nothing imperious in her words. Glenda could not choose but accept this graciousness. She walked to the back room, carrying her new wardrobe. From behind came the erratic pulse of the shears.

Glenda closed the door behind her. She felt comforted. That morning, Doctor Henckell had drawn a hot bath for her. She had been afloat in bliss for all of a half hour, while the men pursued their foreign conversation. Even now, her skin smelled of soap inside the bedraggled dress. Her body felt warm and whole.

As Glenda slipped the dress off her shoulders, there came a soft thud. She looked beside her feet. It was the rumpled, curled manuscript which she had tucked guiltily inside her dress each morning since La Fourchue. When she was ambushed by Bruno, a foreign impulse had seized her and made a thief of her. Now she felt too afraid to return it to Leclair and thereby confess her crime, yet the thought of secretly disposing of it altogether was even worse.

Glenda bent over and picked the papers off the floor. She

wanted to stow them underneath Chloe's garments until she had changed, but now the title page caught her eye and she read: *Ouanalao. A Treatise on the Native Virtues.* Glenda paused, listening for Leclair's footsteps.

From behind the door came the squeaking of the shears. When would she find such another opportunity to put a closed door between herself and Leclair?

She turned the page and began to read.

Ouanalao was the name given the West Indian isle of St. Barthelemy by her native dwellers the Caribs.

Her eye was drawn again to the title sheet where, on the back, he had scrawled a few lines of verse. Some words had been crossed out and others scratched in lieu, which led her to believe that it was Leclair's own handiwork.

> *As I write, so poureth my blood.*
> *Five and thirty years of other pleasures,*
> *Other labours, but now all else is vain.*
> *Ev'ry other commodity giv'n,*
> *Now there is but one. Finite yet bountiful,*
> *It will run out, yet shall I be satisfied.*
> *What remains in me shall be writ*
> *Day by day, and when my ink's run dry*
> *It will be a night to end all nights,*
> *My own substance giv'n and gone,*
> *And thankful unto the end.*

No couplets. Not even a rhyme. Glenda contemplated his verse with some exasperation. It was so ill-crafted, clearly the handiwork of a man who knew more about soldiering than about letters, yet the substance of it was not trivial. She was affected.

Shaking her head, Glenda skimmed the pages and found that the treatise had turned into a diary, the same that she had sampled on La Fourchue. Glancing anxiously at the door, she flipped back to the earlier portion, casting about from page to page until the word cannibalism stopped her short. She began to read.

These same Caribs, of excellent stature and royal bearing, are also known anthropophagi, which is to say that they devour their enemies in shameless orgies of cannibalism. On the isle of Dominica, it seems, a Carib ate a monk and became very ill. For years to come, mariners in the Indies would bring a supply of monks' habits to wear whenever going ashore for drinking water!

Caribs have come to eschew the taste of Europeans which is no great wonder, for how could the feeble, avaricious heart of a European nourish such savages? Here is most pertinent evidence in favour of J.J. Rousseau's critique. A man who can subjugate his fellow men through no effort of his own, merely by the gold paid to his constables, deputies, orderlies and other scurvy lackeys, is a tyrant indeed and Europe is full of them. Not only is oppression a sanctioned science, it's a virulent disease affecting victim and tyrant alike. One is as enfeebled as the other.

But to learn that these same Caribs are wont to dine on the flesh of their neighbours goes against the grain, quite against Monsieur Rousseau's grain. Whence do these untainted souls have their cruelty?

Glenda looked up, sensible that the stillness had deepened. The shears had stopped. She closed the manuscript and hurried across the room, tossing the whole bundle into Chloe's basket. Leclair had told the old woman that he would come back to help her. The treatise would be waiting for him.

Gratified at having found a safe disposal for the papers, Glenda began to dress. Still her thoughts lingered on his argument. The discovery of cannibalism had been a disillusionment, perhaps a blemish on the entire notion of native virtues. Leclair had found his West Indian savage prone to extraordinary acts of cruelty.

The world of reason is small, she remembered him saying. A smaller world within a much larger one. Leclair seemed to be always embroiled in paradox, eyeing the small world from the outside, eyeing it with as much of wistfulness as of contempt. But the small world was all Glenda desired right now. Her thoughts didn't stray into the grim uncertainties of what would follow but stayed in the little room, safe in Chloe's keeping.

03 80

OF THE CONTINENT

ॐ ॐ

UNLEASHED

℘ ℭ

Leclair grabbed the reins of Glenda's mule and guided her off the trail. He made directly for a small bamboo thicket, scarcely a stone's throw away.

Glenda glanced furtively behind her and noticed dust rising off the hillside. When safely ensconced within the penumbra of the vaulted bamboo, Leclair let go of her reins.

He dismounted and tied their mules to one of the trunks. "I want to know who that is."

He turned to the west. Over the next hill was Petite Anse and then Anse Paschal, but that would be another hour or more. The dust was edging down the hillside, on a course that was sure to intercept their path.

For nearly half an hour now, Leclair and Glenda had been riding on the lee side of Pointe à Etages, with only the tell-tale roar of breakers to remind them of the blustering easterlies. They knew their reprieve was soon to end. Just ahead, they could see thistles and shrubbery squirming in the relentless blast.

Glenda kept her eye on the snail-like approach of billowing dust. The high wind gave it nowhere to settle, but whisked it ever higher across the deep greens of the hillside. Her hair was tied back to keep the wind from knotting it. She reached for the kirtle, ensuring that her legs were modestly sheathed in the rust-red buckram.

When she was maybe twelve or thirteen, uncle Heywood had taken her horseback riding on the moors. She could remember the splendour of the wind entering her and living within her for a week afterwards. This was altogether different. Instead of a side saddle, Glenda had to straddle the animal's damp body, clinging for dear life even at a leisurely walk.

By now, her muscles were protesting. Aside from that, she was feeling quite fit, in no small measure owing to the precious boon of a hot bath and fresh garments all on the same day.

"Was it Swedish you were speaking?" she asked, as they peered between the clustered pillars of bamboo.

"Yes, he's a Swede."

"As are you, from the sound of it."

Leclair regarded her with a sidelong glare. She braced herself for a lash of his vehemence but his eye showed no such edge, only a reluctant bemusement.

Glenda plucked up her courage. "I shall address you as Olof."

"It's not my name."

Glenda knew enough to expect no gallantry from Leclair, so she proceeded to steady her hipbone against the animal's neck while pivoting herself off the mule. "If ever there was good in you, it was Olof. So I shall address you as Olof."

Leclair shook his head. "You *are* a silly wench."

He turned away and resumed his distant vigil. "Your biggest sin," he went on, "I say your cardinal sin, is to judge so blithely."

Glenda was content to observe along with him for a moment, feeling his words inside of her. The cloud of dust had arrived at level ground and a dark outline of horseback soldiers was emerging.

"It was pirates who named you Leclair, wasn't it?"

He kept his eye on the troops. "You're full of questions today."

"I wanted to know even before."

"Damned redcoats," he growled. "What are the English doing here? The Swedish garrison is capable enough."

Glenda gazed toward the riders, now approaching in double file on the same trail. They were heading back the way she and Leclair had come, south to Gustavia. The animals were plodding along, quite at their leisure. The soldiers had undone their brass-studded coats and, sheltered from the wind at last, donned their tricorns against the scorching sun. At intervals they turned and spoke softly, each to each, maybe a chuckle or shaking of the head. A bayonet hung from each saddle horn, spearing the dust with its shadow.

"Were you named for your fair skin?"

Leclair answered by raising a hand to her head. He held a pistol. "You've nothing to fear, so long as you don't give us away."

It occurred to Glenda that she hadn't thought, not even for a moment, of looking to these soldiers for rescue. This was disconcerting to her. She looked away from him, fixing her eye on the procession of riders.

"I wasn't named for my skin, no," continued Leclair. "I was struck by lightning."

Glenda turned to him, her eyes narrowing.

"So bright," he went on, "it marked my skin forever."

With his free hand, Leclair reached for the shoulder and Glenda remembered it from the night before. She swallowed hard, not from emotion but from the suddenness of his self-disclosure.

"Papa came up with the name," mused Leclair softly, "so they'd never forget the story. He was an old fox, Papa. He'd cook up a story as good as he cooked up a roast."

But Glenda wasn't listening. The handwriting came back into her mind. His former name. The sallow pages from La Fourchue. The man in Doctor Henckell's story. She had never met him at all, she now realized. His name began with anchor but wasn't spelled that way. She had *seen* the name. It wasn't him she had seen, it was his name. It flashed before her mind's eye, etched with meticulous strokes of ink. *Anckarström.* The name in Doctor Henckell's story. The murder of a king. He that pulled the trigger. Whose name she had seen on La Fourchue, on a score of letters addressed to Olof.

Glenda looked up, dazed. The English soldiers had passed. Slowly, they receded into the speckled terrain of rock and brushwood. The dust whirled against a vivid sky. In the stillness, they could hear waves breaking on the far side of Pointe à Etages.

"I suppose it's you they're after," said Glenda at length.

Leclair lowered the pistol. He stepped away from her, shaking the stiffness from his legs. "They'll be looking for Fenwick's murderer."

Glenda turned to him abruptly. "Fenwick?"

"Yes," nodded Leclair. "Fenwick was shot."

"God be praised for His justice."

Leclair smiled. He was coming up to the part about where he'd been the night before.

CR SO

Big Raoul drops his breeches around his knee. A hush descends on everyone. Though his shoulders cast a shadow across the groin, there's no mistaking the silhouette pointing from his thigh, heavy as the unsheathed erection of a stallion.

She, too, has discovered his swollen organ. Reaching blindly behind her, she gropes at the windlass. Her flailing arm finds one of the two turnpoles of the windlass and she hauls herself away from his reach. But his two hands have her by the waist and, with a jolt, rip her fingers away from the windlass. She appears like an alabaster figurine in his swarthy clutches. Sobbing loudly, she is dragged inch by inch into his groin.

His voice is low and hoarse. "If all you do is take, it proves nothing. It proves you're a thief and that's as much as nothing. Are you listening, Bruno? We're gentlemen all. To rob a woman is a crime. But giving is another matter. Give her what she likes most and you'll own her truly."

He has dragged her, by now, almost out of her dress. The round buttocks and flat, white belly are bared for all to see. His broad fingers, pressed into her midriff, lift her pelvis off the deck while he steers his bulging erection all the way inside of her.

The men are nothing but eyes.

She lifts her head in protest as his mighty buttocks begin to toil. Her head drops back onto the deck, as her breath is sucked in quickly. She tries to raise her head again but lets it flop, and yet again but then no more. His massive ribcage and pelvis undulate with a slow, purposeful precision on top of her. Against the deck, her head bobs up and down as her body rides the to and fro of his buried muscle. No sound comes from her.

Nor a sound from the pirates.

Her head rolls to one side. Raoul toils steadily, muscles rippling across his arched back. Her head rolls to the other side and then back again. Still he persists, pulsing like a jenny from the cotton factory. Her face whips side to side, lips clenched.

He rolls away, his erection whipped from her groin like a wet dolphin's tail.

CR SO

"It's getting worse."

Loman's words broke into Leclair's thoughts. He pressed his eyes shut. When he looked again, he could see better.

Even inside the anchorage, the waves were simmering with mischief. The clouds had closed their ranks, shrouding Anse Paschal in a baleful pall of darkness.

"We could get a hurricane," said Leclair.

Glenda had been observing her own whitened knuckles on the edge of the little skiff since they pushed out from shore.

"We'll make Petit Cul-de-Sac before dark," continued Leclair. "No topsail, no foresail."

Glenda observed him speaking to the back of Loman's head. Loman wasn't saying much, just a vague nod as he pulled at the oars with all his might. As a matter of fact, he hadn't said much of anything even when he stepped ashore to greet them. Glenda had to suppose that yesterday's gruesome battle might weigh heavily on his mind. Perhaps he had lost his closest comrade. Perhaps he was blaming Leclair or simply feeling desolate.

Certainly, in spite of her fresh apparel, Glenda herself was succumbing to the gloom of the elements. That's how she was wont to think of it. Whenever she had been at her own worst, she seemed to recognize her turmoil in nature's looking-glass. After Woolsley's ignoble death, the blistering sun on La Fourchue had revealed to Glenda her own parched soul. At other times, an excess of darkness could, with no further cause, swathe her heart in gloom or, when the rain burst freely upon weeks and weeks of dust, lift her spirit into the treetops. She had always felt as though the elements were her sisters, conjunctive and mutually resonant of her own passions. Until now.

She had never seen a hurricane. This was no sister, nor brother or cousin or anything she'd ever imagined. Hurricane was a word from her uncle's books, a page in one of those exotic travelogues he had always favoured, an oddity perused and given some whimsical explanation over a glass of warm toddy. Hurricane was an element unto itself, a thing to be regarded and feared on its own account. Such a towering majesty of darkness as she had never known. The wind, which had vexed her for two days, was not about to wane. This was, as it would seem, only the beginning.

Glenda looked again at Leclair, whose stern face kept disappearing behind Loman's toiling shoulder. From the looks of it, Leclair took hurricanes seriously. Glenda felt a rush of apprehension as she turned her eye to the ship.

The *Clifton* sat stolidly upon the water, unruffled by the waves that kept teasing Loman off his course. Every sail had been sheeted home and tucked hard to the cross-tree. Yet the booms and blocks groaned ominously. As Glenda ran her eye up the foremast, she noticed the very timbers trembling. Though the storm might not find its way into the anchorage, it was overleaping the low headland and taking blind swipes from overhead.

"Where can we be safe?" asked Glenda.

Loman glared at her with unabashed contempt.

Glenda strained to see past him to where Leclair was seated. "What shall we do?"

"Petit Cul-de-Sac has the best harbour," answered Leclair. "And I want some distance from those English troops."

"They're everywhere," said Loman darkly as they neared the *Clifton*. "Two loaded clippers were docking in town."

Leclair looked down at his buskins and said nothing.

Glenda took a deep breath before she addressed him. "And do you also dispatch royalty?"

Leclair looked up.

"Yes, royalty," she went on. "I mean to say, were you a conspirator against the Swedish king?"

His countenance gave her no inkling.

"And was that what brought you here?"

"I came to this island to –" As abruptly as the words had burst from Leclair, he fell silent again. His eyes narrowed.

If he was keen to correct her, he was far more keen to forego his correction. Loman's interest had been tweaked, though he still made an attempt at indifference.

"Yes," continued Glenda. "Why, indeed?"

Leclair didn't hear their hawser coming. The coiled hemp struck him on the shoulder and fell splattering into the waves.

"Beg your pardon, sir," came Twitcher's anguished voice from the high gunwale.

But Leclair knew that Twitcher had done no wrong. He was angry at himself for giving the woman his attention.

"I don't know why I shouldn't whip you," he snarled at Twitcher.

Loman had grabbed an oar and fished the hawser out of the water. It was time to board. Leclair had his arm out to keep them from ramming the larger vessel. He pulled the skiff around while

Loman held them on a tight leash, until the stern had come half circle and Glenda could've touched the shiny barnacles below the scupper-holes. Her eye travelled along the high bulwark where, fore and aft, every porthole boasted a cannon. Glenda had no desire to remain in the tossing skiff.

When Loman motioned for her to climb, she found a scupper-hole for her foot and proceeded to pull herself up by the hawser. Leclair was right behind, ready to catch her. Twitcher was still peering at them from the gunwale, but made no gesture of a helping hand.

With shoulders aching from her own weight, Glenda thrust an arm over the gunwale. Leclair gave her a final nudge and she rolled over the edge, stumbling on her skirts.

They were amidships, just aft of the mainmast. Leclair stepped onto the deck and came face to face with his men, no more than a dozen, huddled at the forecastle.

"Gentlemen," he called out. "No time to waste. We'll have our council at Petit Cul-de-Sac. Every man will get his due in gold."

Even before he had finished speaking, Leclair's eyes told him otherwise.

A brief silence ensued. Ripper was glaring at him with a new boldness. Big Raoul was seated on the windlass, legs spread wide and massive arms folded across his chest. At his side was Bruno, massaging his scalp nervously.

Leclair began to comprehend what was afoot. Loman was joining them now, as was Twitcher who took conspicuous pains to go unnoticed.

"It's too late to sail," shouted Bruno in the wind, "so we gone ahead with council."

A sudden blast knocked Glenda backwards. Stumbling on her skirts, she had to steady herself against the gunwale.

"You could've been back," went on Bruno, "and we could've sailed if it wasn't for your wench."

Bruno paused again, as though to gauge the impact of his

words.

Leclair felt a shudder racing to his toes and gave his head a shake in order to conceal it. In Raoul's face, he saw no disdain nor even hostility. Only the scar across his nose seemed more pronounced, more pearly bright. Close behind were Rogers and Angus and a handful more.

"I gave Papa his burial," said Leclair, "that's where I was. Nothing to do with the Englishwoman. Main thing is all's here that's alive and we can beat the weather if we sail to leeward of the island."

"Remember the articles of agreement," shouted Bruno. "Never a wench on ship."

"I say he's a coward that has to blame a woman. A chicken-livered coward."

"Hear that?" hollered Bruno triumphantly. "Leclair says I'm a coward."

"I always have," shouted Leclair, "and I don't see much hope of reformation."

"If that makes Bruno a coward, you better count me too," said Big Raoul in a deep, ominous drawl.

Overhead, the tempest outvoiced them all. Leclair was leaning into the wind, feet wide apart.

Glenda had to grip the gunwale with all her might, or she might've rushed to his side. That could only have made matters worse.

"I'll be fair with you," shouted Leclair. "I broke the agreement, 'tis true. For that, I'll give you my stake in the ransom, to be apportioned for each man accordingly. But now's not a time for settling the score. Heave in, Bruno, and prepare to go about! Either we sail now or the storm will prevail and the English will find us."

The pirates stirred uneasily, trading glances each with the other.

"The English!" answered Bruno, still at the top of his lungs.

"The English, yes! We're just done talking about them in council. Who was it got involved with Fenwick, the scum-sucking dog? Who said we should sail his ship instead of our own? Who was it, Ripper?"

Ripper answered while his eye remained on Leclair. "'Twas you, sir, that's who!"

Leclair knew the terrain had shifted. There was no Matt, no Papa.

"We had a vote," shouted Leclair. "Every man had his say."

"And I said no," bellowed Raoul. "I didn't want the English doing our business. And now half of us are dead. Pierre and Matt. All because of your Englishman."

"He's gone too. I shot him last night."

The pirates stared at Leclair.

"For his treachery, for what he'd done to us. I had the pistol hard upon Fenwick's skull and blew out every bit that was inside. Upstairs at the Wall House."

The men were shifting excitedly, clearly gratified by the news.

In the corner of her eye, Glenda saw a small tree thrown and dragged across the rocky shore. She became aware that the air was full of debris, thistle and shrub and larger boughs locked in the jaws of the tempest.

But Bruno drew his cutlass. "That's fine!" he resumed, his voice cracking from the strain. "That's very good. Now they'll be wanting us on account of the ransom, the ship *and* the murder of Fenwick to boot! Well done, captain!"

Raoul's arm went out to Bruno. "Put up your sword," said he. "He's mine."

Bruno was quick to obey though his mouth kept spouting. "We're staying right here. And we'll do our business without you, Leclair. I'm not your anchor boy." He gestured to Big Raoul. "I'm the new master and here's my captain."

Raoul drew his pistols and handed them to Angus. Then he stepped away from the windlass, speaking again. "We could've left you on a little spit of sand halfway to Jamaica. But we're not despicable. We're men of honour and you've wronged us. So we're dropping you here. Our little gift to the English."

He drew his sabre. Ripper had his brace of pistols trained on Leclair.

"Whatever you want from me, you'll have to take," answered Leclair, tossing his pistol on the deck.

Big Raoul was coming directly at him. This man wanted what Leclair had taken from him. Yet, the first usurper had been Raoul. What Leclair had lost to Raoul was lost forever. He had no words for it. A sacred vault. No one else must know. Inside his ribs, the ache was gnawing and wrenching his gut, shooting holy fire into his head. Leclair had his cutlass in hand. With the wind wet across his face, he stepped up to meet the towering adversary.

Glenda closed her eyes.

Leclair made the first lunge. Big Raoul's parry was solid as rock. The clanging report of their blades sent a tremor through the spectators.

When Glenda opened her eyes, Leclair was alive and well, slashing at Raoul with such a vengeance that the giant had to retreat towards the bow. Once again, she was struck by the fluidity in Leclair's arm, the well-engineered continuity of each stroke flowing into the next, affording Raoul no opportunity for initiative.

"You don't know how you've wronged me," hissed Leclair in a cold rage, already short of breath. "These men can find another captain, I don't care. But you're going to die."

All this time, Leclair was expending much effort on beating Raoul back towards the bow. His strength began to flag while Big Raoul remained impervious in his parries. They were only a few feet from the very bowsprit when Raoul was able to get in his first thrusts. Leclair was nimble on his feet and kept out of danger. Big Raoul slashed the air between them, swiping again and again while Leclair dodged him or used his cutlass to deflect the blows.

As Raoul beat his way out of the corner, they had circled each other and were moving aft again. Leclair took a glancing blow on his cutlass. Big Raoul had such force in it that his blade crashed into the carriage of a cannon and stuck. Leclair struck at him but Raoul had let go of his sabre just in time to salvage his hand. Leclair stepped in for the kill.

A cutlass came rattling across the deck. "Kill him!" shouted Bruno.

But Raoul paid no heed. He was readying himself for Leclair, smiling now. "Throw me a pistol," he said, keeping his eyes on Leclair.

In a flash, Bruno tossed him one of his. Raoul caught it with one hand. Bruno had uncocked it first, so Big Raoul took aim at Leclair and drew back the hammer.

In the next instant, a shot rang out and Raoul made a nasty grimace, his pistol lowered. The pirates were stunned.

Turning his head, Leclair beheld an astonishing sight. Glenda was standing alone, no longer by the gunwale but on the spot where he had dropped his own pistol. With both hands she clutched his weapon at arm's length, as though it might bite.

As in a dream, he saw Raoul give a snarl and turn his pistol on Glenda. Leclair let up a furious howl, hoping to divert Raoul a moment sooner than his cutlass could. Leclair made a desperate dash and, indeed, the giant was looking his way when Leclair's blade struck him hard across the ribs. Raoul went down on one knee. A swift kick to the head sent Raoul flat on his back.

Leclair made room for both hands on the hilt and stepped up to his mark. Before anyone could so much as gasp, Leclair's swooping blade had dug deep into the deck. Raoul's neck was on one side of it, his head on the other.

CR SO

CECILIA

℘ ℘

No one moved a muscle.

Even the storm couldn't get their attention.

Leclair hovered over the body, as though waiting for Big Raoul to rise again. For a long instant, the storm didn't exist. Its fury was impotent against this stillness.

Glenda was rooted to her spot. The pistol had slipped from her numb fingers.

Bruno's lips were pressed to a hair's breadth, his eye wracked by unremitting twitches.

The spell was broken only when a wave tilted the *Clifton* a smidge higher. Raoul's head turned slowly and paused, eye to eye with Snake and Rogers. But moments later, as in a ponderous change of mind, the head turned even wider, stretching and therein exceeding all natural compass until, suddenly, it rolled free of the body, the straggled locks bathed with blood.

The movement jolted Leclair, rousing him to his purpose. He stepped over Raoul's chest and, giving himself a good hold, lifted the head by the hair. The pirates were dumbstruck. They couldn't take their eyes off his trophy. Leclair walked away like a prelate swinging his censer of deep crimson. From between the windlass and the foremast, he pulled the iron-shod mallet and a couple of handspikes. Laying the head face-up on the planks, Leclair set one of the spikes to the forehead and, with two quick strikes of his mallet, had penetrated to the back of the skull. He hoisted Raoul's head above his own and nailed it to the foremast with a dozen blows of the mallet.

Leclair stepped back to view his handiwork. With the handspike protruding above the left eyebrow, Big Raoul surveyed his crew. Even in death, his eye had congealed in that brooding, contemptuous frown which had silenced many a protest and overruled many a council. It was useless now, indeed ludicrous since nothing at all remained below the mangled throat, nothing that could give physical consequence to his dire glare. That unrivalled frame was offal now, fodder for kites.

Leclair saw a tear of red trickling through Raoul's left eyebrow and across the luminous scar from the nose. He turned to face the pirates and noticed that their eyes weren't on the grisly spectacle at all. It was him they were looking at.

Glenda never made it to the gunwale. As she ran from that abomination, her stomach rose into her mouth and spewed its bilious stew onto the deck. She stumbled, gasping and choking, reaching for a cannon's carriage to steady herself. She couldn't believe what she had seen. It was of such brutishness, such monstrous wilfulness as passed all understanding. Nothing she had ever heard or read could've prepared her. Only the night before, she had dreamt that this man held her in his arms, carrying her aloft, ever mindful of her sweet repose. This barbarian. This madman. It had been a dream, she reminded herself, a mere fancy.

As Leclair approached, the pirates stood aside. Angus, Twitcher and Loman stepped back, while the rest edged to starboard. It wasn't difficult for Glenda to apprehend why. Advancing slowly between them, Leclair met every eye unflinchingly, but lingered on no man long enough to pay more allegiance than maybe to the planks beneath his feet. Where he had run a hand through his hair, it was smeared with Raoul's blood, as were his neck and sleeve. His face was taut and soaked with sweat, his jowl bulging as in some provoked beast, his shoulders dropped but held slightly forward of the chest in perpetual readiness, each nerve poised for extreme measures. There was about him, then, such a singlemindedness, a degree of self-possession so loathsome, so absolutely feral as Glenda had witnessed in no man.

"I'll heave in, honest I will," piped up Bruno, barely audible over the roaring blast. "Orders is orders."

As the storm tried to gag Bruno, his words were lost to Glenda but presently came weaving back to her.

"...got to do what a man's got to do... Methought the fire inside of you had gone out. I'm thinking the wench has gone and made you soft but I was wrong, God's mercy. The lightning is in you still. You say the word, sir, and I'll heave in the anchor."

Bruno waited for a reply but none was given. Leclair's gaze was opaque. Bruno struggled in his mind with whether his words had delivered him from trouble or perhaps dug him deeper into the mire.

His words left Glenda puzzled. The obseqiousness was easy enough to apprehend but what about the lightning? Like a fire that might leave Leclair's body. This brought to her mind the unexpected account he had given of the provenance of his new name.

She saw him turning now, even as he walked. When Leclair reached the cutlass, he was walking almost backwards with an eye on his ragged throng of bandits. He gave a tug to dislodge the cutlass, sheathing it once again. Then he squatted down, cradling Big Raoul's body by the knees and by the armpits. After a moment's preparation, Leclair rose to his full height with the headless body like a deformed, unwanted child in his arms. He stepped to the gunwale and tossed Big Raoul into the deeps below.

He didn't turn again to the men. He came to Glenda.

"I beg of you," she said, "don't harm me."

When she retreated, Leclair looked at her oddly from under his brow.

"You're mine again," he murmured. "I won't fail you."

He offered her his bloodied hand and, for a moment, she felt as though she were some ragamuffin queen to his poor, defiled majesty. His hand closed around hers. She lifted one foot over the gunwale and, steadied by Leclair's arm, let the other leg follow. She was trembling all over.

But Leclair had swung himself over the gunwale and, clinging now to Twitcher's hawser, he clambered down alongside Glenda, guiding her feet to the easiest footholds. Together they descended once again and climbed into the skittish vessel below. For a minute that seemed like eternity, Glenda waited for the speeding bullet that should cut her short. She couldn't imagine what was taking them so long, nor did she look behind.

All around, chaos prevailed. The air was darkening by the minute as dust mingled with sand and hurtling bits of vegetation to shroud the shoreline in gloom and foreboding. The wailing of wind had become a dull roar, making conversation increasingly impossible.

Leclair used both oars to shove off from the *Clifton*. By now, the anchorage gave no shelter. Waves rammed their skiff from every side, tossing it high in the air only to topple it into the next hole. Glenda held on for dear life.

As they rode the frothing turbulence, Glenda listened for pistols. The storm was bellowing worse than before, but nothing was heard from the *Clifton*. What had deterred those bandits from making a quick end of it? Did they have one more scruple than Raoul had had about murdering a woman? That scruple would spell her salvation. But Leclair would be a different matter. By shooting him, they could've had her all to themselves to use as they wished. Why his men had tarried so reverentially, allowing this lunatic to slip from their grasp, was passing strange.

Glenda turned at last to catch a view of the *Clifton*. No, not a one of them was to be seen. Had they gone under hatches? Or were they transfixed by that gruesome head on the main mast? At every splash of the oars, Glenda had expected to breathe her last. But Leclair's countenance showed confidence, as though he were privy to some secret covenant that provided for their safe conduct.

The eerie feeling returned to her, that same sense of being paired with this monstrous rebel, this mongrel king in some horrible, miscreant act of departure and exile. As though their crude vessel were serving for a royal craft. But this wasn't a leisurely, musical procession on the well-girt Thames, as in the etchings from Squire Heywood's drawing-room. Rather, it was the very heart and craw of havoc, void of any girth of likelihood or decency.

Musing thus, Glenda was quite unprepared when their boat ran foul of a rock, thrusting her from the seat. Leclair lurched sideways, dropping his oar. She was catapulted over the edge. Before she knew it, her head was swallowed by water, a cataclysm of cold water swirling and tugging at her. Glenda opened her eyes and saw, dimly, a world of anemone and coral and sea-urchin swaying and undulating as though beckoning her to kingdom come.

In a matter of moments she broke the surface, gasping and coughing. The waves kept licking her face with brine. Glenda reached for the boat but it had drifted from her. No sooner had she cleared her lungs of the salty wash than a new wave toppled over her head and again she was spitting and coughing. She eyed the light-hued rocks around the lagoon, but no sign of Leclair. Knocking her knee on the rocks below, Glenda was reminded to brace herself for a rough docking. The undertow grabbed her by the waist, sucking her back into the deep. Her ears reverberated with the drone of rolling pebbles.

Again, she was lifted and launched into the shore. Her hands fumbled for a hold. She was able to get onto her feet but, out of nowhere, the undertow had her by the waist and back she went into the frothing deep. This time she went completely under, thrashing madly with helplessness and rage. As her feet found a hold and she tried to stand, Glenda was sideswiped by the next breaker and fell hard upon her shoulder. When the wave withdrew, she found herself high and dry, though soaked to the bone. Sobbing and shouting such words as had never been uttered in her family, Glenda gave up trying to stand. She rolled over on her back and continued to drag herself along while the breakers were bursting all around, each one knocking her for another loop.

Out of nowhere, Glenda became aware that her arm was being pinioned not by a crevice or snag but by an unyielding clutch of fingers. With a jolt she looked up to discover Leclair. Then another wave toppled on her head. Leclair slipped his other arm around her ribs and pulled Glenda onto her feet, still coughing and sputtering. He seemed amused, the fair hair pasted to his forehead. It was the briefest of smiles.

"Come with me," he shouted.

Glenda stumbled again, nearly felled by the force of the hurricane. She was too exhausted to utter even a syllable. She followed Leclair, slipping and sliding on the boulders with the spray lashing her cheeks. The *Clifton* was still at anchor but wilful and rebellious now, rolling scuppers under. Walking in her kirtle was a Herculean task, like hauling a half of an anchor up the hill.

The sun was buried in a pitchy bog of clouds, shrouded ever deeper in dust and the hurtling limbs of tree and shrub. Such a magnificent way to perish, she told herself. Glenda did not doubt that her dear father would be there to greet her, as would grandma Nellie and cousin Devon and even the good Captain Woolsley. All would be well in the end, of that she was certain.

"Where can we...?" Her voice failed.

She slipped and fell. The unrelenting blast made her shudder inside of the drenched garments.

Leclair stepped away from the boulders onto a sloped ledge of mountain which skirted this end of the anchorage, rounding the outside of the headland. Glenda pulled herself together and scrambled a few last yards to get away from the treacherous rubble.

"Is there a shelter?" whimpered Glenda.

Leclair did not look back. He couldn't hear or he couldn't be bothered, and she didn't know which it was.

"Where are we going!" she hollered at the top of her lungs.

Leclair turned briefly and beckoned to her. As they neared the jagged cliff on the south extremity of Anse Paschal, the full cacophony of the hurricane broke in upon them. It was making no sense. He was headed into the eye of the storm. But Glenda had succumbed to an abject slavishness. She tottered along like a drunkard, weaving to and fro and gnashing her teeth as the wind threatened to dump her back among the boulders.

The sea was hurling itself upon the cliff, breakers tripping close upon each other with cascades of wind-blown white. The stampeding air was charged with a single, unrelenting roar. She heard it now. The full reverberation of His unfailing majesty. The heavenly strains unfurled with grace and dignity, sopranos winging their way to lovely, pristine heights while the basses strode stalwartly below, bearing the entire edifice of song on their broad, reverberant backs. *God himself is with us: / Let us now adore Him, / and with awe appear before Him.* Slow and majestic and joyful. She was certain of it now, weaving in and out of the storm. The ultimate procession, impervious to the flailings of the blast. *Like the holy angels / who behold Thy glory, / may I ceaselessly adore thee, / and in all, great and small, / seek to do most nearly / what Thou lovest dearly.*

The wind was gouging her eyes, sharpened with grit, riddled with debris. Through the thinnest of slits, she saw that Leclair had stopped. He had his back to the sea, staring at the bald rock face. It came to her that the hurricane was not in competition with the choirs of her Lord, nor ever could be. It *was* His choir, His marching upon the perjured earth, yet frenzied, yet unhurried. *God himself is with us.* God's visitation upon one and all. Leclair had already had his wits plucked from him, left to stare insensibly at the rock. In all things, her heavenly Father would prevail. *Let us now adore Him, / and with awe appear before*

Him.

All was not as it had seemed, however. When Glenda drew near to Leclair, he beckoned her suddenly to his side. Gasping for breath, she arrived beside Leclair who, holding her by the waist, proceeded to guide her into a dark fissure in the rock.

Next thing she knew, the storm was behind them. A wondrous calm enveloped her cheeks and, for a moment, Glenda imagined that she had reached that final shore. But no, the hurricane was still at their back, echoing inwards to the darkness beyond.

The fissure widened into a gaping hollow that stretched out of sight. Leclair had her by the arm. He appeared to know his way. As they groped along, the rock grew slippery and soft underfoot. Glenda reached out to steady herself. Her fingers found a wall, dripping wet to the touch. She tried in vain to penetrate the darkness. An odour entered her nostrils, sweet and strange at the same time.

Of a sudden, she had her hand full of fur, a small, sleek body squirming in her hand. Glenda gave a frightful shriek and tore the hand away, bumping hard into Leclair. On the instant, the darkness came alive with echoes from an unseen commotion.

"What was that?" she heard him asking.

But Glenda couldn't speak. She was wiping her hand furiously on the kirtle, catching her breath while her heart continued to pound.

Leclair peered into the shadows. "Stay away from the wall."

In the dim light from outside, Glenda lifted her eye to his. "A bit late, aren't you?"

Her annoyance was not lost on Leclair. He blinked with embarrassment. "Bats," he explained. "I forgot."

He took her hand in both of his and examined it. "Must've been asleep or he'd have bitten you. The blood would've brought the rest of them."

Leclair's explanation was cold comfort. Knowing that the furry little creature was a bat did less than nothing to allay her fright. Blood suckers. Trapped in the dark with blood-sucking vermin. Glenda began to look around, lest they should attack her on the instant.

"Let's keep still until they've settled," continued Leclair and showed her a seat upon a pile of rubble.

Glenda folded at the knees. She ended up in a heap on the pale, well-rounded stones. Leclair was next to her, breathing almost as hard as she was.

"They live here," he mumbled under his breath.

Glenda began to look around. She was growing accustomed to the dark and, now, the interior of the cave emerged before her eyes. The vaulted rock was, in fact, draped with hundreds of bats, a stunning charcoal arras of folded wings. They were stirring and fretful from the noisy intruders but only a few had taken wing. Presently they were settling in for a slumber, again, until nightfall. The floor of the cave was awash with their droppings, presumably the source of that high odour.

Her mouth ajar, Glenda turned to the wall beside her and found, again, the entire face of the rock crawling with black wings.

"The tempest can't reach us here," she heard him saying.

But Glenda was eyeing the wall directly above their heads. A crude inscription had been etched into the stone. She tried to determine if it was the rough hand that made it incomprehensible, and then decided it was not in English.

"Look," she said.

Hearing no reply, Glenda turned and found Leclair gazing at the inscription. His countenance had changed, almost sombre now, almost reverent.

"Is it primitive?" asked Glenda with a shudder of excitement.

But Leclair seemed insensible to her words, as though in a reverie.

"Leclair?"

He shot her a glance. Then he spoke without pause. *"Och*

frukten icke för dem som väl kunna dräpa kroppen men icke hava makt att dräpa själen, utan frukten fast mer honom, som har makt att förgöra båd själ och kropp."

Glenda listened to the words. "And is that the inscription?"

Leclair gave a nod, his gaze straying towards the mouth of the cave.

"Pray, what does it mean?"

Without looking at her, Leclair repeated it in English. "Fear not him who can destroy the body. Fear him that can destroy the body and soul in hell."

Glenda looked again at the inscription, scratched painstakingly into the rugged rock. The same words. Waiting for them in this cave. The din of the hurricane was nothing now, banished from her ears. The only sound was his recitation in English, that same recitation which had so maddened and confounded her before.

"What's it doing here?" asked Glenda in a whisper.

"Because that's what they did to her."

Glenda felt a chill that wasn't from her drenched garments or the dampness of the cave. "Did what to whom?" said she.

"To her that lies here." Leclair patted one of the stones upon which they rested.

Glenda struggled to draw her next breath. "You're out of your mind," she whispered, almost to herself.

Leclair turned to her now, without a word in defence. Madman though he might be, his fancies were palpable enough to frighten her.

"Is someone buried here?"

Leclair gave a wan smile. "This is all coral. Nothing but coral for her grave."

Glenda realized that all the stones, every one of these pale stones was coral. A whole cairn of coral, carted from the seashore. They were sitting upon a grave. And she was looking at an epitaph.

"This is your writing?"

Leclair seemed to think a reply wasn't needed. Indeed she knew. At the mouth of their cave, Glenda noticed the light dimming. She couldn't be sure whether it was night falling or merely an escalation of wind and dust.

"Who was she?"

But Leclair was crossing to the far side of the cairn, where the coral reached shoulder high on the dark wall. He ducked out of view from Glenda.

"What did you do?" Then she raised her voice. "Who is it lies here?"

Leclair emerged carrying a large, wide-mouthed flagon made from greenish glass.

"We were newly wed," said he. "Sailing to America."

Although his words fell very simply, Glenda was rendered incapable of further questioning. Her emotions ricocheted pell-mell within her. Leclair had thus admitted her an inch deeper into his confidence.

Glenda watched him untie the leathern seal from the rim of the flagon. Leclair pushed his hand down inside. Through the grimy glass, she saw him fetching a sackcloth pouch tied with thongs. From the pouch, he pulled a small tinder-box. Then he reached again inside the flagon and dragged his fist back out, filled with strips of lichen and wood shavings which he arranged neatly upon the flattened pouch.

Glenda's thoughts kept straying to the secrets of the cairn, but her limbs were too intent on a spark of warmth. She watched in silence as Leclair tested the tinder-box and packed two strips of lichen loosely inside. Again he struck the flint against the iron. A frown came over his face and he tried repeatedly. There was no smoke or spark, just the muted crack of flint upon iron.

"Dear heaven," said Glenda. "If it please you, try again."

So he did, to no avail. Then he used a corner of the sackcloth to scrub both surfaces. Even so, every effort was in vain. Cursing under his breath, Leclair examined the box closely.

"I don't know," he mumbled, rolling the lichen between his fingers. "The dew must've got inside."

Leclair threw down the tinder-box and the kindling, thoroughly exasperated.

"What do we do now?" sighed Glenda, shivering.

In the cave, shadows had deepened. The entrance was barely discernible, blending each minute with the umbrage within. Night was fast approaching.

"We can't remain here," ventured Glenda.

For the first time, Leclair appeared at a loss. "Do you prefer the roaring blast?"

She realized this was his best answer. He wasn't being nasty. He simply hadn't anything better to offer. Just the two of them. Drenched to the bone, with the chill of night creeping up from the raging sea.

Glenda stepped away from him, pacing gingerly through the oozing muck. If she could at least move about, maybe she wouldn't freeze to death.

"I'm going to remove my clothes," she heard him say.

Glenda turned. Leclair had walked towards the other side of the cave where the roof was buckled, sloping to a mere crawl-space.

"You're going to catch a chill," he went on. "For my part, I'd rather be rid of these wet rags."

Speaking thus, Leclair proceeded to divest himself of his garments. Glenda watched briefly, uncertain of her options. He was a mere shadow now, as the cave inhaled the full darkness of night. Soon he would be only a voice to her. And so also she to him. The breeches dropped about his knees, revealing a hint of his rounded buttock. Glenda turned away, her hand to her mouth.

She began pacing again, slowly and deliberately, as she swung her arms about in order to quicken the flow of blood. The tempest, her dripping wetness, his nakedness. What *else* could befall her?

"What became of her?" cried Glenda suddenly.

He wasn't expecting another question. "You mean Cecilia?"

"Was that her name?"

"Yes." And again, almost swallowing the word, "Cecilia."

"And was it *her* father that died from grief?" ventured Glenda quickly.

"Even so."

"What did you do to her?" insisted Glenda, speaking now to keep warm as much as anything.

"I buried her."

Glenda did not believe that he could've so misconceived her question. Surely, he was dodging. "Bruno spoke of a fire that's in you," she said, impatient.

"That was after. When they found me. Raoul had his pistol cocked but it wasn't his ball that struck me. It was lightning. Papa used to say he was there and saw it. They were all watching. Papa, the old fox, told them I was destined to lead them because I lived. Matt said the lightning went inside of me. That's what they thought, even Raoul. They say it's keeping me alive. So long as the fire is there, it's my ship. If the fire goes out, it will be over."

Glenda was listening, her lips ajar. "So a flash of lightning is your name."

"And it blinded me."

"You lost your eyesight?"

"In truth. When I could see again, nothing looked the same."

She looked over. He was visible as a faint suggestion only, a pitchy blur that was deeper than night itself but dissolving soon into oblivion, like a spring lamb inside a sated python.

"And by whose hand did she die?" continued Glenda, a shiver at her spine.

"I was punished."

Glenda wasn't going to let him off. "Her death was a punishment?"

"She paid for my crime."

"What crime?"

"Not a crime at all except in the vengeful sight of God."

"Humble yourself," said she, "and all is forgiven, even this blasphemy."

"I say, He *is* vengeful. He's the defender of corruption and privilege. Behold your own self. He created woman to be a wound perpetual, a sorrow unending."

Glenda welcomed her own anger. It would keep the blood racing.

"I'll not brook those words, sir, without more substance."

She listened for him. There came no reply. Glenda steeled herself, determined to outlast him.

"I was in the crowd that night," said Leclair unexpectedly.

She looked over and there he was, an evanescent phantom, hardly more than a conceit of her imagination.

"We had waited a year to see Anckarström pull the trigger. We made ourselves invisible in the crowd and knew each other only by the full-length black domino. His Majesty took the shot in his back. But I was gone before they could lock the doors. The Chief of Police never got my name."

"You plotted the King's murder?"

Glenda heard him laugh, ending in a kind of whimper. "Oh yes, again and again. Pechlin trained us all, at his dinners, his firesides, his political salons. He handed me a copy of Thomas Paine. But, you see, most of us have been apprehended. They're in the dungeons now or perhaps in exile. They were tried, you see, and punished. But I wasn't on the rolls. I sailed to the far side of the world. So it was left to God."

The storm wailed and boomed through the hidden shafts and ducts of the mountain. Glenda had her arms crossed and tightly wrapped to her ribs. She was savoring Leclair's strange tale.

"And you had thought God's justice might be more clement than men's justice," she concluded.

"I had thought many things. Things I couldn't share with you before. But know this, my dear, I'll not fail you."

She couldn't see him. The darkness was complete. Glenda was unsettled by his words, for she could swear that she had heard those words that afternoon, onboard the *Clifton*. *I'll not fail you.*

And as if to prove her right, he went on. "You're mine again."

‹∂ ∑›

A PURGING WIND

ෂ) ඌ

Hansson was tucked safely in his warm fourposter with Cornelia splayed beneath him in extravagant bliss. It had become a mutually rewarding and frequent arrangement.

"I have no patience for that rogue Bellman," opined Hansson, wheezing with the present labours of his nether torso.

"No?"

"Even at the Wall House a man isn't safe from his ditties."

On top of them, the blankets heaved mightily. Their bed echoed his movements with a steady, creaking pulse. Cornelia, formerly Fridell, was offering up a succession of the loveliest moans and exclamations, spurring him onward. She had lit their lamp and turned the wick down low. A soft spell of amber enveloped the nuptial bed. On the rug were his pantaloons and wig.

"Don't be cross," said Cornelia between moans, her eyes shut all the more to savour Hansson's delightful forays. "Bellman writes for the commoner... Goodness, how you've grown!"

Hansson grinned, redoubling his amorous exertions. From the street came frightful rumbles of the storm. Cornelia raised her ample chin to make room for him in the crook of her neck.

"His sole sport is baseness and depravity," insisted Hansson, beads of sweat rolling off his balding pate.

"Hold me tighter," begged Cornelia, her voice breaking at each thrust from her husband. "My gazelle... ivory gazelle... my intrepid pathfinder! You shall have what you seek."

"Bellman keeps company with slatterns and cretins," gasped Hansson, now flushed and belligerent. "He doesn't know the sublime from the vulgar. His nymphs frolic in the dung."

His ivory loins pursuing the quarry with unrelenting haste,

Hansson nestled into Cornelia's neck. That was where her spasms would begin.

"But my dear," she was crooning at his ear, "it's not Bellman that's made Stockholm so foul. He's just a poet."

"And that's precisely the root! Is poetry a place for filth? We'll end up with nothing else."

His forehead was lodged against her jowl or she might've tried to catch his eye. "But you'll have *me*," she said, switching into English now. "Here we are, safe at home on a such night."

"*Such* a night," he corrected her, choking on his concupiscence.

"Such a night," she repeated hoarsely.

"*Night*," droned Hansson, insisting on the diphthong.

"Night."

He pressed his cheek to her jugular, feeling the beginning of her jitters. It was their moment of triumph, when she would clamp her arms about his flat buttocks and shout with exultation. Hansson, too, closed his eyes and waited for her little quivers to grow into the full quake.

When nothing happened, he looked at her again. Content though she seemed, there was nothing about her face to justify the shaking in her limbs.

"Yea, my brave...gazelle," she panted, "one last...hill to climb!"

He was happy to oblige but what shaking, then, could this be?

Cornelia turned her gaze on the rest of the room. It was quaking. The bed was trembling, a portrait rattling on the wall.

"Pray, not a hurricane?" whispered Cornelia, motioning for Hansson to bridle his lust.

The last word had barely left her tongue when their window exploded in a flurry of glass. Hurtling into the room came a rocking chair. It landed on one of its rockers and slid across the wide timbers before coming to rest between their bed and the door. Still rocking. Hansson and Cornelia were stupefied. Their eyes dwelled on the ghostly rhythm of the empty rocking chair, with the storm snarling at them through the fangs of broken glass.

Hansson reacted to a flutter at the window. Fine garments had plastered themselves to the frame, snagged on the spears of glass, flapping in the wind like pennants. A hooped crinoline came unstuck and soared into the chamber, knocking their oil lamp off the table.

The room was in darkness. Hansson took a dive off the bed and attacked the lamp with his pantaloons, snuffing out a little caravan of flames along the spill of oil. Someone's crinoline, he thought. The storm had pillaged someone's wardrobe, snitched someone's chair. What was it going to confiscate from him and Cornelia?

Beyond the shutters of their chamber, a tiled roof was wrestled loose and hurled across town.

A sheet of laths and plaster found its way to the heights, where it knocked a soldier upon the pate at Fort Gustav. The remainder of His Swedish Majesty's guard withdrew to their barracks.

The hurricane was tugging at St. Barth as though to fleece her of all her greens, leaving only bare bones of granite. Goats were tossed from one pasture into another, or into the sea. Brigantines and schooners were run aground, snatched from human hands and crushed on the treacherous shoals.

At Morne Rouge, the wind heaped sand in dead men's eyes. At Anse Paschal, the mizzen mast cracked and fell thundering onto the deck of the *Clifton*. Everyone was under hatches, waiting to hear the main mast follow. They waited past midnight, but it never did. Loman whispered to Snake that he could hear Big Raoul's head wailing and snarling at the storm and that this was what saved their mast. Snake wasn't sure he could hear it, but the rest of them did. And Snake was deaf in one ear anyway. The hurricane would've crushed them against the boulders, but wasn't able to unstick the anchor.

With redoubled aggravation, the storm lashed out to sea, broadsiding the lone house on La Fourchue. The windward gable caved in, bringing part of the roof along. From within, the sprawling bough shivered and tossed, clawing at the delicate groves of Ovid.

On the rebound, the hurricane pummelled the cliffs at Flamands, whipping the sea into towers of rage. Over the hills, it came upon a solitary cabin nestled on the mountainside. The wind gave a good poke but the walls were staunch. So it crooked itself around the little wooden cross and gave a tug, but the cross stood firm. The storm took another lunge at the cabin. This time, the beams gave a desperate cry and the roof lifted like a hatch.

The wind scoured every nook, knocking over the spinning wheel, huffing the hammock high into the air. Another blast toppled the walls like dominoes. From the wreckage, a plume of sallow pages arced into the night, swirling and scattering upon the air. At last, Olof's argument had given up the quest for coherence, surrendering to sweet obliteration.

Within moments, the cabin was a shambles. The storm ploughed through the debris, clearing away enough to find her. But no one cowered under the rubble. The floorboards were laid bare, pots and brooms and clams and rice flying every which way. But one of the boards had shifted, leaving a tell-tale gap. There would be no escape, no respite. The plank was tossed blithely aside and other boards flew up, revealing the shallow vault. The wind thrashed about, peevish and disgruntled. She wasn't there. The rocky trench was empty, except for a dozen stout bags.

Outfoxed by an old woman. The storm let loose at the sackcloth bags but they were stashed so snugly, bulging so boldly as to defy a mere hurricane. The ducats jingled merrily.

In the village below, Winnie sat by her fire. Across from her was Chloe, blue hands crossed on her lap and fast asleep.

CR SO

On the second day, we came under attack.

The master told us there was a canoe on our stern, four or five men, no more. The crew opened fire and dispatched one or two of the wretches. But the rest were safe behind our aft-castle, well below reach of the stern-chaser. Post-haste, they had wedged our rudder. A clipper sailed out from a jut of land, overtaking us and peppering the sails with fire. The captain put up a fight, but we were doomed. We could neither give speed nor alter our course. I had been seasick and hiding away beneath the galley, so as not to sicken Cecilia with my foulness. Of a sudden, the ship was quaking from cannon fire and I heard the captain hollering. I had no idea what was afoot.

Glenda listened as the words were formed, in twos or fives or singly, from the darkness. His deepest darkness. A darkness which Leclair inhabited as comfortably as though it were a second skin.

Barrels and sugar crates had been stacked up everywhere. My nostrils were numbed by the foulness of bilge-water. From above came someone's laugh, but no more screaming. No more pistol shots. I needed to find Cecilia before they did. I groped along in the dark crawlspace, trying to imagine what I was going to see. A warm drip caught me on the cheek, someone's blood. I couldn't get my breath, scrambling on hands and knees. At last I found the stairs.

Beside the hatchway was the doctor, his throat slashed and still throbbing. I said a prayer, then, for my soul and my dear wife. The main hatch was before me. It hadn't been opened, but overhead the pirates shuffled to and fro. I charged and primed my pistol, knowing full well that firing it would bring them all upon me. I picked a cutlass off the floor. When I stood up, I was looking down the barrel of a pirate's pistol. If this pistol went off, everyone would be alerted and I would be dead, that much was certain. The fool wretch was reeking of rum and I was able to slash him on the hand.

Leclair's voice was quite close to her now, echoed by the hollows of the cavern. He wasn't stationary. He was walking about, to ward off the chill or perhaps driven by the torment of memory.

I ran him through with my cutlass. He stumbled back, still staring after his missing fingers. I needed him dead or he would give me away. But he stumbled on, still on his feet, refusing to drop. And I had to dig the blade deeper and deeper, pushing him back, the two of us tangled and dancing to our death. At last I had him against a bulkhead and the cutlass... Yes, well. No matter...it's no matter... Now all my prayers were for Cecilia alone. I climbed the stairs to gun deck, possessed of the darkest dread. The corridor was quiet. All the ruckus came from out of doors, at middledeck. I ran to the second door on the left and threw it open. Our cabin was empty. The oak chest hadn't been touched. For a moment, I couldn't move. The narrow chamber suffocated me. Only my pounding heart. Through the bulkheads I heard their clamour, deafening. And most dreadful.

The sacred vault. In this indiscriminate darkness, his walls were crumbling. Bleeding into the night. Inside became outside. Or maybe a deep contraction, inhaling all the world into his sanctuary.

Glenda couldn't see herself, couldn't even summon a vision of how she would appear in a looking-glass. She knew that he was using their only glass, the indiscriminate darkness itself, to conjure her image. And it wasn't Glenda. Who was she, with nothing in her eye except night? Night mirroring night.

I stepped back into the corridor, walking as in a dreadful sleep. The ruckus drew me towards middledeck but I climbed to the higher deck instead. All caution was gone. I had banished all care except for one name alone. On quarter deck were the mariners, our good mariners slain and their limbs most woefully abused. It was twilight. We were on a course for the shore, entering a lagoon with white sands. I dropped to my knees and crawled forward. On the far side was the forecastle and in between was middledeck, coming into view as I reached the foreward edge. I dropped flat on my face, shutting my eye against the sight. Every other thought had fled. There could be no more thought, only seeing, only drinking of this poison. I wormed my way to a fallen body and peeked from behind it. No turning back, no turning aside. It was plain to me.

Glenda heard him speak through gritted teeth, his voice growing hoarse and grim. But there he paused and she felt as though her heart might stop, so well had she attended to his story.

"Olof?"

She thought she heard the pad of his feet. Or maybe it was some debris being whisked along by an errant gust of the storm or perhaps the rustling of bats' wings, for surely they would know enough to have kept still on a night such as this.

"Olof? What's the matter?"

But he wouldn't talk.

Glenda felt as though whatever was unfolding in his mind's eye had to be viewed in silence or it might blur. As though he were using the very silence to summon up the reality of every detail. An exquisite form of self-torment which took precedence above all else.

Exasperated, Glenda groped about until she had found the bumpy slope of the cairn. She eased herself down and slumped forward, crushing her bosom upon her knees. Without his story to goad her appetite, Glenda was reminded suddenly of her fatigue. She was alone. Olof had stepped into some other room and shut the door behind.

She ran a fingertip slowly over the goosebumps on her arm. Her own wrist so slender and cold. Her aching mind was dragging itself back into her body, almost shocked to find it so sodden, so decrepit, so laden with despair. In her ear the abject ululation of wind, inexorable, interminable.

She couldn't see them. A thousand eyes watched from the walls of their cave, those scurvy little beasts waiting for her to bleed. They watched her squirming and rocking herself. But she saw nothing, couldn't stare them down. Didn't want to. Wouldn't want to have to.

Her flaxen hair was tangled now and dull. Emilio had gathered his fist full of her hair and pulled, forcing her head backwards.

With a start, Glenda was wide awake. She had snoozed, though not deeply. These few words had pierced her slumbers like fire. She had no sense, now, of how long she had been dozing, maybe half an hour, maybe moments. What did it matter?

This folding at her neck had pried her lips apart. I heard her gasping, almost choking. They had dragged her down upon a coil of hawsers. Loman had her by the arm and Twitcher held the other, pulling them almost from their sockets. She was on her stomach, the rose-coloured dress tossed in folds across her back. From the edge of the rose fabric, her nakedness shone forth, so fair, without all guile and past all remedy. She had her knees spread wide on the deck and Emilio was... He had her from behind, holding her by the waist, so surely and rudely having his way.

Olof's voice had tightened to an excruciating knot and trailed off altogether. If he was sobbing, Glenda couldn't hear it for the din from outside.

"She did not give herself willingly," was all Glenda could think to say.

You haven't the faintest notion. Have you known how she felt? Or the bursting, the shattering that took place within my chest? You cannot possibly. She did not concede, 'tis true, but she felt his lust, the raw insistence from Emilio, more than she had ever had from me. I saw him flailing hard against her and all of them, piss-drunk, taking up the rhythm with grunts and groans and clapping of their hands. That was my Cecilia. He clutched her to his groin and spilled himself in Cecilia. I remember how her head drooped between her shoulders, hair like tangled sunbeams on the coils of shiny hemp. Emilio rolled off her like a sated goat.

Glenda had enough. In a matter of moments, her appetite had turned to a sickening surfeit, a fatigue without end. She stared in front of her, uncertain of where Olof's voice would come from next. Pray that he would speak no more.

She was wracked by a long tremor as his words came back to her. Emilio had done this. That boy at Morne Rouge, lying beside her with a pistol shot between the eyes. The boy who had been sent to fetch her in Gustavia. Had done this deed while even younger. And Twitcher had pinioned Cecilia together with the other one, whatever his name was. They were his own men. But he wasn't Leclair then, Glenda had to remind herself. He had been a victim of these same men.

Everyone had a turn. Or most of them. Matt came back for more.

Glenda was curled up on her side, holding her stomach. "Not Matt. No, not him! He wasn't like the rest."

Not like the rest, no. Nothing like the rest except he'd guzzled rum with the rest. Ever since they dropped anchor in the lagoon.

Olof waited for Glenda to fathom this before he spoke again.

He never got his second chance, though, because it was the captain's turn.

"The captain?"

Raoul. He scorned them all. Puppies, he called them. Untaught puppies. And they were stinking of rum and having a good laugh. Matt egged him on, saying are you man enough, Raoul, are you a man for it? So Raoul dropped his breeches. That's when they stopped laughing. I saw Cecilia, her eyes wide with fright. She had seen what Raoul had for her and grabbed for the windlass to get herself to safety. But Raoul was quick. He drew her close, hauling her free of the dress. Give us a bit of a show, said someone.

"No!" cried Glenda. "No more!"

To rob a woman is a crime. But to give is another matter. Give her what she likes most and you'll own her truly.

"Hold!" wailed Glenda, pressing a hand to each ear. "I won't hear it."

It's what Raoul said to them. Give her what she likes most and you'll own her truly.

Olof had come to her now, close by her side. He wasn't visible, yet she imagined the heat from his body in the air beside her. His voice was that of a ghost, veiled and private almost past recognition.

That's what he gave Cecilia. She lifted her head in protest but he topped her, thrusting with all his might to show those puppies a lesson. Still she raised her head but still he prevailed, using his flesh so precisely to win her for himself. I looked at her, then, and knew she'd lift her head no more.

"Monster! He killed her. But you've got him now, his head on a stake, the foul wretch, and so he breathes no more!"

But hear me closely.

Out of nowhere, Olof's hand touched her at the shoulder, holding her with such imploring gentleness as she could not rebuff.

Here is the wound whereof I've spoke before.

Uncovering her ears, Glenda let go of herself and fell softly towards him. Her cheek flopped against his chest, her arm across his naked belly. All cares were gone. She had no more.

Here is the wound. For though Cecilia had been used most

foully, she was breathing still. There's a thing, you see, that women do. A way the woman moves to give unto herself the pleasures owing to a man…

Olof paused, overcome by the closeness between them. Glenda lay silent upon his chest, her head like a dead weight riding on the ebb and flow of his breath. She shut her eyes, as though to remove herself from someone she couldn't see anyway.

Do you follow?

Glenda made no answer. An honest reply would've bespoken her virtue, of which she was proud, as much as her naiveté, which was another matter. She had often sought to overcome the latter without forfeiting the first. Glenda knew not, now, whether simply to feign indifference or to admit to her curiosity. Her cheeks were burning from the boldness of his words.

A man will take his pleasure with a woman until his seed is spent. But I've known women who learned to do the same for themselves. In sooth, it's not like… It's strange indeed but, though they have no seed to spill, there's a tremor, a peaking pleasure the same as in a man.

Olof had paused again, expecting her to break away. Glenda was all ears. It was an initiation she didn't want to be without.

Raoul knew it also. Cecilia's own will was no matter to him. He knew how to ply her flesh to unchasten her mind. I saw her head roll side to side, her eyes shut and lips tightly pinched. My Cecilia. He spited her spirit into pleasure.

"Your eyes deceived you. She was warding him off."

I saw it plainly. She made no protest.

"Her strength was gone. I tell you, she was insensible."

No! Not insensible when her face could show so much.

"By what measure could you read her so? What schooling made you a master of her face?"

I did not want it to be true. And so Raoul was done. He had taken her. Forever taken her from me.

"I was hidden," she heard him whisper.

Again, Glenda had been off somewhere, not exactly sleep but some stupor lasting perhaps an hour. His skin was wet, her hair still sopping, dampness everywhere. Her fingers had dug into his hipbone.

"Yes?"

"All that time, I was in hiding."

Glenda struggled to reach wakefulness. "Where?"

"I was up above, remember, on the quarter-deck. I wouldn't show myself to them."

She thought about it for a moment. "But there was nothing to be done."

"Yes."

"Was there?"

"No."

They lay together, breathing in the darkness.

"The story grew more painful, more hideous by your own fancy."

"I was there." And again, "I was there."

In vain, Glenda searched for the magic word.

"It's already done," he groaned. "There was only the once." And again softly, "Only the once."

Glenda removed her hand from his hipbone. "You were afraid."

"Lousy, white-livered craven."

"Do you mean yourself?"

She felt his chest heaving suddenly. Then it trembled from several rapid, shallow breaths. Glenda didn't need her eyesight to know he was weeping.

"You were alone," he sobbed at last. "They had you all to themselves. And I let them do it."

The coral rocks had bruised Glenda. She felt them prodding at her skin. It was the bones rising, the old bones risen from their grave, passing from coral to flesh, making their home in her.

"They would've murdered you," she said.

"But I didn't even try."

She hesitated. "You were afraid of dying."

"Yes. I let them have you."

Her hand lashed out. A muffled crunch.

With astonishment, Glenda felt her fist striking him on the head, again and yet again. She did nothing to prevent retaliation, gave no thought to her own safety. Both of her arms were thrashing blindly in the dark.

With each blow, she found his body still waiting, each thump swiftly following upon the other. Head or shoulder, cheekbone and ear and collarbone, Olof didn't seem to flinch. Once or twice she heard him gasp for breath but he didn't raise a finger. Her fists pummeled him with a fury that knew no fatigue.

She felt him strangely altered, the shock of a slick membrane, shrouding himself in wings, a nimble rush of wings between her wrists, brushing her elbow, fastening to her waist. The dark was spiraling, tossed with invisible speed. Glenda lashed out viciously, slashing and scratching.

He had brought her this far, only to step behind the arras. An impenetrable, winged commotion. The allegiance of bats. Olof had donned his black domino. She flogged the tumultuous darkness with her arms. So this was it. Had the arras been all of a piece and stationary, Glenda could've torn it aside. But even so, it would surely be futile. He would be gone already. Behind the charcoal, nothing. Olof's trump.

Only a hole, a hidden hatch into the mountain.

When Glenda awoke, their cave was flushed with daylight.

Directly before her eyes was Olof's belly, crowned by a tuft of reddish hair from which protruded his male organ, lolling to one side. Here was an end to all modesty, an abrupt dismissal of her past. As she allowed herself to ponder the intricacy of veins and creases on his dainty, shrunken skin, a merriness stirred within her. Before, when she could not look upon him, he had made a study of her nakedness. But now he was sightless. Her turn had come. Her smile reached everywhere except her face.

Then she heard the silence, a vast, encompassing silence. Glenda retrieved her arm from under his shoulder and pushed herself gently up to sitting. No, she hadn't lost her hearing. The hurricane really had passed.

Olof was blissfully oblivious to the world. She looked and looked again. His face was puffy and blood from one nostril had dried on his lip. Like a bad dream, the drear stretches of the night came back to her, fathomless, sightless, unthinkable.

She contemplated Leclair without remorse. She had never seen him thus. Oddly, something new had settled upon his brow and in the corner of the mouth, something that belied his bruises. There was to his repose a tenderness or wholeness, as though a mask had shattered and, in the chinks, revealed the living flesh beneath.

But Glenda's empty stomach was fast becoming a distraction. "Olof."

With the light of day, it had become awkward to reach out and touch him. She put her hand gingerly to his shoulder, fingers traversing the glassiness of his old burn. Suddenly she was afraid. She had been this close to Matt on the mountain when he breathed his last.

"Olof."

He stirred, one arm groping briefly.

"Listen."

Olof's eyes opened, first one and then the other. He looked at her without speaking.

"Do you hear?"

Olof gave a loud snuffle. He turned towards the entrance. After a moment, he stumbled to his feet and went looking for his wet breeches.

"They'll be coming for me," he mumbled over his shoulder.

"Could you find me something to eat?"

As Glenda looked about, she saw everywhere the charcoal arras of wings, hundreds of furry little snouts all turned discreetly to the wall, a thousand little eyes and ears who would guard Olof's confession, except to squeal and screech to one another where no human ear could follow.

Olof returned from the inner cave, dressed and brandishing his cutlass. He was shivering. "The only disadvantage of removing these wet rags is having to put them back on."

She smiled. "I'm sorry for what you've been through. But you didn't finish the story."

He turned to her, faintly puzzled.

"You said Raoul wasn't the death of Cecilia."

"He might as well have been." Olof gazed abstractedly at the corals beside her. "She must've bled all night. By morning she was dead. They threw her overboard. That's when they discovered me."

Glenda was ahead of him. "And that's when Raoul had you walk the plank."

He nodded, indecisive for a moment. "He never knew what he had done to me. I never told him about Cecilia."

Glenda heard him with a grim sense of wonder. Observing the softness in his eye, a thought crossed her mind. What if this was it, the thing that had been foretold? Maybe it was the lightning itself that had passed, finally, from Olof's soul.

"Papa offered to go find her body. Once I could see where I was going, I brought her here."

Glenda could imagine no greater abandonment than the bloated half-body which had lain beneath this coral, a thing more foul and putrescent than the sum of all that bats' dung, a thing so desecrated that no redemption had been possible until each bone was bare.

"For my king I took many a wound but none like this. None could be like this. The soul has its torments, and the body has wounds of its own. But he that uses the body to destroy the soul, he is the canker in God's creation." Olof drew a deep breath. "He is the pith and form of Satan."

Olof walked to the mouth of the cave and stood with his back to her, framed by the light. Glenda struggled for something to say.

"What happened to her was a monstrous pity."

They were silent. From outside came the solitary cawing of some bird.

"And, you know," she added, "what happened to you is no less of a pity."

Glenda bit her lip, doubting that the words had come out right. But then she knew, without question, that this was precisely what she had needed to tell him.

Glenda got to her feet slowly, chasing the numbness from her limbs. She bent forward until her hair hung limp before her eyes. Using her fingers, she began the arduous task of teasing the strands apart from each other.

"That canker is everywhere in Europe," she heard him saying. "Do you know of Voltaire?"

"I've read *Candide*," said Glenda with some offence.

"Well, the same Voltaire has called Sweden the freest nation in the world. And Rousseau looked to the Swedes for the example of democracy. When King Gustav was a boy, all his tutors were taken from him. New ones were appointed, true Swedes that would show him respect for the common man and shield him from the follies of divine right. The education of a child is a political matter. You're a tutor. You need to know this. 'Twas Rousseau that said it, and he said whatever education cannot amend, violence will. But nothing could help King Gustav. There again, the flesh was weak. The vanities of the theatre, you see, and all of the frippery and gluttonous appetites that cleave to a royal throne. All is corrupted. Mercifully, there's a wide sea between Europe and Tom Jefferson."

Glenda's stomach was crying out, but she was unsure of how

to turn his talk from politics to breakfast.

"I'm sure I shan't forget what you've told me," she said meekly, hoping it would satisfy him.

"Teach those children well," said Olof as he left. "Don't add to the dungheap."

She brushed her hair aside and looked around, but he was nowhere.

α ε

IN THE WAKE

ℬ ℭ

The voice that reached Glenda's ear was not Olof's.

Neither was it in her dream, which had slipped away at the first sound from outside. It was, possibly, an hour or two since Olof had stepped out of the cave. She couldn't recall the dream but a sadness lingered in her bosom. Not fear or evil, but nevertheless affecting her deeply.

Two or three voices were heard, speaking quietly near the mouth of the cave. Glenda was sitting bolt upright, still on the cairn where she had tried to make herself comfortable again after fastening her damp hair away from the face.

Maybe the pirates had rowed ashore. Glenda stumbled to her feet, hurrying towards a narrow alcove that would conceal her in shadow. After only a few steps, she heard a scraping of boots echo across the cavern. A shadow had leapt along the jagged floor, ending on the far wall.

Glenda turned to discover a soldier, fully attired in King George's red uniform. His musket was already levelled, as he stared cagily into the darkness. She glanced about her, looking for any evidence that might lead to Olof. If they were looking for her, all would be well. But if they found Olof, he would hang.

The soldier must've seen her, for he called out. "Someone to see you, ma'am."

It couldn't be. Her heart jumped into her throat. Olof had stepped out to do some foraging, or so she had told herself when she curled up on the rocks. He would bring whatever was to be had, maybe mango, hopefully a coconut. They would eat together. But now? He was back and surely shackled, destined for the gallows on St. Kitts. How could everything have turned so abruptly?

"Someone here to see you, ma'am," insisted the redcoat, stepping closer now. "You best come with me."

He stepped aside and Glenda walked, in a daze, into the daylight. Behind her, the bats shuffled and squeaked. Her thoughts coursed aimlessly this way and that, preparing to see Olof in cuffs, to say those few words which could suffice forever. She was even reminded now of her intended assignment on St. Kitts, imagining the townsfolk as Leclair would step up to his noose.

What she saw next made her forget everything else. Standing on the rocks, flanked by a dozen soldiers, was a dashing figure who had not entered her mind except as a broken corpse on some distant shore. She was looking at Devon Heywood, as dapper and as comely as ever she had known him of yore.

"Dear God," said he, fastening his gaze upon her. And then again, "Oh dear God."

She could only imagine what it was in her appearance that had prompted her cousin's dire tones, but whatever it was must've been apparent to one and all. Without another word, two of the soldiers rushed to her side, catching her by the arms as her knees began to fold. They propped her up gently, while Devon approached.

"Cousin," he burst out, folding her sopping wreck of a body in his arms. "My dear, dear, dear cousin."

Glenda hung limp in his embrace, tears blurring her sight and streaming onto the dark green frock-coat. All her words stuck in her throat.

"Thank you, Lord," she heard him saying. "I told Him I had to find you and He was my guide."

Glenda blinked away the tears and, over his shoulder, peered across the anchorage. It was empty. There was no sign of the *Clifton*. The entire shoreline was a shambles, the rocks littered with splinters of trees, of shrubs, even of roofs and, yes, a cartwheel. But the pirates were gone, whether devoured by the madding seas or perhaps shrewdly heaving in and skulking off at dawn.

It was no matter now. She was going home. Devon held her gently away from him, his hands at her shoulders. "You need a good leg of lamb."

Glenda looked up, her eyes red but smiling. All she could do was nod.

"Have you escaped the pirates?"

Again she nodded.

"Their captain is well known," continued Devon. "He will hang."

"God save you, Devon," said she.

He looked startled, as though her voice were a miracle. "But what were you doing in that cave?"

"I was marooned. Maybe a week now," said she, pausing for a moment. "The captain would have no woman on his ship."

Devon shook his head in frustration. "Let's come back for Leclair," he said, turning to his officer. "The lady needs a medic."

The officer quite agreed and gave orders to his men. Glenda was on Devon's arm, crossing the rugged rock. Though cloudy, the day was warm and sultry but Glenda couldn't stop shivering. She kept an eye on the troops returning to their horses at the top of the footpath. They had no one in custody. Olof had eluded them.

A terrible joy filled Glenda, rippling through her feeble heart. As they scaled the path, her head went back against Devon's shoulder.

He noticed her smile. "My turn to smile," said he. "And I won't rest until you've told me everything."

Glenda thought about that. It wasn't going to be easy. Sooner or later, she would need to understand what, indeed, had happened in her.

CR SO

Devon held the door as she stepped up into a clarence that would drive them to the wharf. It was mid-morning on a resplendent day touched by early autumn. Glenda felt almost out of place in the new rose-coloured taffeta that rustled between her fingers as she looked for the footrest. She stepped into the shady carriage, tucking the dress about her on the seat.

Devon, in a rare moment of indecision, couldn't seem to decide whether he should nestle next to her or take the advantage of facing her from the opposite seat. After a moment's fluster, he sat down across from her. Glenda felt disappointed but not surprised for, in the past two days, her cousin had grown more and more circumspect. He appeared to be listening always for innuendoes or hidden messages in her reports. It was in keeping that he should now forego the intimacy at her side in favour of the greater visual command of facing her, where she couldn't elude his eye by turning to the window.

The coachman gave a loud snarl. With a jolt, wheels began to turn and the horses' hooves pounded the paving stones. They were leaving the large brick house which had accommodated them that entire week. As it turned out, the hurricane had blasted Devon's previous lodgings, so they were obliged to take a referral to P. J. Rydström on Smedsgatan. This blotchy, choleric fellow was a ship's pilot and newly appointed customs examiner who had regaled them daily with stories about the roguish commerce of Gustavia. Of course Devon had made his usual inquiries into the cotton market.

Whenever the conversation turned to Glenda's convalescence, Rydström had proven himself every inch a gentleman. A hot bath was drawn for her each morning and Rydström had taken upon himself to fetch an assortment of medicinal salts and vapours. For this, Devon was much beholden and had insisted, the night before, on paying a handsome premium for their rooms, to which their host had willingly acceded. They would not see him again, for he had an appointment to bring a Dutch merchant into the

Carènage and from there report to the customs house. But he would see them from his window, he had assured them, and would be sure to wish them godspeed. For the moment, St. Kitts was forgotten. At three bells they would sail for England.

Gustavia had been sorely maimed by the hurricane. Some quarters reminded Glenda of a battlefield. A rubble of tiles where roofs had been. Entire houses knocked sideways into their neighbours. Large wooden homes blasted as though by gunpowder, with nothing remaining except a reservoir and brick-and-mortar foundation.

From Smedsgatan, the coachman turned left at the waterfront and they rode along a wide esplanade which bore the name Västra Strandgatan. This was looking very familiar. A veritable forest of ships' masts, comprised of all the trees of the nautical landscape, schooners, barques, caravels and other smaller craft in the foreground, lining the timbered wharf, while the larger species rode at their anchors in the distance, brigantines, frigates and a stately galleon.

Dock workers and street mongers hurried about their business, laughing and hollering. Glenda had walked these very stones with Papa. She recalled their landing, and how Big Raoul had locked horns with Leclair as the *Clifton* dropped anchor. It came back to her now, more terrible and prophetic than before. And how she had tagged along with the old sea-cook on this very esplanade, still thinking it was all a brief accident.

"You look ever so much better," said Devon.

Glenda met his inquiring eye. Again, he was straining to show her a smile. They had not spoken during the ride. He had his own struggle, it seemed, even as Glenda had hers. On the third day, once they had agreed that St. Kitts might be too much for her, Devon began his queries. He had been very solicitous of her welfare, seeking to ascertain precisely what attempts had been made on her virtue in the company of such felons. Glenda had told him, straightforwardly, that she had been attacked, in

Devon's presence, by Big Raoul and that, following their capture, she was nearly ravished on La Fourchue and certainly would've been, were it not for Leclair's protection. But answer him though she might, nothing seemed sufficient to allay Devon's doubts.

He would go about his errands for an hour or more, only to return with further queries, asking perhaps about her sensations during the assault or if Leclair had wanted her to himself. About her sensations she was clear and unequivocal. But Leclair's motive, on the other hand, had confounded her and was only now becoming more intelligible, since their refuge in the cave. Her earlier surmise had begun to fit with Olof's hidden story and, in the course of a week, she had now learned to think of him as a man of rhyme and reason not so different from others.

The trouble was, Devon would not take it kindly. Any intimation that Leclair wasn't a mere felon could only fuel Devon's doubts and redouble his inquisitiveness. This wasn't the only trouble, however. Glenda found it difficult to speak of Olof without an admixture of sympathy which was becoming all the more difficult to disguise. Hence, she must avoid an answer altogether by pleading utter ignorance.

"You've not said much," ventured Devon in a kindly voice.

"Forgive me. I'm so tired."

"How can nature so deceive! Yet your eye has found its sparkle, yet your cheek is sanguine but you're not well."

"I pray, dear cousin, do not think worse of me. The body hurries before, the soul comes after."

"Quite so," he nodded. "Quite so."

Devon's attention wandered off through the window, lost in the clamorous bustle outside.

Glenda guessed that, once again, her words were being weighed and measured. The more she assured him that she had been safe under Leclair's wing, the more he brooded; precisely what had Leclair *done* for her?

As she observed her cousin's ailing soul, it was as though his fears grew familiar. In his worst moments, Devon must've known what Olof knew. Maybe some day she would tell her cousin what had possessed, and very literally *possessed* Leclair on that distant day of their capture. Maybe she would find the words and the courage to impart to Devon why Leclair had staged an assault by Raoul and had cast himself as a witness, rather than claiming her for himself.

The menace that Olof had known from another man was not unlike that which haunted Devon now. Fear him who can destroy the *soul* in hell. By what coincidence Olof had stumbled upon these words and how he had come to adopt them was unknown to Glenda. By one vertiginous reversal of fortune, Olof had tasted the horror that is a woman's lot, and known what it is to be utterly overpowered and wanting for protection. Rather than face such defencelessness, he had banished it. That's what had prompted him to sign on the account. It had made him into a pirate.

Not a day had gone by when she didn't ponder Olof's fate, or even look for him in the streets. Before she would go to sleep, she had tried to imagine the possibilities. Was he dead? Devon had had several reports from the English troops, including a capture of four pirates, but none about Leclair. Yet he might have died, even by his own hand. The lightning had saved him, only for as long as it ruled his body. Without it, he had come eye to eye with his guilt. Olof might be incapable of his own sorrow. She had feared the worst.

But on the day before, as she was dressing herself to join Devon for lunch, a knock had come upon her chamber door. Preparing her sweetest smile for him, she was startled to find the maid standing there with a small basket of mangoes.

"For you, ma'am."

"How sweet," had been Glenda's reply, assuming it was another favour from their host.

"A gentleman stopped by."

"A gentleman?"

The maid squirmed. "I asked his name but he just shook his head."

The maid hesitated. "I paid no heed to his roguish garments because being as his errand was with you, ma'am, surely he's a gentleman on the inside."

Back inside her room, Glenda had sat upon the bed with the basket on her knee. When Devon's knock came, she had stowed the basket in the window without disturbing the fruit and that's how she had left it this morning.

But Devon had proceeded to announce his plan. Before setting out to find her, he had asked her mother's blessing on their marriage. The dear woman had dropped her needlework, he claimed, and smiled for the first time since her daughter's disappearance.

Perchance Devon had delayed his announcement these five days in hopes of overcoming his own doubt but finding that no amount of questioning could suffice for the task. Or did he hope to sway her away from other thoughts by such a definitive scheme?

Glenda had been greatly cheered by the news of her mother's rallying spirits. This may account, in part, for why she had accepted, on the spot, his offer of marriage. And Devon would love her all the days of his life. He was so confident of his role in the new wave of commerce sweeping across the seas, so effective and all-of-a-piece as that poor demented Swede could never be. She felt embarrassed even of the comparison.

On a couple of occasions, she had allowed herself to wonder what it would be to love such a man as he. She had smelled the salt water on his skin. Daylight had ambushed her with a blunt view of his uncovered body. For an instant she had even sensed what it meant to own his love when, in utter distraction, he took her for Cecilia. What had possessed her, even for that moment, to play along? Did it warrant the name of playing? Glenda had always known the meaning of compassion. What she had not known was the passion.

"There it is," said Devon. "That's the *Esperance*."

Glenda peered across the bright waterfront.

"Look," he said, pointing. "Second from the right."

Across the water, their ship was riding at anchor. Flat-bottomed skiffs were standing by to shuttle passengers from the wharf.

Glenda gave a smile, while a dull panic rose from within. Had Olof stopped, arms full of mango? Had he watched the soldiers at the mouth of the cave? Who was to say if he had cowered in the shadows, watching from the perpetual cavern of his bleeding soul, blinded yet again as they whisked her away?

Glenda's eye roamed far and near. Among street mongers and seamen, labourers and merchants she sought his face. It was not a sensible thing, to be sure, but she couldn't desist. Or was it not his intention to return to her at all?

She recalled their parting. Don't add to the dungheap. His last words to her. Was he on his way to France to join the ranks of exiled revolutionaries? Or would he walk off a ship at Boston, blend into the crowd and build a better world in New England? This uncertainty, these limitless possibilities were not a way to end anything. It would be the most difficult part about forgetting him.

She could dedicate her own work to the teachings of Rousseau, indeed would be glad to do so. She could advocate for a child's right to grow their heart along with their intellect. But was that enough? Don't add to the dungheap. Was she to forego children of her own? To deny Devon a son? Such thoughts would pass, she told herself, even as a delirium, a tropical disease that must dissipate some day, but not before she had quit these craggy shores, not before she had purged herself of the insuperable mischief of wind and waves, rid herself of it not only in the flesh but in the seat of her soul.

Until the clarence came to a stop, Glenda searched the crowd for a sign of Olof, one last glimpse of the chiseled face, the sunbleached locks. She knew better. He would not come to her in thoroughfares or public places. But she would look the world squarely in the eye, the green sprouting face of the mountain, the leafy green forever endangered by shadow, forever receding into the insatiable shadow of its own interior. He would be with her there. He would be her pilot, day by day, in the thick of the dungheap.

And the green, the struggling green would prevail.

ॐ ॐ

ACKNOWLEDGEMENTS

The Intended was written with support from the City of Toronto through the Toronto Arts Council. For this, I am much obliged.

John Hunt, Autumn Barlow and the entire team at John Hunt Publishing were a delight to work with. They are to be commended for the path they've chosen in the new literary marketplace.

I would like to thank Thelma Barer-Stein at Culture Concepts Books for her caring and insightful work with the manuscript.

I am also grateful to my comrades in the Bloor West Writers group in Toronto, whose feedback and engagement were a guiding light.

I had great help from two books in particular. "Historien om Sverige" by Herman Lindqvist (Norstedts, 1997) gives a dramatic and yet scholarly account of King Gustav III's era, in the years leading up to the French Revolution. "Den svenska kolonin S:t Barthelemy och Västindiska Kompaniet fram till 1796" by Ingegerd Hildebrand (Lindstedts Universitetsbokhandel, 1951) is an academic dissertation with a wealth of detail and insight about Sweden's colony in the West Indies.

Many thanks to my brother Alf Hornborg for tracking down Hildebrand's book and giving me access to it.

My appreciation, also, to the Black Cultural Centre for Nova Scotia and their helpful consultation about the African diaspora in 18th century Europe.

A lively, informative chapter on the Swedes in St. Barth is to be found in Alf Åberg's "När svenskarna upptäckte världen" (Natur och Kultur, 1981) and it gave me much to draw from.

I have also consulted Dr. Christopher Carlander's travel diary "Resan till S:t Barthélemy 1787-1788" (Christer Wijkström Publishing, 1978) and "Svenskstad i Västindien" by Gösta Franzén (Almqvist & Wiksell, 1974).

The real-life anecdote of Aaron Åhman and his wilful wife was drawn from "Ön som Sverige sålde" by Bengt Sjögren (Zindermans Förlag, 1966).

In chapter 3 "Olof's Love," the lyrics sung by Olof are from "Liksom en herdinna" by Carl Michael Bellman, in my translation.

The hymn "God Himself is with Us," heard by Glenda in the church, was written by Gerhard Teerstegen in 1729.

The historical anchor for my book is two-fold – the assassination of the Swedish monarch Gustav III and the founding of a Swedish colony in the West Indies during the 18th century. King Gustav did not die until some time had passed, and many conspirators fled the country. I was going to say "...and the rest is history" but no, the rest is fiction!

**TOP HAT
BOOKS**

Historical fiction that lives.

We publish fiction that captures the contrasts, the achievements, the optimism and the radicalism of ordinary and extraordinary times across the world.

We're open to all time periods and we strive to go beyond the narrow, foggy slums of Victorian London. Where are the tales of the people of fifteenth century Australasia? The stories of eighth century India? The voices from Africa, Arabia, cities and forests, deserts and towns? Our books thrill, excite, delight and inspire.

The genres will be broad but clear. Whether we're publishing romance, thrillers, crime, or something else entirely, the unifying themes are timescale and enthusiasm. These books will be a celebration of the chaotic power of the human spirit in difficult times. The reader, when they finish, will snap the book closed with a satisfied smile.